A GRAVE IN THE COTSWOLDS

Undertaker Drew Slocombe is not having a good day. His business is failing, the car needs an MOT and he's driven 120 miles to the Cotswolds to carry out the late Greta Simmonds' final wishes. Unfortunately, when he gets there, a string of bureaucratic mistakes means that he's now the chief suspect of a murder inquiry. Thea Osborne and her loyal spaniel Hepzie are house-sitting at Greta Simmonds' house, which is currently between ownership. Then the discovery of a body in a nearby field finds her embroiled in a murder investigation once again.

A GRAVE IN THE COTSWOLDS

A GRAVE IN THE COTSWOLDS

by

Rebecca Tope

Magna Large Print Books
Long Preston, North Yorkshire,
BD23 4ND, England.

British Library Cataloguing in Publication Data.

Tope, Rebecca
  A grave in the Cotswolds.

  A catalogue record of this book is
  available from the British Library

  ISBN   978-0-7505-3475-8

First published in Great Britain in 2010 by Allison & Busby Ltd.

Copyright © 2010 by Rebecca Tope

Cover illustration by arrangement with Allison & Busby Ltd.

The moral right of the author has been asserted

Published in Large Print 2011 by arrangement with
Allison & Busby Ltd.

LP

Magna Large Print is an imprint of Library Magna Books Ltd.

Printed and bound in Great Britain by
T.J. (International) Ltd., Cornwall, PL28 8RW

For Judy Buck-Glenn
in gratitude for your interest
and encouragement

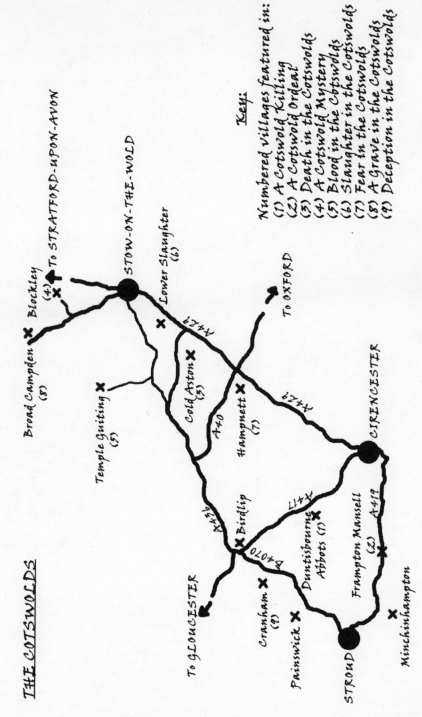

THE COTSWOLDS

TO STRATFORD-UPON-AVON

Broad Campden (8)
Blockley (4)
STOW-ON-THE-WOLD
Lower Slaughter (6)
Temple Guiting (5)
Cold Aston (3)
A429
Hampnett (7)
A40
TO OXFORD
A429
Birdlip
A436
A417
Duntisbourne Abbots (1)
Frampton Mansell (2)
A419
CIRENCESTER
A4070
Cranham (9)
Painswick
TO GLOUCESTER
STROUD
Minchinhampton

Key:

Numbered villages featured in:
(1) A Cotswold Killing
(2) A Cotswold Ordeal
(3) Death in the Cotswolds
(4) A Cotswold Mystery
(5) Blood in the Cotswolds
(6) Slaughter in the Cotswolds
(7) Fear in the Cotswolds
(8) A Grave in the Cotswolds
(9) Deception in the Cotswolds

Author's Note

As in all the other Cotswolds titles, the setting is in a real village. But as before, the actual buildings and people in the story are imaginary. Furthermore, the personnel on the Gloucestershire County Council have been wholly invented for the purposes of this fiction. Drew Slocombe's Somerset home, however, is in an invented village, surrounded by other invented places, making the interface between real and imagined impossible to follow on a map.

Chapter One

The roads grew increasingly narrow and undulating, the closer I got to the village of Broad Campden. The strange intimacy of travelling with a dead woman in the back of the car joined with the timeless effect of the towering trees and long stone walls, the combination making me quite light-headed. I found myself muttering out loud, addressing my silent passenger in none-too-friendly terms.

'What a place to bring me,' I accused her. 'Why couldn't we have stayed in Somerset and done the business there?' I groped once again for the map beside me, checking that I really did have to take the right turn shortly before the town of Chipping Campden. Yes – right, and then right again after passing through a small village, and then left into a small sloping field on the edge of a wood. Three cars awaited me, and I greeted their occupants with due dignity, straightening my tie. It was windy, the trees tossing loudly overhead.

Broad Campden was a mile or two away from Chipping Campden, in the middle of the Cotswolds. It was a region I hardly knew at all, the road map on the passenger seat a vital part of my equipment as I transported the dead woman in her cardboard coffin to her place of rest. Cardboard had been selected after an exhaustive discussion about the coffin, a year before. 'Willow,' she had said, to begin with. 'I hear there are lovely willow coffins available.'

'There are,' I had agreed, 'but they're extremely expensive.'

When I told her the price, she gulped. 'And that's with only a modest mark-up,' I added. She had not questioned my integrity; it was my own sensitivity to the practices of some undertakers that led to my saying what I did.

I really had not expected to be handling Greta Simmonds' funeral so soon. She had seemed to be in good health when I met her, and I had wondered why she was so intent on arranging and paying for her own funeral at the relatively tender age of sixty. Childless, retired, and passionately committed to all things Green, she was a type that I recognised. We had got along well, and I was sorry when her family contacted me to say she had died.

The funeral had come at a bad moment, and I was in no mood for the task that particular week. It was going to take all my most conscientious efforts to conduct things as they should be conducted, for a number of reasons. It was sixty miles from home, for one thing, and poor Karen, my wife, wasn't happy about being left on her own with our children. I took no pleasure from driving, and had little anticipation of a warm reception from the family. The dead woman had been emphatic about wanting me to dispose of her body according to sound ecological principles, while admitting that her relatives were unlikely to be very cooperative about it. I had been visited by her sister and nephew, who had stiffly agreed to the day and time for the burial,

16

casting their eyes to the ceiling and sighing heavily as they did so. Now they were gathered, along with another nephew and a handful of friends, in the windy little field, where Mrs Greta Simmonds was to be interred.

The great majority of the funerals I conducted were in the land at the side of my house in Somerset. I had been running Peaceful Repose Natural Burials with my partner, Maggs Cooper, for nearly five years, building a quiet reputation for reliability, sensitivity and frankness. I told people how they could reduce costs, how they were still permitted under the law to opt for a range of alternative burials, and I invited them to take control of the process as much as they wished. As a result, Maggs and I earned an embarrassingly small income, but made a lot of friends.

Greta Simmonds had been unusual in several ways: her insistence on the precise position of her grave, in this obscure corner of the Cotswolds; her comparatively early age; her wry acceptance of the need for a minimum depth for the grave in order to safeguard her from scavengers. 'You know,' she had said, with a little tilt of her head, 'I'm not sure I would mind if some hungry vixen took part of me home for her cubs. What's the difference between that and providing nourishment for a lot of fat pink worms?'

I had been careful to retreat from that line of conversation. People were almost never as sanguine about their own dying as they might appear on the surface. I had diverted her to the question of timing. 'Statistically,' I said, 'you are quite likely to live another thirty-five years. You need to be

17

sure that your money is safe, and the funeral costs secured, however far in the future it might be.'

Her smile suggested that she knew something I didn't. 'I don't think we need worry about that,' she said. 'We don't make old bones in this family.'

As any undertaker would, I had inwardly permitted myself to hope she was at least more right than I was. With risibly low interest rates, and every prospect of rising costs and changes in regulation, the sooner I could gain access to her cash the better. But I squashed the thought. I liked this woman far too much to wish an early death on her.

She had paid for it all, up front, quite content to trust me with her money, thrusting the carefully drawn-up agreement into a large shoulder bag.

That had been fifteen months earlier and now she was dead. I was shocked when her sister, Judith Talbot, telephoned me with the news, and harassed by the implications. Maggs had been on holiday at the time, with Den, her husband. They'd gone to Syria, of all places, and I had a nagging worry that I might never see them again. I had to arrange the Cotswold burial for the day after they came back, dropping everything into Maggs's lap only hours after she crawled off an overnight flight from Damascus. But we both knew this was the way it went. She made no complaint, helping me to slide Mrs Simmonds' coffin into the back of the vehicle and waving me off with a good grace.

To our disappointment, natural burials hadn't caught on as well as I'd hoped when Karen,

Maggs and I began the business. If anything, it had gone backwards – we'd had fewer customers over the past twelve months than in the year we started. It was galling in a number of ways, not least financial. If it weren't for the compensation package we got when Karen was shot, we'd have had to wind everything up and do something else. Even the stalwart Maggs's meagre salary would have been unaffordable.

All of which meant, of course, that I was in no position to turn away work, even if I had not been obligated by my agreement with Mrs Simmonds. Maggs assured me she could watch out for Karen, as well as keeping everything going in the office. She'd done it plenty of times before, after all. And I could do the funeral on my own, since three somewhat reluctant pallbearers had been dragooned into helping out when it came to the actual burial. It was a far cry from the days when I worked for a mainstream undertaker, with no fewer than five members of staff always in attendance.

The dead woman's two nephews and brother-in-law helped me to carry her to the grave in a corner of a field that she told me had been hers for decades. I had, with some difficulty, arranged for the necessary digging to be performed that morning, by a man from Blockley, who still dug graves for some local undertakers. He had promised to return as soon as the funeral was over, to fill it in again. I deftly arranged the pulley ropes around the coffin, and we lowered it in without mishap. There was no vicar or other officiant. Mrs Talbot, sister of the deceased, produced a sheet of

19

paper and read a poem by Sylvia Plath which Mrs Simmonds herself had chosen. I hadn't heard it before, and forgot it as soon as it was over – but it was a relief not to have to endure the ubiquitous lines by Henry Scott Holland which claim that the person in the grave isn't really dead, but just in the next room. That had never worked for me.

I was unsure of Mrs Talbot. She showed very little sign of distress at the loss of the person she must have known for her entire life, longer than anybody else, in fact. She stood straight-backed and British, reading the poem with no trace of a regional accent, wearing a well-cut dark-blue suit and expensive shoes. Her elder son, Charles, kept close, flicking frequent glances her way, as if needing to follow her lead. Mr Talbot was silent, detached, as if wondering quite why he was there at all.

And then a little surprise sent ripples through the modest assembly. The younger son, still in his teens, cleared his throat, and moved a few inches closer to the open grave. 'Auntie Greta,' he began, looking directly down at the coffin, 'I've got a message from Carrie for you. She says she wishes she could have been here, and she's going to miss you a lot. We both are. You've been the best auntie anybody could ever have. You were the bravest, funniest, cleverest person in our whole family...' here he glanced defiantly at his parents and brother, 'and it's a bastard that you went and died, when we still need you. But you've got what you always wanted, and that's a good thing. Rest in peace.' He choked out the last words, and retreated to the edge of the group, turning his back on us all.

A long silence followed. I waited for the mother to go to her unhappy boy, in vain. The father was equally unresponsive. I almost went to give him a hug myself, but resisted. After a minute or so, a small woman I had not managed to place in the general scheme of things strolled calmly to the lad and laid a hand lightly on his arm. I couldn't see the look they exchanged, but it seemed to be right.

The funeral was over. I filled in the minimal paperwork required by the law. Mrs Talbot – Judith – came up to me, looking relieved. 'Thank you, Mr Slocombe,' she said formally. 'I think we've satisfied my sister's wishes, haven't we?' As I had seen before, when she and Charles had come to my office, there was irritation lurking just below the surface. She had actually said, on that occasion, 'When my mother died, we had a cremation. For myself, I think that's by far the most sensible option. But I'm afraid Greta hated it. That's why we've got all this carry-on now.'

'It's what she wanted, Mum,' Charles had said, more than once. Until the funeral I had not met the husband or the younger son. Nor the two middle-aged couples whose names I didn't know, and who seemed to find the whole experience altogether fascinating. One wife kept nudging her husband and whispering. Nor did I know the pretty woman who had gone to console Jeremy Talbot. Throughout the burial, she had hung back, giving the impression she thought she ought not to be there.

The wind blew fiercely from the east, and I hoped I wouldn't have a long wait for the grave-digger to arrive, it being unthinkable to leave an open grave unattended. To my relief, I glimpsed a man in heavy boots, leaning on the gate, when we began to straggle back to our cars. He was with two young people, who I took to be idle onlookers, curious as to what was taking place in this quiet corner. Having checked with Mrs Talbot that there was nothing more she required of me, I approached the gravedigger, exchanged a few words, and paid him in cash.

Behind me a voice spoke. 'Er ... would it be OK if I helped?' he said.

I turned to see that Mrs Simmonds' younger nephew was addressing the gravedigger. 'It'd be good if I could see her covered up,' he continued. 'And my brother, if he wants to.'

The gravedigger nodded understanding. 'There's a spare spade in the van,' he said easily, as if this was no new experience. He gave me a quick wink, full of a wisdom and tolerance that made me think he would be exactly the companion young Jeremy needed.

I had some doubt as to whether Charles Talbot would be similarly moved to assist in the filling of the grave, though. He had not looked to me like a man who could abide to get his hands dirty. Then I wondered how Jeremy would get away, if he stayed behind while his family all departed. My little flock of mourners still felt like my responsibility while any of them remained in the vicinity of the grave.

'How are you getting home?' I asked Jeremy.

'On the bike,' he said, as if this was obvious. He indicated a blue racing bicycle, leaning against an oak tree, on the verge outside the field gate.

I smiled, and waved him a final farewell, turning to go straight home again. And I would have done, if it hadn't been for the small woman standing slightly apart from the others, watching my face so intently. I smiled, pleased to have a chance to learn more about her.

'That was very ... different,' she said, holding out a hand. 'I'm Thea Osborne. I was looking after Mrs Simmonds' house when she died. I feel sort of *involved*, although I'm not really.'

I took her hand self-consciously. People were not always comfortable shaking hands with an undertaker. They expected something bloodless, perhaps faintly redolent of formaldehyde. Thea Osborne did not appear to have any qualms. 'Did you not know her at all?' I asked.

'No, not really. I only met her once, when she gave me my instructions about the house. Then she went off to Somerset and died.' She shook her head ruefully. 'That's never happened to me before.' She spoke as if a lot of other things had happened, and this was something new to add to a collection. Here, I thought, was a woman who had seen things that many others had not. A woman like Maggs, who could confront the truth without flinching. A rare creature. Then she added an extraordinary remark: 'At least she wasn't murdered.'

I laughed. 'Why – do you often encounter people who've been murdered?'

'Actually, yes. It happens rather often. Partly because my ... um ... former boyfriend, I suppose you'd call him, is in the police. So are my daughter and my brother-in-law. And there's something about house-sitting that skews the balance of the status quo.'

'Oh?'

'I mean ... it creates opportunities, leaves a vacuum, changes the pattern in a community.' She shook her head. 'I'm not really as fey as that sounds. And it might not even be true. Every murder has its own set of motives, after all.'

'Well,' I echoed her own words, 'at least Mrs Simmonds wasn't murdered. It wasn't even much of a coincidence that she'd prearranged her funeral with me, and then died twenty-five miles from my house. She was visiting her former home, apparently. I assume those are friends of hers, from the place she lived before she came back here.' I tilted my head discreetly towards the two couples who had been amongst the mourners. They were looking back at the new grave, quietly talking.

'No, they're locals,' Thea told me. 'But I agree it's a very thin turnout. I'm glad I came.'

'There's not usually a crowd at these natural burials,' I said. 'They tend to be rather discreet.'

'So *you* knew her?' she said.

'No better than you. She came into my office a year and a bit ago, and made arrangements to be buried here, where she lived as a child. I didn't realise it was now her full-time home.'

'She inherited it ten or fifteen years ago, apparently, when her mother died, and let it out for a while. That was when she was in some kind of cooperative place in Somerset. Which I suppose you knew.'

'They call it co-housing. Horrible word.'

'Indeed. Odd, don't you think, that she left it? People generally expect to stay for ever when they join something like that.'

'Ructions,' I shrugged. 'It can't be easy to get along together in that sort of set-up.'

'Well, she seemed nice enough. Unusual. Interesting.'

We were scattering stray comments back and forth, the wind making us uncomfortable. Skirts were whipping around female legs, which I suspected would normally be encased in trousers of some kind. 'After all, not many people plan their own funeral when they're only sixty – especially not a funeral like *this*.'

'I had the impression of someone rather, well, *forceful*. I made some joke, if I remember rightly, about her living another thirty years or more.'

'She seemed quite healthy to me,' Thea agreed. 'But perhaps she wasn't. Perhaps she knew this was likely to happen.'

'According to the certificate, she died of an occlusion.'

Thea Osborne blinked. 'I don't know what that is.'

'A blockage, basically. Generally impossible to predict. Very quick.'

'Oh. So she approached you because she wanted a woodland burial, and fixed up all the details – is that right? That weird coffin, for a start. Don't you have to make some special application to use something like that?'

I smiled. 'Actually no, hardly at all. You don't really want to know the whole story, do you?'

'Not if you can't be bothered to tell me.'

She meant it literally – not in a nasty way, but giving me permission to save my breath, if that's what I preferred. I saw her looking around at the people in the field. She had the air of a person slowly coming to understand that her role was over, the last line delivered, and all that remained was to leave.

The Talbots had begun to get into their somewhat elderly BMW, apart from the boy nephew who was hanging back as if wanting time alone. I wondered fleetingly about his bike and where he would go on it. The family lived miles away, somewhere the far side of Oxford. Was he intending to cycle the whole way? I watched the family for a moment. 'Who's Carrie – do you know?' I asked Thea.

'What?'

'The boy said something about Carrie, in his little speech.'

'Must be a girlfriend, I suppose.'

'And why isn't she here?'

She looked at me with a parody of patient understanding. 'I don't know,' she said.

'Sorry. I wasn't really asking you. Just wondering. It's funny the way families get to you, in this business. You want to figure all the relationships out, and understand the patterns. Loose ends niggle at me.'

'I know what you mean,' she said. 'I'm the same, but in my case, it's just idle curiosity. I really should get myself a life, one of these days.'

I had no answer for that, other than a string of inappropriate questions that I would have liked to ask her. Like, was she married? Where did she live? Why was she doing house-sitting, of all things? Instead, I stuck firmly to the matter in hand. 'Is there a get-together somewhere?' I asked, thinking I would have heard if this was the case. Mourners were moving off slowly, apparently with nowhere definite to go. Nobody had said anything about adjournment to a local hostelry, or glanced at watches as if due somewhere.

'Doesn't look like it. How sad.'

It was time for me to go. The melancholy little funeral had given me scant satisfaction – the woman had died too soon, with only the teen-aged nephew showing any sense of loss. Every death should be important; the survivors should acknowledge that the pattern had changed. The permanent hole left by the deceased should be given its due recognition. In this case, I sensed surprised relief amongst the relatives, except for Jeremy, and an almost careless reaction from the middle-aged couples in attendance, who were purportedly local friends. Nowhere could I see evidence that Greta Simmonds' death caused much more than a momentary pain to most of the people who knew her.

'Oh, look!' said Thea suddenly, as I started to walk away from her.

I turned, following her pointing finger to a tree that stood at the edge of the field. Four big magpies were lined up along a bare branch, staring down at the grave.

'Four means a parcel or something like that,' said Thea.

'Pardon?'

'"One for a wish, two for a kiss. Three for a

27

letter, four better." I always thought that meant a parcel.'

I smiled at her naïvety. Magpies were scavengers, and already they had detected the presence of decomposing flesh. I tried to catch the eye of the gravedigger, who would be well aware of the need to proceed quickly with his duties. 'Maybe somebody's going to win the lottery,' I said carelessly.

I walked to the gate, where my vehicle was parked on a wide grass verge. I still sometimes called it a hearse in my own mind, but in reality it was a large estate car, with the rear seats removable to leave space for a coffin. Standing beside it was the young couple who had been chatting to the gravedigger, the woman sideways to me, the man behind her with a hand resting on her shoulder. She was light-skinned, in her early twenties. He was tall and black and a few years older. They were talking about my car.

'Is this your motor?' asked the man, unsmilingly.

I admitted ownership readily enough.

'Are you aware that three of the tyres are illegal, and the road tax expired over two weeks ago?' asked the girl.

They weren't in uniform. It did not occur to me that they were police officers, so I laughed. 'The disc's in the post,' I said easily. 'And the MOT is due next week. I'll sort it all out then.'

'Not good enough, I'm afraid, sir,' said the man. 'Might I see your licence and insurance documents?'

The penny dropped. 'Good Lord, are you police?' I asked.

'That's right, sir. PC Jessica Osborne, and

Detective Sergeant Paul Middleman.'

'Osborne?' I had automatically filed away the name of the small woman I had been chatting to at the graveside. It's a habit with undertakers – people's names acquire considerable importance in my line of work.

'Right.' The girl gave me no encouragement.

'There's a lady called Osborne over there,' I continued, pointing into the field.

'She's my mother,' said PC Jessica.

Chapter Two

Thea Osborne argued strenuously on my behalf, but her daughter stood her ground. 'I do not believe the law says he can't drive home,' said Thea. 'That's idiotic.'

The girl sighed melodramatically. 'If he lived just a few miles away, it would be different. But no way can I let him go sixty miles on those tyres. They're *bald*, Mum. They could cause a serious accident.'

Both women looked at me, with very different expressions: the mother with exasperated sympathy, and the daughter with officious scorn. There was little similarity between them anyway – Jessica stood three or four inches above Thea, and was nowhere near as pretty. I was still wrestling with the fact that Thea was old enough to be the mother of this strapping PC – she must have been twelve when she had her, I thought. Or maybe she

29

was a stepmother, or adopted the girl as an older child, when she was still in her twenties.

I repeated my feeble defence. 'I knew they were a bit dodgy, but I was waiting for the MOT. I haven't had them all that long. I thought they must have a bit of life left in them.'

'And the tax?' queried Jessica.

'I applied for it on the computer, four days ago. It'll arrive on Monday, I expect.'

'You were two weeks late applying, then?'

'I suppose so. They give you a fortnight's leeway, don't they?'

She rolled her eyes. 'Mr Slocombe, sir, that is a complete myth. Besides, today is the sixteenth of March. Your tax ran out on the twenty-eighth of February. By any reckoning, you are overdue. As well as that, the usual procedure is to have the MOT test *before* renewing the tax.'

'Yes, yes, I admit everything,' I pleaded. 'But *please* let me go home. My wife's not well. She'll need me to be there this evening.' I was over-egging it, almost starting to enjoy the whole episode. There was something pleasingly ludicrous about an undertaker being given a rap for an illegal motor. I could see that Thea was aware of some of this – that she felt, like me, that such details were beside the point. A woman had died and been buried, there were wars going on and whole populations starving. The minutiae of vehicle regulations counted for little in the larger scheme of things.

'Besides,' Thea persisted, 'you're not in uniform. Doesn't that mean you're not entitled to throw your weight around like this?'

'Don't be stupid.' Jessica was clearly losing any cool she'd retained till then. 'If I observe a felony taking place, whether in uniform or not, it's my duty to confront it.'

'Bollocks,' said Thea, earning herself my eternal affection. 'You just enjoy the effect it has on people.'

'I'm sorry,' said the daughter, inflating her bosom with dignity and turning back to me. 'But the law's the law.'

'So, what must I do?' I enquired humbly.

'Kwik-Fit will still be open – you can go and get new tyres, and be on your way in an hour or so,' said the girl briskly.

And it'll cost me money I didn't have, I calculated gloomily. The credit card could stand it, just, but I'd vowed to myself not to use it again until the end of the month. The business survived only by virtue of a constant juggling act with the finances, and although I had been able to access Mrs Simmonds' carefully secured money, things were still very tight.

'Right,' I said with a sigh. 'Where's the nearest one, then?'

They didn't know. They weren't local. Jessica and her boyfriend had invited themselves over to join Thea for a meal in Chipping Campden, all three of them staying in Mrs Simmonds' house (which I thought slightly dubious, but it seemed they felt perfectly justified) overnight, before departing to their respective homes next day. 'Or we might even leave it till Sunday, if the weather improves,' said Thea, happy to share their plans with me. Her daughter rolled her eyes again, obviously thinking I had no need to be told about their personal arrangements.

I was uneasy, even agitated. Money trouble always sent me into a spin, and I also had the worry of Karen and the children expecting me home. Plus there was my usual reluctance to finally detach myself from the person just interred. Normally, this was accomplished quite gradually and painlessly, because they were buried in the field behind my house, and I could stroll around the graves every day and commune with them as much as I liked. This time, I believed I would never come back to this remote little village, never revisit my onetime client, to check that all was well with her. Daft, I know, but there's something about the dead that makes it difficult to abandon them completely. I liked to know I'd done a good job; that nothing had disturbed their resting place. I worried for Mrs Simmonds' remains left alone in this corner of land, with careless relatives and uncomprehending neighbours, and the constant niggling worry about foxes and dogs that came from the shallower graves employed for ecological reasons. Mrs S might have earned my respect when she said she quite liked the idea of an arm or leg being taken away by a vixen as a hearty supper for a nest of fox cubs, but I had no intention of letting such a thing happen.

I was also annoyed – as anybody would have been – with the young police officer, who I could not help feeling had been showing off for the benefit of her boyfriend, if not her mother. The detective beau further confused me by appearing sympathetic towards my predicament, whilst studiously remaining silent. Where Thea was rapidly becoming a confirmed ally, he seemed, if not quite on my side, then far from impressed by the eager Jessica. The criss-crossing currents of emotion and motivation made me feel tired. The cold wind kept blowing, with a few drops of rain in it, hitting the side of my face. All the mourners had gone, leaving us, a motley foursome, to bid a final farewell to Mrs Simmonds.

'Oh, for heaven's sake,' burst out Thea, after a moment or two of silence. 'You started this, you sort him out.' She was addressing her daughter. 'Find out where he can get some tyres, and show him how to get there. The whole thing is completely ridiculous, and you know it.' She gazed impatiently at the sky, as if appealing for celestial witnesses. 'Since when did the police become so hopelessly sidetracked by stupid little details like car tyres? No wonder you get so little respect from the public. This is a prime example of where it's all gone wrong.'

Detective Paul cleared his throat warningly, and his eyes widened. He was big, and muscular, filling the blue rugby shirt he wore with bulges that could only come from serious physical power. I imagined him felling a runaway criminal with a forceful tackle that showed no concern for subsequent cuts and bruises.

Jessica's bosom heaved again, and she clenched her lips tightly together, before managing to speak. 'Mr Slocombe, it's up to you what you choose to do next. I'm going to file a report to say I cautioned you about the condition of your vehicle and the failure to show a valid tax disc. If you report to a police station within forty-eight hours, with proof that the tyres have been replaced, that will be enough. No further action will be taken. Do you understand?'

She was polite and calm. I nodded weakly, feeling I'd had a reprieve from a prison sentence. 'Thank you,' I said. 'Do you want me to sign anything?'

'That won't be necessary.'

'Well, goodbye then,' I said, looking hard at Thea Osborne, wondering if I had caused a major family rift, and whether there was anything I could do to mend it. 'Thank you very much. I mean – it was nice to meet you. I'm sorry if I've made you late.'

'It was a very nice funeral,' said Thea gently. 'Dignified but human. Just the sort of thing I'd like to have myself.'

'Oh, God, Mother,' groaned Jessica. 'Don't start on that now.'

Somehow they appeared to have evened things up, to have established a balance between them that was free from animosity. I smiled carefully.

It was close to two o'clock, the burial having begun at twelve-thirty, and somehow the subsequent business having occupied nearly an hour. Nobody had had any lunch, especially me, and my stomach was complaining. The grave was already being discreetly filled in again by the efficient local man, assisted by young Jeremy, and there was absolutely no further reason to stay.

'I'd better get on, then,' I said. 'I've kept you for ages, haven't I? I'm so sorry. You must be hungry by now.'

34

Nobody replied, but Thea met my eye with a little nod of understanding that seemed close to an apology for her daughter. I went back to my delinquent vehicle and climbed in. There was a Mars bar in the glove compartment, and I retrieved it and tore off the paper before trying to start the engine. All I needed was the overzealous police constable to get me for eating while driving. According to Maggs, that was one of the latest batch of misdemeanours you could be stopped for.

The country lanes were confusing, and I forgot to check the map before finally setting off. All I knew was that I needed to head south, and my sense of direction was just about reliable enough to ensure I got that much right. I remembered passing through Stow-on-the-Wold on the way up, so hoped to find a sign directing me back that way, once I'd reached a more major road.

All of a sudden I felt any sense of urgency fall away. Karen was quite capable of collecting the kids from school and giving them their tea. Maggs would handle any phone calls or visits to the office. It was Friday, and although my life hardly followed the normal working pattern, there was still the general air of relaxation, if only because we could forget about school uniforms and packed lunches for a couple of days.

It was over three years since Karen had come home from hospital, pale and fearful after being shot in the head at close range. Nothing vital had been destroyed, and at first the doctors had assured us that her periods of blankness and problems with eating and sleeping were the result of

35

trauma, rather than physical damage. The very fact of her still being alive had carried us through several euphoric weeks. And she did slowly get better, although the lack of appetite persisted and the resultant loss of weight alarmed me. She had always had lovely creamy shoulders and neck, well padded for a child's head to rest on. She had been strong and nurturing, a perfect wife and mother. The new Karen was very different, her efforts to play the same role as before often painful to observe. I watched her self-assessments, whereby she calculated how much energy she had that day, and where the priorities should lie. She tackled everything head-on, from some deep sense of obligation, but there was no joy in her. It took me a long time to see that the euphoria had been all mine, and that my wife was no longer sure about the purpose of being alive.

The only answer she could find to that question lay in the children. Stephanie and Timothy, who had been four and three at the time of her injury, needed her irrefutably.

I decided to stop at a pub for a sandwich and drink before joining the M5 and pressing on home, if I could find one still serving food at that time in the afternoon. A detour on a whim down a small road leading to a village, the name of which I never noticed, took me to a plain-looking hostelry, which offered me a choice of ham or cheese in white or brown. I drank a large quantity of very expensive apple juice, and hoped I could reach home before my bladder started to bother me.

The motorway was busy, it being a Friday after-noon, but nowhere near as bad as it would have been a year or two earlier, before failed busi-nesses, high-priced fuel and general economic gloom took so much commercial traffic off the roads. No longer did people head in their thou-sands for the South-West the moment a nice weekend was promised. Admittedly, this rush had never really gone mad until after Easter, but given the reduction in lorry movements, and the near disappearance of small vans dashing hither and yon on mysterious business, the traffic kept moving very nicely.

Home beckoned strongly on the final stretch. The children would greet me like Irish setters, as if I'd been away for months. Karen would smile and tell me about her day. Maggs would wait in the background, and then fill me in on any dev-elopments. I had never seen myself as a patriarch, but nonetheless, there was a pleasing sense of being absorbed into a world of women and child-ren, all focused on me. The hunter coming home, the returning warrior, the breadwinner with his sack of sustaining goodies over his shoulder.

And so it proved, with only minor deviations. Karen had a headache, which was not unusual, but pained me to witness. Her hair, once thick and tawny, had thinned and faded after the removal of much of it in the hospital. Her suffering head throbbed almost visibly, the crease in her brow suggestive of a heavy weight crushing her crown. Stephanie had lost another tooth, the resulting gap somehow ghastly in my once-perfect little daughter. She and I had enjoyed a close bond from the outset, when Karen returned to teaching and I was setting up the business. My little toddler girl would play calmly in the office while people came to discuss burials. Looking back it felt like an idyll in every respect.

Timothy had been in trouble at school – again. He could never explain his sudden bouts of violence against other children, but we assumed it could only be a legacy of Karen's injury, an inchoate rage against the loss of the trouble-free life we had known in his first years. When I suggested that it might simply be that he was too young to be confined to a classroom and expected to conform to the rules of an institution, no matter how benign, Karen defended the system, from her standing as one-time professional teacher.

I went to my office, to find out how my weary colleague had fared. Maggs had nothing to report, which in itself was a disappointment. She smiled determinedly, and asked about my trip to the Cotswolds.

'I got into trouble with the police,' I said, anticipating her reaction.

She eyed me attentively, her brown face slightly tilted. 'Speeding?' she guessed.

'Nope. I wasn't even in the car at the time.'

'Tyres,' she nodded, pleased with her cleverness. 'I knew they weren't legal.'

'Right. And tax. It was a policewoman, at the funeral. Sort of. Her mother was actually there first, and she came along later, for some reason. With a detective boyfriend.'

'Bummer,' said Maggs carelessly. Like me, she

had a healthy disregard for life's trivialities. The small stuff passed us by where other people seemed to find it desperate. They would fight over who did the washing-up, or whether the toothpaste was in the right configuration. We chose instead to focus on the larger issues of grief at the utter finality that came with death; the future condition of the planet; the obligations we had shouldered in our work and our relationships. Maggs and Karen and I had been a forceful trio when we founded Peaceful Repose, carrying all before us. If Karen and I had grown tireder and older since then, Maggs continued just as before, an indispensable inspiration and support. Even now, after twenty-something hours with no sleep, she was reliably focused.

'It's daft, though,' I persisted. 'When the city centres are impassable and the youth of today are feral monsters, why waste time on model citizens like me?'

'Forget about it,' she advised. 'And have a nice weekend. I'll see you on Monday.'

'Yes ... you too,' I said, never doubting that I would indeed see her on Monday.

I went back to take over from Karen. She had put some potatoes on to boil, but done little else towards preparing us a meal. 'Chops?' I suggested, looking in the freezer.

'If you like.'

'I'll turn the spuds off for a bit, then, or they'll be done too soon.'

'OK.'

I flew around the kitchen, thinking about the

food. I could gather some mint from the garden, and fish some frozen runner beans out for the veg. It was simple, basic stuff, which Karen could have done standing on her head before she was injured. Now she so easily lost focus, so that peeling and boiling potatoes could seem to her all that was required for a family meal. We had often sat down to unadorned pasta, or a large quantity of grilled bacon with nothing to go with it. I had quickly learnt to have instant sauces, frozen peas, tins of beans and sweetcorn and soup stacked in the cupboards ready to add to Karen's partial meals. I had also acquired a microwave oven, despite a strong resistance to that sort of cooking. Karen and I had been united in choosing a simple life-style, with slow cooking, home-grown vegetables, minimal use of technology. It went with the ethos of the business, after all. But much of that had changed over the past three years. The world itself was in deep confusion over the demands of the environment, the global recession, the price of oil – the word *ecological* had begun to seem old-fashioned, along with *alternative* and even *organic*. *My* children were catching up with the digital age, while Karen and I struggled to cling to the ideology that had been so important to us.

After the meal, I put the children to bed. They shared a room, and I read them a story sitting on the edge of Stephanie's bed. It was a chapter of *The Jenius* by Dick King-Smith, an old favourite of my daughter's. But I noticed that it was Timmy who listened more intently, laughing at the witticisms, his eyes fixed on my face as I read.

'What are we going to do tomorrow?' Stephanie

40

asked me as I tucked her in.

'I don't know. What do you want to do?'

'Go swimming!' shouted Timmy.

Stephanie and I both groaned theatrically. Timmy's passion for water was inexplicable to us both. Trips to the local swimming pool were strictly limited to times when it was inescapably Timmy's turn to choose what we did. Karen carefully monitored the fairness of such decisions.

'Not your turn,' said Stephanie emphatically.

'Yes it is.'

'We went swimming last weekend,' I said. 'And you lost your rucksack – remember?'

It was chastening to see how his face fell. 'Oh, Tim,' I said. 'Don't worry. It's the holidays next week – we'll go swimming *three times*, I promise.'

'Daddy!' protested Stephanie. 'That's too much.'

'Maggs can take me,' my little boy suggested. 'She *likes* swimming.'

It wasn't true. Maggs had no more fondness for the noisy, chlorine-imbued atmosphere of the local baths than I did. But she liked Timmy, and put herself out for him as she had never done for his sister. Maggs, more than anybody, had noticed how badly Timmy had been cheated by the injury to his mother, and had swiftly, unobtrusively, done her best to fill the gap. The bond between them was seldom openly acknowledged by any of us. It was simply taken for granted as one element in our lives.

'Don't bank on it, Tim,' I cautioned. 'She's only just got back from holiday, and she'll have a lot to do. I think we'll just have a lazy weekend. We could go for a walk and see if we can find catkins

41

and sticky buds.'

Neither child manifested any enthusiasm for my suggestion.

Chapter Three

It was nine-thirty on Saturday morning when a sharp rap sounded on the front door. We almost didn't hear it because Timothy was shouting and Stephanie had the TV on far too loud.

A policeman stood there, and I sighed impatiently. 'For heaven's sake,' I snapped. 'Give me a chance.'

'Mr Slocombe?' he asked calmly.

'Yes, yes. Look, I'll get the tyres replaced today, OK? There's no need for all this harassment.'

'Sir, this is not about tyres. It concerns a burial in Gloucestershire yesterday. I understand that you were responsible for it.'

'What? Yes. Mrs Simmonds. So what?'

'There has been a complaint, sir. From the council. They contacted the police with a view to pressing charges.'

My impatience escalated. This was familiar territory. 'The burial was entirely legal,' I told him. 'The council has no jurisdiction over what was done. Believe me, I know my rights on this. It's my business, after all.'

'The council owns the land, sir. You have committed a trespass.' His face relaxed a little as he heard his own words. 'Quite an unusual trespass

42

at that,' he added.

My mind was racing. 'But it's too late,' I protested. 'You can't just move a grave once it's been established. There's nothing to be done now.' I suspected that I knew the law on this matter better than this officer did. 'There'd have to be an application to the Home Office for exhumation. Nobody does that lightly.' Indeed, such a procedure was the stuff of nightmares – literally. It was one of my greatest dreads.

'We need you to explain that to the man from the council,' he agreed. 'He might listen to you.' His expression suggested that this was unlikely, and I sighed.

'So I'm not under arrest, then?'

'Trespass is not a criminal offence, sir. But the ... well, *delicate* nature of this case means we would prefer for you to come and talk it through with Mr Maynard, face-to-face. Get the whole matter settled quietly.'

A suspicion struck me. 'He wants us to *pay* for it – is that what you're saying? He'll leave the grave undisturbed if we pay some sort of rent for the land?'

'Not for me to say, sir.'

I was inwardly cursing myself from the moment of the revelation that the land had not belonged to Mrs Simmonds. It had not occurred to me to ask for proof of ownership, which seemed idiotically sloppy, in retrospect, although Mrs Simmonds had clearly said the field was hers. She had deceived me, I realised, with a sickening sense of having been betrayed. If she had admitted that there was the slightest chance of local council involvement, I would have refused to accede to her wishes. The first rule of one-off natural burials in anything other than a cemetery or churchyard was – Don't Tell The Council. Don't ask their permission, don't casually phone them to check that it's all right with them. Leave them out of it. Generally speaking, burials fell under the jurisdiction of the Parks and Recreation Department, often headed by an earnest little jobsworth who would seize this deviation from the usual run of daily paperwork with relish. Mythical regulations about waterways and notifiable diseases would surface and proliferate until any chance of conducting the proposed burial vanished under the weight of obfuscation. There would have to be specialist reports on the density of the soil, the potential consequences for rare moths or molluscs, the appalling difficulties involved in parking eight or ten vehicles on the roadside for the funeral, delaying everything so drastically that the proposal could only be abandoned.

And the law was, in effect, on our side. Once the burial was accomplished, it was pretty well permanent. Retrospective complaints could safely be ignored. Usually. The fact that this land was unconsecrated meant an exhumation could be more readily carried out than if the grave had been in a churchyard, although it would still be a serious procedure, with any amount of paperwork. I became aware of a dawning collection of doubts. I had made a mistake, a gaffe, and was already quailing inwardly at the potential consequences.

The police did not drive me to Broad Campden

44

in a locked car with a stout female officer beside me. They let me go by myself, in a car with expired road tax and bald tyres. The man on my doorstep insisted I had to go and hear what Mr Maynard had to say. 'He said he'd meet you by the grave at eleven-thirty. I think that gives you plenty of time, doesn't it?'

'Can't I just phone him?' I pleaded.

'Sorry.' He shook his head.

'It's Saturday. Why isn't he at home planting potatoes?'

A shrug suggested that I was wasting time for both of us. 'All right,' I conceded, as if I had a choice. 'Let me go and tell my wife.'

Karen took it serenely. 'What a pain,' she said. 'When will you be back?'

I visualised the tedious drive, an hour and a half each way. 'Hard to say,' I replied. 'But definitely long before dark.' Darkness fell at about seven, the equinox less than a week away.

The children had no plans for the weekend. They would watch too much television, but also play with the chaotic jumble of toys in their bedroom, Stephanie herding her Playmobil figures on and off the brick trains that Timothy fashioned for them. Karen might read to them or organise some cutting and sticking, or drawing. Or she might not. They were unlikely to go outside, any of them. Karen had once grown most of our vegetables, but somehow that had all withered away since her injury. If I had been at home, I might have taken them on a walk by the old canal, watching the nesting birds and pointing out the new spring flowers. My mother had done the same for me and it must have been in the blood.

So I drove all the way back to Broad Campden, where the council officer had arranged to meet me, the police liaising between us in a way I found surprising. Until, that is, I realised that they hoped this would see the end of their involvement. From their point of view, I was the best chance of calming the whole thing down, and leaving poor Mrs Simmonds where she was.

Mr Maynard was waiting for me, standing in the gateway to the field, on the spot where policewoman Jessica had planted herself in order to chastise me about my car. The associations were unfortunate, rendering me more defensive than was useful. A strong wind – even stronger than the day before – was blowing, ruffling my hair and providing an irritating background noise as it swirled through the surrounding trees. I spotted one magpie, riding a wind-tossed branch with apparent enjoyment.

'So!' the man from the council began with an air of infuriating triumph. 'This is Mr Drew Slocombe, is it?' The invisible third person to whom he appealed said nothing.

'Good morning,' I said, refraining from offering him a hand to shake. 'I gather there's a problem.'

He was a weedy man, with a round head on which the hair had receded to an oily semicircle. His eyes were small and round, his chin unobtrusive. But his mouth was fleshy, his lips damp. 'This is a *travesty*,' he shrilled at me. 'A travesty!' He waved an outraged arm towards the grave. I had to admit it was a good word.

46

'I don't really think so,' I said mildly. 'It was what she wanted.'

'Without any consultation, without due care to ascertain ownership of the land,' he accused. 'You simply took her word for it, and went on your own selfish way, out to make money from a foolish woman's whim.'

He had combined the most pertinent point with a fatuous and offensive imputation. It meant I had to take him seriously and not seriously at the same time, which very much threw me off balance.

'I don't think Mrs Simmonds was foolish,' I said. 'She had a fine regard for the environment, and her own clear values. She faced up to her own mortality, which I found admirable.' It was a clunky little speech, and I was not proud of it. There had been a time when I addressed groups about natural burials, with some impressive rhetoric.

'The land was not hers,' he shouted, bringing his face close to mine. 'You have committed a definite trespass on council property.' We were standing a few feet inside the field, thirty or forty yards from the grave itself. I had the impression that Mr Maynard was reluctant to go any closer, that the mere fact of it made him nervous. He wasn't unique in that, of course, but it did nothing to increase my scant respect for him.

'So I am now given to understand, although I imagine it was a genuine mistake. I presume she must have rented it? In fact, I'm sure she thought she had the right to use it as she did. I gather she inherited the house years ago, but only moved here fairly recently. She must have been told the land went with it in some way, even though it's so far from the house.' Why couldn't I just say it straight? *She must have thought it was OK to be buried here.* Instead I went on the attack. 'Are you perfectly sure it belongs to the council? It seems very odd to me. After all, if Mrs Simmonds had been paying rent on it, she would know it wasn't hers to do as she liked with.'

'Yes, of course I am. I know all the details, thank you very much.'

'Then it must have been a misunderstanding. Age-old usage, missing paperwork – that sort of thing.'

'That is not the point. The *point* is, the land is now valueless. Useless.'

My heart gave a lurch out of all proportion to his actual words. I had managed to convince myself during the drive up to the Cotswolds that whatever happened, I would not be personally liable, but now that the conversation was turning to economics, things began to feel scary. 'Well...' I began, not knowing what I meant to say, 'well, I don't think there was any need to involve the police. There are various things we can do, if we think about it calmly. You could fence off the grave, and put the rest of the field to whatever use you want.' Besides, I wanted to add, it is a very *little* field. Barely two acres, I would guess.

'But it's *sick*,' he blurted. 'Insensitive and disgusting and sacrilegious. A travesty,' he repeated, for good measure.

'No,' I argued, finally on firmer ground. 'It is none of those things. It's perfectly normal and

48

natural, and if you have a problem in acknowledging the basic facts of death and decomposition, then I feel sorry for you.'

His beady eyes narrowed and the lips grew even wetter. 'Mind what you say,' he warned. 'You have not heard the end of this. I intend to apply for an exhumation order, with all costs awarded against you, Mr Slocombe. You personally.'

'Don't be ridiculous,' I said. 'You petty little man. Haven't you got anything better to do with your time than interfere in something you don't even begin to understand? Can't you see this for what it is? An innocent mistake was made, and nobody loses by it. I can't believe you received very much in rent for this scrap of land. In fact, if it was properly investigated, I wouldn't be surprised to find she paid you nothing at all. After Mrs Simmonds' mother died, I just bet you forgot all about it, and never collected any rent.' A thought struck me. 'And how did you find out about the burial so quickly?'

'One of the mourners telephoned yesterday afternoon,' he said, looking rather pale at my attack. 'They were worried about the legalities, as well as the sheer lack of dignity in the whole sordid business.'

I knew it wasn't worth arguing any further with him. If he saw a simple natural burial in a small Cotswold field as sordid, there was no hope for him.

But the argument was not entirely within my control. 'So?' he went on, quickly reviving. 'The situation is completely unacceptable. What do you propose to do about it?'

'Me? Nothing whatsoever. It's too late to do anything. Besides, it's not up to me, is it?'

'It most certainly is. Either you reimburse the council for the full market value of this property, or we take the whole business to a higher authority. Personally, I want this abomination removed immediately.'

Higher authority always meant God to my ears. If Mr Maynard proposed to consult the Almighty, I didn't think I had much to worry about. Quite obviously, God was on my side, even if it had been a secular funeral.

I snorted sarcastically, which wasn't very wise of me. The man from the council had no tolerance at all for being mocked. The wind continued to blow, buffeting us quite violently at times, before pausing to recoup its strength. We were partly sheltered by the hedge, but such was the force of the gale that it got into every corner of the little field, a separate entity that seemed to involve itself in our argument. The entire conversation had taken place with raised voices, which had the effect of making everything more aggressive than it might otherwise have been. A few minutes later, it occurred to me that we could have been heard by anybody standing on the road, or on the other side of the hedge in the scrappy woodland adjacent to the field. If not our actual words, then the fact of raised voices and confrontational stances would have plainly revealed a serious disagreement was under way. At the time, that didn't worry me at all, and it certainly didn't worry Mr Maynard.

'Oh!' His minimal chin reared itself to its full

extent. 'Oh, so you think this is funny, do you? I can assure you, Mr Slocombe, it is very far from amusing.' I waited for him to say *travesty* again, but he disappointed me. 'You are so patently in the wrong that words fail me,' he sneered. 'I can see we're getting nowhere here. There will be a letter from our solicitors in the post first thing on Monday.'

'It won't do you any good,' I retorted hotly. 'Do what you like, you won't get any money out of me. You might try Mrs Simmonds' family, although I very much doubt that you'd have much luck. Give it up, Mr Maynard. It isn't worth the taxpayers' hard-earned cash, for a tiny patch of land you'd forgotten all about until now.' A new thought occurred to me. 'Besides, you'll probably find that she had squatters' rights over it, anyway, if she'd been using it for more than seven years.' I was on doubtful ground here, but knew vaguely there was some such rule.

'Twelve,' he snapped. 'It's twelve. And she would have to be able to prove constant usage through-out that time. In any case, she *was* paying rent, which means she knew for a certainty that she was not the outright owner of the field.'

'Difficult,' I agreed, with another reckless smile. Somewhere in the past thirty seconds I had opted to fight openly for Mrs Simmonds and her chosen burial spot. Something inside me had clicked into battle mode, and I was feeling good about it. 'Let the best man win, then, as they say.'

'You'll regret this,' he warned loudly. 'I'm going to make you very sorry you ever got involved.'

'And let me tell you,' I said, even louder, finally

51

losing my temper, 'that I don't intend to let you win. People like you don't deserve to have any authority; you understand nothing about what really matters. You should all be swept away, if you want my honest opinion.'

We had begun to move back to the road by this time. At my parting shot, Mr Maynard had already turned his back and begun to march stiffly off, in a northerly direction, towards the village of Broad Campden. A car came towards us and slowed to a halt beside my vehicle.

'What's all this, then?' came a voice I recognised.

I turned to meet the enquiring gaze of Police Officer Jessica Osborne who, if anything, appeared to like me even less than she had done the day before.

Chapter Four

I made it worse for myself by sighing, 'What on earth are *you* doing here?' It seemed a reasonable question at the time.

'I don't have to explain myself to you,' she snapped. 'Besides, I should be asking you that question. I thought you'd gone back to Somerset.' Really, I said to myself, this was one very unfriendly girl. What had I done to deserve such disapprobation? Then I remembered my illegal car, and felt a small but real panic. However decent and competent a person you might be, there was no redress against police harassment. They could do exactly what they liked to you, so long as it didn't leave too nasty a mark.

'There's a problem about this field and who owns it,' I explained, tilting my chin to indicate the receding figure of Mr Maynard. 'That's a man from the council, who summoned me back here to be informed that the whole business has been a travesty. But I really don't think there's any need for you to get involved.' As before, she was not in uniform, but dressed in a red sweat-shirt. When she got out of the car I saw she also sported a pair of black jeans. She really was nothing at all like her mother.

And why *was* she there, anyway? There was no sign of the detective boyfriend.

'Hmm,' she said, unhelpfully. 'I did wonder.'

'Pardon?'

'I wondered how legal this burial was. Mum assured me you should know your own business, and there couldn't possibly be anything dodgy about it.' She looked at me with a false innocence that I found extremely irritating, but at least she wasn't quite so hostile as she'd been at the start.

'There's nothing illegal about it,' I said. 'At worst it's a trespass. That stupid idiot is overreacting, as they generally do. It's a pity, though,' I admitted, running a hand through my hair. 'If only for Mrs Simmonds' sake. Anyway, I have to go. This was a very inconvenient interruption, driving a hundred and twenty miles for a ten-minute argument. The whole thing could have been done by phone.' The enormity of it hit me for the first time, causing a wave of rage against the infuriating council official.

53

'It's outrageous,' I spluttered.

'You can't just turn round and go straight home again,' she said, with a much softer tone. 'You'd better come back to the house with me, and have some lunch or something.'

I blinked. Was this the same bossy young police officer I thought I knew? 'Well...' I prevaricated. 'I shouldn't, really. If I get cracking, I can be home again soon after one.'

'Up to you,' she shrugged. 'We're probably leaving this afternoon, as well. But you ought to have a look at the village, first. It's really interesting. Paul and I walked around it after breakfast, and now I'm off for a look at Blockley.'

'On your own?'

She shrugged. 'Paul isn't very interested. I know Blockley, you see,' she added. 'I stayed there with my mum, just about a year ago.'

She was confiding in me against her better nature, the way people often did. I was good at simply absorbing revelations and vague musings like this. I watched her face, which had relaxed and softened as she spoke. 'A man was murdered,' she went on. 'I hadn't realised until today how close the two places are. You could walk from here to Blockley and back in barely an hour.'

I reminded myself of why I was there. Mr Maynard had marched off, his head bent against the wind, and I wondered why he had no visible car to drive away in. Did he perhaps live in Broad Campden? I felt quite glad that he had not stayed to include Jessica in our confrontation.

'No,' I decided. 'I really think I ought to head for home.'

'Up to you,' she conceded. 'But I think I'll leave Blockley for another time. I might go and have a proper look at your grave instead, now it's been filled in.'

As I opened the driver's door of my car I remembered again that there was history between Officer Jessica and my humble motor. Keeping my back to her, I waited for the heavy hand, the stern words. They never came. When I glanced back, she had gone into the field, and was disappearing towards the grave, which we had very considerately tucked into a corner out of sight of the road. I got in quickly, and started the engine.

But something held me back, and I switched it off again. Was I simply going to drive all that tedious way home, with nothing resolved? Mr Maynard would be true to his word, despatching legal threats to me at Peaceful Repose, and disturbing my serenity for the following weeks and months. Wouldn't it be better to face up to the situation now, and try to get it settled? And where better to start than with an officer of the law, who might yet lend a helpful word, if I managed not to alienate her any further?

I got out of the car and waited, watching the wind tossing the tops of the leafless trees, thinking how typically March it was and finding some small consolation in the cycle of the seasons and the bigger picture. It seemed a long time before Jessica came back, but was probably less than five minutes. 'Still here?' she asked me, unnecessarily.

'I don't suppose you know Mr Maynard from Parks and Recreation, do you?'

She stared at me blankly. 'Of course not. How

would I?'

'No ... silly question. I just thought, as you were in Blockley recently ... well, you might have come across him somehow. He was phoned by one of the mourners at yesterday's funeral,' I went on. 'And he wasted no time in causing trouble. He's one of those people you feel should never have been born. It's impossible to imagine him doing any good in the world.' I was speaking as much to myself as to her, venting my spleen with no sense of caution.

Jessica fixed me with a clear greeny-brown gaze. 'You can't say that about anybody,' she told me seriously. 'That's a fascist remark.'

'I know,' I said. 'It indicates the strength of my antipathy towards him. You should have heard the things *he* said.'

'I can imagine how it might have been. Council officers do tend to miss the point at times.' She smiled at me, and for the first time I caught a flash of her mother in her. 'It's a nice grave,' she added, and I felt she'd awarded me some kind of major Brownie point.

'Thanks,' I said.

'It'll be a shame if they have to disinter her. Although...' she looked thoughtful, 'it might be interesting to observe, I suppose. If they did it soon, it wouldn't be particularly gruesome.'

'It wouldn't be soon, though,' I said. 'Even if I didn't put up a fight – and I will – the paperwork would take ages.'

'You're just like my mum,' she sighed. 'Always looking for a fight. It's people like you...' She didn't finish, but just threw me a dark look that conjured street protests and fathers for justice climbing up public buildings and causing embarrassment. I had heard the police viewpoint before, and was seldom tempted to sympathise.

'Speaking of your mum,' I said, 'is she still at Mrs Simmonds' house?'

'Yeah. She doesn't like to leave until she knows who's responsible for it, although I told her she ought to go home today. They've already turned the phone off, and the electric's likely to go at any moment. She says she was booked until this time next week, so she doesn't have anywhere else she needs to be, and she might as well stay on for a few more days. The fact is, she'll do anything to avoid going home.'

'Oh?'

'Mm. My father died three years ago, and she lives in the same cottage – the one I grew up in. She won't admit it, but I think the memories are still bothering her a bit too much for comfort. She's been doing this house-sitting lark for a couple of years, and never seems to get sick of it. She's got the dog, of course.' It was a disjointed bit of explication, but I thought I'd got the basic picture.

'Dog?' I said.

'Hepzibah. It's a cocker spaniel.'

'And people let her take it with her when she's looking after their houses?'

'Evidently. She specialises in looking after pets, and Hepzie's very easy-going. She gets along with most things. The worst was a parrot in Lower Slaughter, apparently. And there was a nasty moment with a snake at one point. Usually it's

57

dogs and cats, and she's fine. Mum can sweet-talk people into agreeing to anything, if she sets her mind to it. You wouldn't expect anyone to ever hire her again, the things that keep happening, but they seem to think it'll just make her all the more capable. That's if they get to hear her history, of course. I don't think this Simmonds woman knew about any of it.'

'Sounds intriguing,' I said, my head full of exotic animals and mysterious goings-on. I also noted that once again Jessica was confiding in me.

'Please come and have lunch with us,' she invited, again. 'I was probably a bit out of order about the car yesterday.'

I suspected her mother had been giving her a telling-off about it, and she was hoping to earn forgiveness by being nice to me, now she had a second chance. I had little sense that she approved of me any more than before, but the persistence of her invitation impressed me.

'Oh, all right then,' I said, pushing aside all thought of Karen and the kids missing out on my company.

She turned her car around first, waiting while I did the same, and then leading me a surprisingly short distance to a picture-book thatched cottage facing onto a quiet lane, a few yards off the main street of the village. Through the bare trees behind the house, I could glimpse the land sweeping downhill in a grand slope, with a classic farmstead at the bottom. As I got out of the car, Thea Osborne opened the front door and stood there, the sun on her face, looking young and pretty and cheerful.

58

She was obviously astonished to see me, as I squeezed my car into a space behind Jessica's, tilting her head in wordless enquiry. A dog came past her, trotting towards us, a long plumy tail held out horizontally behind, and sniffed my legs as I emerged from the car. I bent to pat its soft head. 'Shouldn't cockers have docked tails?' I asked, stupidly, trying to work out what looked wrong about the animal.

Neither woman answered me, but Thea rolled her eyes as if I'd said something annoying.

'I found him arguing with a man from the council about the new grave,' Jessica explained briefly. 'He'd been summoned back here to answer some questions. I asked him to join us for lunch.'

Thea grimaced in an exaggerated wince of sympathy, but said nothing. I remembered the detective boyfriend, who was probably around somewhere. What was I doing here, I suddenly asked myself? I'd walked into something I wasn't prepared for, on a number of levels. I had not been adequately prepared for Mrs Simmonds' funeral, to begin with. Nor the attentions of the police when it came to my delinquent car. Nor the fury of Maynard-from-the-council. Nor the sweet smiles of Thea Osborne. I felt myself floundering. 'I ought to phone Karen,' I said, to nobody in particular, having consulted my watch and found it was already five to twelve. 'She'll be wondering when to expect me.'

'Your wife,' said Thea, with a little nod. 'The phone's been turned off, and my mobile's with the wrong outfit, apparently. I can't get a signal without going up a hill.'

Jessica threw her mother an exasperated look. 'Why don't you use the Blackberry I gave you?' she demanded. 'That would work here. You should throw that old thing away.'

'I will,' Thea promised with a disarming smile. 'I did mean to, but I forgot to bring it. It'll take a while for me to get used to it.'

We tried my phone, and found that Thea was right about the signal. I looked round at the scenery, wondering where I could go for better reception, since it was clear that the police officer had no intention of lending me her mobile. 'Have I got time to walk up there?' I asked, pointing across the road. 'There seems to be a footpath going that way.' The path led alongside a very substantial brand-new house built of yellow Cotswold stone that I thought warranted a closer inspection.

'No problem,' said Thea. 'And when you come back, we can all go to the pub.'

And that meant spending money, I realised with a silent groan. Perhaps, after all, I should simply go home and do my best never to revisit Broad Campden.

I walked down the little lane and emerged quite soon onto rising ground. Looking back, I got a fine view of the new house, as well as another one of similar age, further along. I tried to imagine life in this tiny settlement, where people could afford to live in mansions with electrically operated wrought-iron gates, and pay a gardener to keep the topiary under control. The views were of tilted fields, bare hedges and leafless trees. Overhead, the clouds were being shredded by the wind.

There was no sound of traffic, or voices or dogs. Even without the wind, I suspected the place would lack all the usual noise of normal life.

I had to walk to the very top of the field before my phone would work. I called Karen, who sounded distracted, even though she assured me the children were fine, and her headache had gone. 'Oh, but Maggs wants you,' she remembered. 'There's been a call from somebody in a nursing home.'

Aha! Here was my excuse to skip the pub lunch. I could easily plead sudden urgent work, with Maggs unable to remove a body by herself. But first I ought to phone her, to check that Karen had the right story. It wasn't certain that anyone had died at all.

Maggs did not answer her mobile, so I left a message and then waited on the hillside to see if she would call back. It was no hardship, on that sunny March day, to do nothing for a few minutes. The wind was quite violent, apparently having shifted to the south or west, since there was no longer the easterly chill in it, and I enjoyed a sense of exhilaration as it tossed my hair about and swished the treetops. The hedge that ran alongside me sported patches of celandines and violets and the grass had begun to grow at the base. I meandered aimlessly as I used the phone, straying along the edge of a narrow piece of woodland. Strange little towns with names like Chipping Campden and Blockley and Paxford were scattered about within a mile or two – places I had never seen and which conjured another world where prosperous medieval Englishmen strolled

61

down the main streets haggling over the price of wool. Just to my right somewhere was Mrs Simmonds' grave, although I had lost my bearings so completely that I was far from sure of the direction or distance.

Maggs took just over five minutes to get back to me. 'Where are you?' she asked, before I could put the same question.

'In a sloping field, on the edge of some very nice woods, in a tiny Cotswolds village,' I said. 'Where are you?'

'In a lay-by, on the way to Ottery St Mary. Remember Mr Everscott?'

'He died?' We had both liked Mr Everscott, who was ninety-three and wanted to cause the least possible disturbance by his death. He had hated being in the nursing home, where they spoke baby talk to him and teased him simply because he was the only male. It was a small place, decently run, but nothing could make him like it.

'Yes, and they want him removed right away. I said I was on my own, and they said they've got somebody there to help me.'

'He's not very big,' I remembered. 'But you shouldn't have to go by yourself.' For the second time in two days I was reminded of the plentiful staff at the undertaker where I had formerly worked. There had always been a team on standby, ready for just such a call.

'But I've got the car!' I remembered. 'How are you going to manage?'

'Den let me have his, with the trailer, but he says it's just this once and I can't have it again.' Den Cooper drove a two-door Yaris, into which a dead body could in no way be fitted. But a trailer!

I groaned. 'Maggs – we can't remove him in a trailer. That's awful. What are you thinking of?'

'No, it's fine,' she promised. 'It's got a proper cover, and is just long enough. I don't know why we didn't think of it before.'

'Somebody's going to have to help you get him in. It won't be dignified. They'll tell the opposition and we'll be a laughing stock.'

'Drew!' she interrupted. 'Trust me. It's fine. Stop agonising. I'll make a virtue of it. It can be part of our image.'

The only image that I could come up with was of the cover blowing off the trailer on the dual carriageway, and poor Mr Everscott finding himself bowling along the road like a tree trunk lost from a timber truck.

'No,' I said. 'It can't. You can do it this once, if you're very careful, but never *ever* again.'

'That's what Den said,' she replied dolefully. Then she cheered up. 'Why are you in the Cotswolds again, anyway? Did something go wrong?'

'You could say that. I'll tell you all about it when I see you. Meanwhile, I'm going to have lunch in a pub with a nice lady. Two ladies, actually, and probably a man as well. And a spaniel, I expect.'

'Lucky you. But that doesn't explain why you're in a field.'

'Signal problems,' I said shortly. 'It's lovely here,' I elaborated, looking around again at the landscape. 'Very Cotswoldy. Mrs Simmonds' house has got a fabulous thatched roof.'

'Thatch isn't typical of the Cotswolds,' Maggs told me.

'How in the world do you know that?' It was a daft question – Maggs knew a million pieces of trivia like this. She seemed to absorb them through her skin, because I never saw her reading.

'I just know,' she said, as always. 'But there are a few villages that buck the trend – you must be in one of them.'

'I suppose I must,' I agreed. 'Well, I should let you get on. Pop in and see Karen when you get back, OK? She had a headache yesterday.'

'I won't be back for hours, probably. It's a fair old way, you know. When are you getting home?'

'I doubt if I'll be able to rush this lunch, but I'll try to leave by two, and be back around three-thirty.'

'Hmm,' she said, in her uniquely Maggsian manner. 'Sounds as if you like it there.'

'It's Saturday,' I defended.

'Right, and your poor wife's got to entertain two kids all day. Just like a man.'

I remembered Timmy's hope that Maggs might take him swimming, but refrained from mentioning it. It was bad enough that she'd been called out on a Saturday, when she must have a thousand things to do at home. 'So what's Den doing?' I asked, instead.

'He's still catching up with sleep, but this afternoon he's doing the garden,' she said. 'Digging out buttercups, I think.'

'Go!' I ordered. 'No more chit-chat.'

Her answering snort was perfectly reasonable, I acknowledged. I knew I had a bad habit of staying too long on the phone, somehow not liking to sever the fragile link between myself and the other person.

I found a gateway onto the road, went up to the junction at the top and turned right, my mind on Mr Everscott and the most likely day for his burial. Maggs and Den were more than I deserved, I reflected, not for the first time. They put their weekends aside when the business demanded, sacrificing normal married life without a murmur. Den's suggestion of the trailer was typical – his practical nature would quickly identify the solution to the problem of Mr Everscott. He had been a police constable when I first met him, but had resigned shortly before Karen's shooting, for reasons I never entirely grasped. His romance with Maggs had been sweet to watch, their wedding, only a few months earlier, a triumph of originality. The trip to Syria had been a kind of delayed honeymoon. Karen was already predicting an imminent announcement that a new little Cooper was on its way – but somehow I had my doubts. Maggs might be fond of my Timmy, but children in general appeared to leave her cold. I also selfishly dreaded such a distraction. As a mother, Maggs could not possibly hope to be such a reliable colleague in the business as she currently was.

My route back to the cottage seemed further than I expected, which turned out to be because I was going in the wrong direction. I'd reached an unfamiliar row of houses, the road dipping downhill, and swung round, trotting back in a state of embarrassment.

'Where on earth have you been?' asked Thea Osborne, when I eventually got back to where my car sat outside Mrs Simmonds' cottage.

'Sorry,' I panted. 'Have I made us late?'

'You've been more than half an hour,' Jessica accused. 'We didn't know what to do.'

I didn't like to admit my stupidity, so shrugged and mumbled something about needing to sort something out at home. My idea of skipping the lunch and going back right away seemed to have evaporated. With a new funeral coming along, I would be more solvent than expected – enough to afford a pub lunch, so long as I didn't have to treat everybody.

We turned right at the main street, walking in an untidy group, Thea's dog straining at the lead, dragging her ahead of the others. The boyfriend was with us, as expected. Paul something – Middleman, I remembered after a few minutes – was young and relaxed, smiling a lot and giving Jessica fond glances. Twenty years earlier, he would have been horribly aware of sharp looks coming his way from locals, an alien in this impeccably white English village; but now he strolled easily along – just as Maggs would have done, skin colour a matter of utter irrelevance.

Maggs was mixed race, adopted out to a sensible couple in Plymouth, who raised her to ignore all issues of skin colour. No nonsense about culture or heritage for them – they simply cherished her for the amazing person she was, and shrugged away the ignorant and unkind remarks sometimes made by schoolmates. This Paul was very much blacker than Maggs, but he appeared to have arrived at the same confident attitude to life and I found myself liking him for this reason alone.

Because, I was slowly beginning to realise, there were not many other reasons to like him. He talked about a stag party he had recently been invited to, where monumental quantities of alcohol had been consumed, and the groom had been left tied to some railings outside his grand-mother's house, stark naked. Paul thought that was funny. I found myself musing on the differences between men – the cads versus the decent blokes, in the lingo of the Thirties. It was not a new topic for me, and as usual I came to the conclusion that you were formed by the sort of women there were in your life. A good woman could rehabilitate the most dreadful bounder, given a chance. But that didn't explain why the decent ones remained decent, even if harnessed to a sarcastic nagging slut. That, presumably, was down to their mother, who sowed the seeds of right thinking so firmly they could never be uprooted.

I found myself catching the eye of Thea as she turned her head to see if we were keeping up with her. She had listened quietly to Paul's story, re-vealing nothing in the back view she kept to us as she trotted along, but somehow I knew she hadn't liked it. Jessica had giggled in the right places, for which nobody could really blame her.

Now, in Thea's eyes, I saw my own feelings re-flected. For good measure, she rolled them upwards in the universal sign of scorn, but she hadn't needed to do that. I had already decided that she was a kindred spirit, the previous day. I did something I couldn't remember ever having done before, and winked at her, wondering how she would take it. Her answering grin came as a relief.

We walked about half a mile to the Baker's Arms, passing several beautiful buildings on the way. A long, low one on the right, calling itself the Old Malt House, was a very upmarket guest house, according to the sign. Then a small fairy-tale church, opposite a high wall topped by a hedge with birds and other things created out of its greenery. The pub came next, on the right. We all filed in, only to be told that dogs were not permitted in the bar. Crossly, Thea led us to a chilly little arrangement outside, just beyond the kitchen, where some sort of creeper provided a bit of shelter. 'It'd be lovely in June,' said Jessica.

Thea ranted briefly about society's ridiculous change of heart concerning dogs. I paid a visit to the loo, pausing to admire a large wall hanging depicting the pub. 'Distinctive,' I murmured to the woman behind the bar. 'Is it a tapestry?'

'It's actually a rug,' she said wearily. 'A local woman made it for us, ages ago.'

It then turned out that credit cards were not acceptable, so we had an undignified scramble for cash, with Paul producing a meagre sixty-five pence. 'I don't really do cash,' he said, as if it were an obsolete practice. I emptied my pockets, managing to produce enough for myself and a little bit over.

Finally we got the food, which I spoilt for myself by a growing feeling that I should not be there. I should be at home, dealing with family and business, garden and car tyres – not indulging in this strange interlude with people I was never going to see again. We spoke briefly about the grave and its transgressions against the council, but Thea waved my worries away with an airy dismissal of petty bureaucracy. 'They're just trying it on,' she said. Jessica tried to put the official view, but was out of her depth when it came to the legalities. I knew a lot more than she did on the subject, but refrained from making this too apparent.

Another person with pressing worries was Thea. 'I was booked to stay here for another week,' she said. 'And now I don't know what to do. They tell me the house belongs to the older nephew now, Charles Talbot, but he doesn't seem interested. He hadn't seen Greta for five years, and he's in the middle of a horrible divorce. I couldn't get a straight answer out of him when I asked what I ought to do.'

'Have you been paid?' I asked.

She shook her head. 'That's another thing,' she said.

'Well of course you should pack up and go,' said Jessica. 'If you don't even know whether you'll be paid, it's crazy to stay on.'

'Except it's rather nice here,' I commented. 'You could see it as a free holiday, I suppose.'

'Right!' she agreed fervently. 'Especially as they say the weather's going to pull itself together.'

'Don't you get lonely?' I asked rashly, imagining the solitary vigils in the various houses she was commissioned to take care of. 'The days must seem long at times.'

'I do in some places,' she admitted. 'But only in

69

short bursts. There are always animals to look after, and Hepzie's good company. And people come to visit.' She smiled at her daughter. I noticed she did not include Paul in her smile, and wondered if this was his punishment for the distasteful little story he'd just told, or whether she had a deeper animosity towards him.

'Well, you'll do as you like,' said Jessica, more in calm acceptance than any kind of huff. This was not a daughter who felt she should control her widowed mother's life, I suspected.

'Of course I will,' said Thea. 'Doesn't everybody? What else would I do?'

'The right thing,' chipped in Paul, crassly. 'Follow the rules.'

'With some people, it's the same,' I could not resist saying. 'I mean, what they want to do *is* the right thing.' I looked at Thea, and clamped down on the obvious remark that she was one of those people.

'That's Mum,' laughed Jessica, with a swift look at her boyfriend. 'But in this particular case, there's no clear rule to follow. Is there?'

It fizzled out at that point, with Paul ordering another pint, and Jessica resignedly foregoing any alcohol at all because she was to be the driver on their journey back to Manchester.

'I must go,' I said, without moving. 'Duty calls.' I threw Paul a conciliatory glance, which he ignored. 'I hadn't planned to come up here again today.'

'I still don't understand why you had to come back in person,' said Thea. 'You could surely have talked to the council man on the phone?'

'Throwing his weight around, that's all,' I said. 'You're quite right – it could easily have been done on the phone. He didn't even have a proper look at the grave.'

'Will they really get you to move the body?' Paul queried, with some relish.

'They might try.'

'The man's an idiot,' said Thea. 'That's obvious.'

I laughed at her plain speaking, but forbore to agree. The silent presence of Jessica was making me uneasy. She was bound to be on the side of the council. I looked at her, hoping she would say something light and good-natured. She did not meet my gaze. After our talk outside the grave field, I had thought we were making headway, but it seemed she still had severe doubts about me and my character.

'Have you got any more funerals this week?' asked Thea, sensitively changing the subject.

I told her about Mr Everscott, and she became quite energised, asking a stack of questions about my life and work, Karen and Maggs and the children. Her interest warmed me, and made it even more difficult to leave. But by then we were back on the road, walking in unambiguous pairs. I even took the dog's lead, and firmly reined it in, to give Thea a chance to listen to me properly.

On the way, we walked down a track beside the little church we'd seen earlier, to look at an ancient Quaker meeting house. It was locked, which we all agreed was not in the right spirit at all. As we retraced our steps, Jessica ran up the little path to see if the church was open. A second

71

locked door set us off on a discussion of petty crime versus open access, a conversation that went nowhere. Across the road we admired again the long curving wall made of the local stone, topped with a magnificent length of topiary hedge, which we could not properly see. It was twelve or fifteen feet high, at least. There was something medieval and forbidding about it. The contrast between the Quaker modesty and this piece of ostentation was unsettling. There were no people around. 'Might as well get back,' said Jessica. 'Not much more to see here.'

When we got back to the cottage, the sun was shining, but the wind still strong. We stood indecisively at the junction with the small side road containing the cottage. 'That's the road to Blockley,' Jessica told Paul, pointing ahead and to the right.

I tried to puzzle out the geography. 'The grave's down there, isn't it?'

Jessica gave me a withering look. 'How can you not know?' she demanded.

'These little lanes are very confusing,' Thea defended me. 'It took me days to get it all straight. It's one of those places where it can be quicker to walk across the fields than meander round the lanes by car.'

Jessica seemed unconvinced. She actually marched across the road diagonally, to where the Blockley turnoff was. 'There!' she pointed. 'It's about half a mile down there. We drove up here only a couple of hours ago.'

'Yes,' I said, following her. 'I realise now. I came back up there, after making my phone calls to–'

72

'Hello,' she interrupted. 'Something's going on.' Following her gaze, I noted a couple of cars parked oddly further up the road.

'Nothing that need concern you,' said Thea, who had drifted after us, with the dog. 'Stop being a police officer for one day, can't you?'

But Jessica and Paul had already loped off to investigate, and we stood watching them. It was all going on about two hundred yards away, by a wooden gate that I rather thought was the one I had used to emerge from the field into the road, after my phone calls. I saw Jessica jerk herself upright in an assertion of her professional status. I saw Detective Paul reach for a phone in his pocket, and wave instructions at the three people assembled by the gate. He called to a fourth, somewhere out of sight, who suddenly materialised as if he had been sitting or kneeling and now stood up.

'Oh, my God,' said Thea. 'It can't be. Damn it, it is. Something awful's happened.' She looked down at her dog, which met her gaze. 'Brace yourself, Heps. Here we go again.'

'What?' I demanded. 'What do you mean?'

'I'll go and find out,' she said. 'Can you hold Hepzie?'

She trotted along to join the others, while I followed hesitantly with the spaniel. 'There's a dead man in there,' said a shrill woman, waving at the patch of scrubby woodland beyond the gate. 'I heard his phone going off, and when I looked, I could see his legs. My husband went to see. He says it's horrible.'

Already she was repeating words almost drained

of meaning, the shock alone giving her voice its high tones. She must have recited them to the two people from the second car, and then to Jessica and Paul. The picture she painted was clear enough, though – except she and her husband must already have been parked, with the engine off and the window open, if they were to stand a chance of hearing a ringing phone. Jessica evidently had the same thought at that moment.

'Had you stopped here for some reason?' she asked.

'Yes!' The woman's excitement was at fever pitch. 'David thought he saw a green woodpecker in that tree, and stopped for a better look. It flew away, just as he wound his window down.'

David was leaning against the gate, looking grey. That left me and Paul to be masterful and manly and all that stuff. Paul was looking at his phone in a dazed sort of fashion, which gave me a flicker of satisfaction. Even he couldn't order up a signal at will, it seemed. But then he began keying in numbers and I realised he was connected after all. I handed Thea's spaniel back to her, and strode to the gate, pushing my way through the opening, which was less than a foot wide.

'Hey!' said Officer Jessica. 'Where do you think you're going?'

'For a look,' I said. 'Why not?'

'It might be a crime scene. You'll contaminate it.'

'And what if the man isn't actually dead? You're standing back when you might be saving his life. Who said anything about a crime? Maybe he just had a heart attack.'

'You won't say that when you've seen him,'

74

croaked David, the birdwatcher.

'I order you to stay this side of the gate,' said Jessica, sounding more like the military than the police.

I paused, but already I could see what David meant. A fully clothed man was lying on his side only three or four yards away, with his face towards us. The top of his head was thick with blood, which had made a pool like a ghastly halo around him. His lack of protective hair made the wound somehow more terrible. At least two things indicated that he was unarguably dead: firstly, his wide-open staring eyes, and secondly, the clotting of the blood on the wound. His heart could not be beating – if it had been, the blood would still be flowing.

But these details occurred to me slightly later than the most startling and major observation. I knew this man. I had seen him only a few hours previously.

It was Mr Maynard, council officer, responsible for Parks and Recreation.

Chapter Five

If I hadn't been so annoyed with Jessica's heavy-handedness, I might have told her immediately who the victim was. Instead, I backed away from the gate, hands melodramatically raised as if she were a Wild West sheriff pointing a pistol at me. Perhaps this piece of foolish play-acting brought about the subsequent avalanche of trouble that landed on my head. At any rate, I couldn't help feeling that quite a bit of it served me right.

As it was, PC Jessica Osborne went to the gate herself and took a good long look at the corpse. I quickly understood that I had underestimated her powers of observation. 'Isn't that the man you were with this morning?' she said slowly. 'I remember that jacket.'

Which was more than I did. His clothes had made no impression on me whatsoever. 'I'm afraid it is, yes,' I said. 'Mr Maynard.'

'What? Who? What do you mean?' demanded Thea, who had been hovering on the grass verge with her dog. 'It can't be someone you know, surely?' She stared from me to her daughter and back again.

'The man from the council who was making a fuss about the grave,' I explained. 'Who summoned me here in the first place.'

'And who you might well want dead,' said Detective Paul, with reliably bad timing.

'Good God,' I huffed scornfully at him. 'You think *I* killed him?'

The resounding silence on all sides made my internal organs quiver. Every single person – and the dog – looked at me.

'Of course not,' said Thea. 'You couldn't possibly have done. That's obvious.'

'Is it?' said Jessica slowly. 'He was gone for half an hour, right here. He's just told us he came past this exact spot. He looked flustered when he came back. When I met him this morning, it looked to me as if he'd been in an angry argument with this man. Hadn't you?' she challenged me.

I could not have said anything even if I'd wanted to. I was sandbagged, stunned. I even wondered whether she might be right – had I gone mad for a few minutes and bashed the annoying Mr Maynard on the head? Enough of Jessica's accusations were true for me to feel there might be something in the idea that this was my work. I had indeed been on this precise spot, approximately two hours earlier.

Thea was scrutinising me with an uncomfortably probing stare. 'He'd have been more flustered,' she said. 'He'd never have acted so normally over lunch.'

'How do you know?' Jessica demanded.

'So – prove it,' Thea challenged. 'Where's the murder weapon, for a start?'

Jessica beckoned her to the gateway and pointed. I followed, peering over Thea's shoulder. A large stone lay a yard away from the body. 'That?' snorted Thea. 'It's just a stone. It hasn't even got blood on it.'

'It wouldn't, if it was only used once,' said Paul. 'The bleeding wouldn't start instantly. Blood would indicate repeated blows.' I could almost visualise the page in the textbook he was quoting from.

'But Drew can't be strong enough to make such a wound. He's probably not even *tall* enough,' my defender protested. I was warmed by the use of my first name, while thinking, yes, I probably was both strong and tall enough for the deed if I'd been sufficiently determined. Mr Maynard hadn't been very tall, after all.

77

'This is not the way it should be done,' Jessica recollected herself. 'We have to wait for the proper procedure.' She gave me a narrow stare. 'But I will have to report what I saw this morning, as well as the fact that you walked this way earlier on.'

'I can see it looks bad,' I said, aiming for a reasonable tone, the sort that an innocent man would use.

We'd been there perhaps ten or fifteen minutes, at most, eyeing each other warily, and studiously avoiding any further scrutiny of the corpse. I found myself wanting to give it a decent covering, to engage my normal undertaker's stance and remove the vulnerable body to a place of safe keeping. I felt a burgeoning pity for the wretched man and his soulless beliefs about burial. All too grotesquely soon, he was going to be the occupant of either a grave or an ashes urn. There was something fateful in the sudden turn of events, as if he had brought ill fortune upon himself by his opinions.

Which was, I realised, rather the way Jessica Osborne saw it. The man had argued with me, and now he was dead. How could there not be a connection?

The backup began to arrive, summoned by Paul. Cars, people, a few more onlookers – all slowly assembled and disposed themselves in a more or less organised fashion along the verge. Only a tiny handful possessed the authority to pass through the gate onto the patch of land where the body lay. I found myself joining the two women who had been there from the start, asked by Jessica to stay in their car, even though they insisted they had seen nothing but Mr and Mrs David, clearly in some distress. 'We should never have stopped,' the older one said crossly. 'This has nothing to do with us. We tried to call 999, but we couldn't get a signal.'

Innocent bystanders, I thought, detachedly. Just utterly bad luck to be passing at that particular moment. But then, why *did* they stop? 'Do you know them?' I asked, indicating the Davids, wondering whether I was allowed to address witnesses. Nobody made a move to stop me.

'Her, vaguely, by sight,' said the cross woman. 'We live in Chipping Campden, and I think she works in a shop there. It is her, isn't it?' she said to her companion.

'What – in the chemist, you mean?'

'Right. Don't remember seeing him, though.'

I looked again at the older couple. He had binoculars slung around his neck, a bizarre detail given the circumstances. Perhaps he had glimpsed the murderer speeding off across the fields, while scanning the area for his woodpecker. His wife was well turned out, her hair neat and her shoes clean. They appeared to be content to stand patiently by, awaiting their moment in the police spotlight. I moved towards them, trying to focus on their plight, thinking I might ask them one or two questions, just for politeness' sake, but before I could speak, a newly arrived policeman approached me and politely told me to remain where I was, until a more senior officer arrived and questioned me. My head throbbed with the strangeness of what was unfolding around me.

Thea attached herself to my side, the spaniel sitting quietly at her feet, licking a paw as if nothing interesting were going on. Thea's spaniel was already a permanent part of my image of her, a kind of daemon, automatically going everywhere with her. Except she had not been at the funeral the day before – left in the car or Mrs Simmonds' house, I supposed.

'Murder,' I managed to mutter. 'Murder most foul.'

'I wasn't going to look,' she said. 'I forgot, when Jessica said about the stone. It's pretty awful, isn't it?'

I nodded. 'Poor chap.'

'I suppose you're used to it – seeing broken and bloody bodies, I mean.'

'Not really. I mean ... you could never exactly get used to it, and I've never encountered one so ... well, *fresh.*'

'Mm.' She turned away, her lips pulled back, her nostrils flexing, creating a vivid expression of disgust and distress.

'I didn't do it, I promise you.' It seemed important to say it, to make every effort to keep her on my side. 'The thing is, he probably had quite a few enemies if he was the same with everyone else as he was with me. I suppose I shouldn't say it, but he did seem a bit of a pest.'

'But it happened *today,*' she almost moaned. 'That's the trouble.'

'Yes. And your daughter's convinced she's solved it before he's even cold.'

'I'm so sorry. Jessica isn't really as – well, *rigid* as she seems. She's actually perfectly nice.'

'I believe you,' I said with a tight smile at this endearing attempt at fairness. 'I'm sure it's all my own fault.'

'Don't be daft,' she smiled back.

But I meant it. It did feel as if I'd brought it all down on myself somehow or other. I *should* have made sure the car was legal, for a start. As I traced events back, this seemed an important element. With new tyres and current tax disc, Jessica would never have spoken to me. I would have bade farewell to Thea with no further conversation, and therefore not have been invited to join them for lunch. And I definitely should have checked that Mrs Simmonds was the rightful owner of that field. That, more than anything, now appeared crucial. I'd been sloppy and negligent, and see where it had got me.

I shrugged. 'Logically, I think I'm right,' I told my new friend. 'But thanks for sticking up for me.'

We walked up and down the road, with an idea of keeping the dog occupied, but could not avoid repeated glances at the crime scene. One of the first procedures was to erect a sort of tent over the body, which was made difficult by the strong wind, corners of it flapping wildly. I found myself hoping that any particles that might have come from me during my earlier encounter with Mr M had already blown away. At least, I thought glumly, there could be none of Mr Maynard's blood anywhere on my person.

A man arrived and, after a few false starts, was accosted by Jessica and apprised of the situation. She indicated me, where I remained on the verge, beginning to feel rather shivery. He walked

81

up to me, his eyes narrow. 'Detective Inspector Basildon,' he introduced himself. 'I understand you are Mr Drew Slocombe.'

'Right,' I agreed, resisting the impulse to put out a hand for him to shake.

'And you can identify the deceased?'

I shrugged self-effacingly. 'Mr Maynard from the council – that's all I know.'

'And that's very helpful, sir.'

'And I might as well tell you I walked through this gate, over more or less the exact spot where he is now, at about twelve-fifteen today.'

'Thank you, sir,' he said, with an impressively straight face.

'I'm an undertaker, and I live in Somerset,' I carried on, intent on getting the basics out of the way. 'I conducted a funeral here yesterday, in a field a short distance from this spot. There was a problem over ownership of the land and I was called back today – a round trip of a hundred and twenty miles – to be told off by Mr Maynard. Officer Osborne witnessed Mr Maynard walking away after our conversation, and I told her afterwards that I wished people like him didn't exist.' It felt wonderful, like drinking whisky on an empty stomach. The detective scribbled busily on a notepad. 'You can check the last part, because he used the police to get me back here. I mean ... a police officer came to my house this morning and told me I needed to come and speak to Mr Maynard face-to-face.'

'That must have been annoying,' he said, with a straight look.

'Very,' I said. 'But not to the point of committing

82

murder. I expect I should add that I absolutely did not kill him.'

'You'll appreciate that I can't comment on that, sir.' I wondered, with a belated pang of anxiety, just how much of police work these days was performed by computers. Would there be a box to tick that said *Suspect seems genuinely innocent,* even if there were glaringly incriminating means, motive and opportunity? They'd have the evidence of my footprints beside the body, my stupid absence to make needless phone calls, my rage against the deceased. A computer might think that was ample proof of my guilt. I expected to be arrested there and then.

But the detective inspector remained calm. 'Could I take your address and other details, sir? I'm sure you'll understand that we will need to speak to you again, given the circumstances.'

It was a relief not to be driven away in handcuffs, so I rattled off my address and phone numbers with alacrity. 'I can go home, then, can I?' I asked.

He frowned at the page in his notebook. 'Might be best if you stick around here for a day or so, just to be on the safe side. We'll need a full interview with you, later today. Please do not change your shoes or any other clothes.'

'I couldn't if I wanted to,' I said. 'I haven't brought anything with me.'

'Well, we'll make it as soon as possible. We'll be setting up an incident room somewhere close by, to make it easier for the local people. Do you know where Mr Maynard lived?'

'No idea, but I suppose it's around here somewhere. He didn't appear to have a car when we met at the grave, so it's probably within walking distance.'

'Thank you, sir,' he said, with one eyebrow lifting at the way I was practically doing his job for him. I was being a trifle *too* cooperative, I feared. Falling over myself to assist the enquiries might lead to an interpretation of guilt as much as strenuous obstruction would have done. I quailed inwardly at the impossibility of my situation. Whatever I did would be open to suspicious interpretations, if there was already a presumption that I was guilty.

'Those people don't know him, then?' I asked, indicating Mr and Mrs David and the women in the car. They'd been kept hanging about for well over an hour by that time.

DI Basildon merely shook his head and pursed his lips, to indicate that I had no business asking such questions.

I reviewed what he had said to me. *A day or so* was alarmingly vague. Where was I going to stay? 'Until when do I have to stay here, exactly?' I pressed him. 'If you interview me today, can I go home after that?'

'Impossible to say,' he smiled. 'Depends what we find here, for a start. Early days,' he added inscrutably and very annoyingly. '"Assume the worst," is my advice.'

I looked to Thea, as the most reassuring face I could find. She didn't fail me. 'You could stay in Mrs Simmonds' house with me, I suppose,' she said. 'There are three bedrooms, all ready to use.'

'Now, there's an offer,' said the policeman,

every bit as crassly as Detective Paul would have done if he'd heard Thea's words. Already the damage was done.

I shook my head regretfully. 'I can't do that,' I said, thinking of how Karen would react if she heard I'd been alone in a house with a woman as lovely as Thea Osborne, for a whole night. People assumed the worst, just as this DI bloke advised them to. And their thoughts changed the reality; they jumped into my own head, whether I liked it or not. 'There must be plenty of B&B places around here.' My mind was buzzing with worries, self-reproaches and obligations. 'I told Karen I'd be back before dark,' I said, to nobody in particular. I hated to break a promise – an undertaker above all had to be reliable.

The DI moved away to speak to Jessica, and then the women in the car, who were finally given permission to go on their way. Mr and Mrs David were also permitted to drive off, with promises of a call by a police liaison officer very soon, to make sure they were all right. It was an improvement, I supposed, on the olden days when witnesses were left to their own devices, regardless of the trauma they might have suffered. The police force was awash with a range of civilian and semi-civilian personnel who participated in almost every aspect of the work, with the idea of keeping everybody happy. My friend – and Maggs's husband – Den Cooper had found himself just such a post after leaving his job as a full-time police constable. A bit like a dysfunctional marriage, where the couple can't live together, but neither can they live apart, with Den incapable of abandoning law enforcement altogether.

'Come on,' Thea urged me. 'At least come back to the house for a cup of tea – assuming the power's still on. I've had enough of this. I don't want to be here when they remove the body.'

Remove the body was the phrase used by undertakers. Had she uttered it by chance, or did she know the routines and practices of the funeral business from personal experience? I remembered that she was a widow, with several close connections to the police force. Even so, it seemed surprising to me that she should use those words. It was tempting to think she had done it in order to offer me a kind of solidarity, an antidote to the isolation I was feeling.

As always, I found myself wondering about my alien status in society. I could go along for weeks, thinking I was just a normal bloke, chatting with ordinary people, taking the kids to school, going to the shops, and then something would happen to remind me that I was actually a pariah. I handled dead bodies; I kept them in a room that was part of my own house. I performed mysterious and dreadful acts on their lifeless corpses, seeing them naked and undignified. Even the vibrantly alive young mums at the school gate were aware of this, and kept me subtly at arm's length. I think every one of them had visualised herself in one of my coffins, helplessly at the mercy of my sinister tools. 'Thanks,' I said to Thea. 'That sounds nice.'

It wasn't until we were in the house that I had another good look at Thea as she bent down to unclip the dog lead from her spaniel's collar. Her face was at an odd angle, foreshortened, giving her an elfin appearance. But it was the fact that her lips were quivering that really struck me. When she stood up again, she dashed a finger under one eye, and sniffed.

I had seen enough women close to tears to grasp instantly what was going on. 'Are you OK?' I asked.

'Oh, God, I'm sorry,' she mumbled. 'Take no notice. Don't, for heaven's sake, be nice to me or I'll be a complete mess.'

'Easier said than done,' I warned her. 'Besides, crying doesn't bother me. Don't bottle it up on my account.'

She laughed then, a little explosive laugh that seemed to disperse the oncoming tears. 'I'm fine, really. I just felt so sorry for that man, bleeding to death in a gateway. Somebody must have hated him intensely to do that to him.'

'I can't pretend to have liked him,' I confessed. 'I thought he was a hidebound little time-server, with a complete absence of common sense.'

She laughed again. 'None of which would make you want to kill him,' she said with total confidence.

'No more than I wanted to kill your wretched Jessica,' I ventured, aware of stepping over a line.

'I told you – she's not usually so bad. Trying to impress the boyfriend, I suppose.'

'Wasting her time there,' taking another step into forbidden territory.

'In more ways than one,' she agreed. 'I liked him at first – you know how it is. The mere idea of her having a handsome black boyfriend went to my head. It's only now I've started to see him for what he really is, to my shame. And I don't think he's actually very nice. There's a coarseness to him, somehow.'

'I noticed,' I said.

'It makes me feel lonely,' she said softly and completely ingenuously. It was as if she had only that moment identified the feeling.

I thought about it. 'Yes,' I said. 'I know how that goes.' My own little moment of insight had struck me between the eyes. That was what *I* had been feeling, ever since Karen's injury, without ever putting a word to it. The shock of this shared revelation made me weak.

'I suppose it's the same for everybody,' said Thea bravely. 'When it comes right down to it. Like Mrs Simmonds. She was definitely lonely. You could see it in her eyes.'

It was a clever move, and I followed it with a mixture of relief and disappointment. At least, I hoped I did. 'Are you really staying another night here?' I asked. 'Don't you want to go home?'

She brought her elbows tightly into her sides, clutching herself in an agony of indecision. 'Oh, I don't know. It is rather bleak here. Charles is sure to get everything turned off at any moment. But now this has happened, I don't think I can leave. I know it's none of my business, and I'll only get in the way, but I think I will have to hang on, just for another day or so.'

The tea never happened. Restlessly, we went outside again, into the empty village, where the wind still blew. I was tense, she was indecisive – we walked, without the spaniel, down a stony path towards a big field. She pointed ahead and told me Chipping Campden was less than half a mile away. 'Have you met many locals?' I asked her. 'Anyone you think might have done the dirty deed?' The silly phrase was my deliberate attempt to lighten the mood.

'One or two. I've been here a week, and we've done the walks, and been to Chipping Campden a couple of times. But the chances of my having encountered the actual killer must be tiny. I don't imagine I'll be involved at all. I used to go out with one of the West Midlands detective superintendents, you see. I got myself pretty much embroiled, once or twice. Then a new one turned up, a woman, and she and I get along pretty well. She's clever, but wonderfully human. It might be her again, I suppose – as the SIO, I mean.'

'SIO?'

'Senior Investigating Officer.'

'Ah.'

There was a wistfulness to her, her voice trailing away as if still too shocked or upset to follow a thought through to the end. I was curious to understand her world – dog, daughter, weird rootless job, as well as a second reference to a former boyfriend and intriguing implications concerning the female detective, which made me wonder whether I was being told something significant. Jessica had told me about Thea's dead husband, but I had not properly considered the grief and suffering she must have endured, the loss of the future she had no doubt envisaged for herself. Had he been in the police as well? I was gathering myself to ask her, when my mobile burbled at me.

Chapter Six

'How did that happen?' was my first question.

Thea grasped my meaning immediately. 'We're on higher ground here,' she explained. 'It only needs a few feet, apparently. The signals seem to come and go according to the wind direction, or something.'

If only she'd told me that before, and sent me along this lane, instead of across the road to the field adjacent to the scene of a murder, things might be very different. I quelled the thought, and answered the phone. It was Karen. 'What's happening?' she asked. 'Will you be back for supper?'

Supper? I looked at my watch, for the first time in many hours. It said three fifty-five. I stared at it stupidly. It couldn't be so late. 'Sorry,' I said. 'I lost track of the time.'

'You're still there, then.'

'I'm afraid so. There's been an ... incident. The police want to talk to me. It looks as if I'll have to stay the night.'

'Where?'

'I'll find a B&B. This place is full of them.'

'Oh, Drew. How much will that cost?'

'Fifty quid probably. I'll try to get one for less.'

'They don't like singles. My mother was telling me – they often refuse to take somebody on their own.'

'That's crazy. Besides, it's out of season. They'll

be glad of the business.'

'Most of them are probably closed. What *happened*, Drew? Is all this about that grave? I don't get it.'

'It is, sort of. It's all got very messy. I'll explain everything when I get home. That'll definitely be tomorrow.'

'It's going to rain all day tomorrow,' she said bleakly. My wife was an avid follower of weather forecasts, checking online as well as staring intently at the TV weather maps. It was her last little ritual before going to bed every evening. And now what she was telling me was seriously bad news. A wet Sunday with two energetic kids was nobody's idea of bliss.

I groaned, remembering that I had the car, so she couldn't take them out, even if she'd wanted to. 'Shut them in their room,' I advised. 'Let them entertain themselves.'

'Right,' she said sarcastically. 'And how long do you think that'll work?'

'I'm really sorry,' I said again. 'But it's beyond my control. I'll try and get away in the morning. It might work out better than I think. I'll make a call now, and see if I can get some sort of promise that I won't be needed. It's all a bit unpredictable at the moment.'

I could almost feel the hot breath of her long sigh down my ear. 'I thought we weren't going to have this kind of thing any more,' she said. 'I thought we were just going to be quiet and ordinary from now on.'

'We *are*,' I assured her loudly. 'I didn't *do* anything. It's a complete coincidence.'

'What is?' Where once she would have spoken sharply, reading my mind and getting the truth out of me, now she sounded tired and slow. She sounded as if she did not actually want the whole story, had no spare energy with which to be interested in my troubles.

'Don't worry about it,' I said gently. 'It's all going to be fine. I'll do everything I can to get home quickly. Tell the kids I won't let them play with the Wii if they're not good.' Karen's aunt had bought us the thing the previous Christmas, for some incomprehensible reason. I hated it, but both my children found it so compulsive that Karen and I had agreed it should be rationed.

She laughed faintly. 'Fat lot of difference that's going to make.'

'Well, it's worth a try. I'll make it up to you when I do get back. You won't see or hear them for at least three hours, I promise.'

Thea had walked on, discreetly removing herself to look over a stile into a field while I was trying to pacify my abandoned wife. But I suspected she would have heard most of my end of the conversation, even so.

'Poor old Karen,' I said, having joined her. 'This isn't fair on her.'

'How many children?'

'Two. Stephanie and Timothy. Seven and five-nearly-six.'

'Nice,' she nodded.

'She finds them a handful. They never stop, you see. Always wanting something to happen. They seem to get louder, too, as they get older.'

'Do they fight?'

'I guess it sounds worse than it is, but yes, they fight. They argue at the top of their voices and get each other into trouble. Karen used to be a teacher – she thinks everything should be educational. Makes it harder for herself, I suppose.'

'Used to be?'

'She can't work any more. She was injured, three years ago. She had some brain damage.'

'Oh, God. How terrible! You ought to get back to her. Why don't we phone the police and insist they let you go? They can't force you to stay here, unless they arrest you.'

I had forgotten, for several minutes, how I stood in relation to the police. 'They might arrest me if I do that,' I said.

'I wonder where Jessica and Paul have got to. They were going back to Manchester this afternoon. All their stuff is still in the house. I suppose they're lending a hand with the enquiry somehow.' She frowned. 'Maybe they'll stay another night, after all.'

'They won't be part of the investigating team, though, surely?'

'No,' she said distractedly. 'They're with Manchester. It wouldn't work. Besides, what do they know about Broad Campden or the Gloucestershire Council? Nothing at all.'

Suddenly there was a flurry of flapping dog, and Thea's Hepzibah was scrabbling at her legs. 'They must have let her out,' she said, pushing the dog down. 'Yes, there's Jess, look.'

Thea's daughter was at the bend in the lane, waving to us. It was only twenty-five yards away,

93

but I felt as if we were being contacted from a great distance – reeled in from our little interlude, and forced to rejoin the real world.

Back in the cottage, Jessica and Paul were both voluble, competing to speak. Their excitement seemed to energise the air all around them. Even in Manchester, sudden violent deaths must be quite a thrill, rare enough to cause ripples and invoke little-used procedures.

'Have they taken him away yet?' I asked, knowing it could often be several hours before the body was removed.

'Just,' nodded Jessica. 'They've been very quick. It can sometimes be a whole day.'

'Indeed,' I agreed. 'I'm amazed.'

'Actually, I think they were a bit *too* quick,' said Paul. 'I'm not sure they did a thorough job. The SOCOs were only there for half an hour.'

'You think they should examine every blade of grass and bit of twig for a hundred-yard radius, do you?' said Thea, aggressively. 'What's the point?'

'Don't be silly, Mum.' Jessica was more uncomfortable than I had yet seen her. 'You know it isn't like that. But they need to look for footprints and signs of a struggle. It's a lot more difficult outdoors, especially with this wind blowing, and we thought they'd give it a bit longer, that's all. They did take a lot of photos,' she conceded. 'And the scene is being guarded, so they can come back later if necessary.'

The young police officer looked at me. 'They want to know who was at Mrs Simmonds' funeral,' she said.

'Oh? Well, I suppose that makes sense, after

what I told that Basildon man.'

'You think there's a connection, then? Between the murder and Mrs Simmonds' funeral?' Thea was frowning at me.

'The connection is me,' I explained, with a twinge of embarrassment.

Jessica made a wordless sound. When I looked at her, she appeared to have something like admiration in her eyes. Hope flared that she no longer assumed that I was a killer.

'You told him about that, then?' she asked me.

'Of course. I wanted to be helpful.' I tried to suppress the fluttering fears that swirled inside me. 'I expect my footprints are right there beside the body. I walked through that gate, before lunch.'

'Oh Drew!' moaned Thea. 'You didn't, did you?'

'You were gone such a long time,' muttered Jessica. 'We'll have to be honest about that.' She sounded slightly defensive, glancing at her mother as she spoke. Was she worried that she'd made things even worse for me? 'And I had to tell the DI about the argument. I know I didn't overhear any actual words, but the way he was marching off, it was obvious he was angry.'

'Don't worry about it,' I said. 'I already said we had words.'

'Sometimes, Jess,' Thea began, 'you do worry me. Can't you *see* that Drew's not a murderer?'

'I never said he was. But if there is a link between Mrs Simmonds' grave and this murder, Mr Slocombe is that link, as he just said himself.'

'But loads of other people might fit just as easily,' Thea blustered. 'After all, yesterday's funeral wasn't exactly a secret.'

'Well...' I began, 'we do try to keep them quiet, actually. It's part of my job, warning people not to spread the news. Neighbours tend to get very upset.' I recalled a back-garden burial of six months earlier, where the whole thing had been arranged as if it had been a bank robbery. We had performed the interment after dark, as quietly as was humanly possible. 'I have to admit I prefer it when they use my land. I know that's going to be OK. In any case, Jessica's right – Mr Maynard told me one of the mourners called the council because they were uneasy about the grave.'

Jessica nodded in satisfaction, before turning to Thea. 'How did *you* know about it?' she asked. 'The time and place, I mean.'

'The sister, Mrs Talbot, phoned me, the day after Mrs Simmonds died, to say they were going to see the undertaker about a natural burial. After all, I *was* looking after her house. I said I'd like to be at the funeral, so she called back when it had been arranged.' She gazed around the room with a little frown, as if she'd forgotten where she was, for the moment. 'She said she supposed she would have to honour her sister's wishes, but as far as she was concerned it was sacrilegious. "But then Greta always had been a strange person, with even stranger ideas."' The quotation marks around this little speech were entirely audible.

I laughed. 'Oh yes – that sounds exactly like Mrs Talbot. She said it all to me as well. And Mr Maynard would certainly agree with her about the sacrilegious bit.'

Then I thought about the handful of mourners at the graveside. 'Those two couples – her friends.

Do you know them?' I asked Thea.

'I know the Watchetts,' she nodded. 'They dropped in here for coffee on Wednesday, to see if I was all right. They're quite a nice pair, and they seemed to like the whole idea of the green burial. I thought they might ask you for your card, actually.'

I shook my head. 'I got the impression they didn't much like it after all, when it came to the point. I can only assume it was them or the other pair who called the council.'

'The others are Graham and Miriam Ingram,' said Jessica.

'How on earth do you know that?' Thea demanded.

'Because while you two were strolling around the village just now, Mr Ingram showed up at the scene of the murder, and spoke to DI Basildon.'

'You're joking!' I spluttered, trying to envisage the wildfire village gossip that must have spread before such a rapid volunteering of information could have been possible.

'I was a bit surprised myself,' admitted Jessica. 'After all, the body hadn't even been formally identified.'

'I bet that means they were the ones who contacted the council. They'd have been waiting to see what he would do about it, and rushed out for a look as soon as they heard something had happened.' I paused, before asking humbly, 'I know I'm being dim, but could you tell me exactly how far it is from the grave to the place where he was killed?'

Jessica savoured her moment of superiority,

before saying, 'I would guess about a third of a mile. It's along the same road, further towards Blockley.'

'Thanks,' I nodded. 'And we know he was walking back along that road, after meeting with me. He left about ten minutes before we drove up here. Why didn't we see him in the road? He couldn't have got back that quickly. Where did he go?'

'Wait,' Jessica pleaded, confused. 'This is important.'

'I know it is,' I said feelingly. 'So?'

'He must either have taken a detour across the fields, or gone home and out again,' she surmised. 'Because he couldn't have already been dead, or you'd have seen him when you went out to make your phone call.'

'Maybe he was there and I didn't see him. Maybe I didn't actually come out of that gateway at all, but a different one. I really wasn't paying much attention.'

'Drew!' said Thea impatiently. 'You can't afford to be vague about it. Are there any other gates along there?' She asked the question generally, but none of us knew the answer.

'We should get the times straight,' suggested Paul, who had been paying close attention. 'Mr Slocombe ... when exactly did you meet Mr Maynard?'

'I don't know exactly,' I snapped. 'I left home just before ten, so it was probably eleven-thirty or thereabouts. We talked for ten or fifteen minutes, then Jessica turned up, and we all headed back here, towards the centre of the village. Jessica and

I were driving, and Mr M was walking.'

'It was five to twelve when you went out to make your phone call,' said Thea. 'We were hoping to set off for the pub by quarter past, and you didn't get back here until twenty-five past.'

'We don't know where he lived,' Jessica reminded us. 'He might have been going across the fields.'

'So where did he leave the road?' I wondered. 'Last I saw him, he was marching along, on the right-hand side, facing the oncoming traffic. I remember thinking he was just the type to stick to the rules. But the murder was on the left side of the road – the west, I mean.'

'Maybe the killer was somebody he knew, who lured him off the road, and into that quiet corner, before bashing him,' said Thea. 'That makes sense.'

'He'd have had to do it in those ten minutes before we drove up the road,' said Jessica. 'That's fast work.'

'But if I did it, he must have been walking pretty slowly to arrive at the spot at twelve-ten, or whatever, to coincide with me,' I said, already thinking it was only too possible. If Mr Maynard had paused to admire a view or have a discreet pee, or check a misplaced road sign, he'd have been at precisely the right spot at the right time for me to slaughter him. The only puzzle was – where did he disappear to, when we might have expected to see him on the road?

'Well, your interview's not going to be until tomorrow,' Jessica concluded. 'I suggest you get your facts straight before then. And yours as well,' she told Thea. 'You'll be able to go to the incident room together, won't you?' She gave her mother a meaningful look. 'They're using that hall in Blockley again.'

'Oh, God,' groaned Thea, much to my confusion.

'What?' I asked.

'We had to go there last year, that's all. I was house-sitting in Blockley, and the man next door got himself killed. Jess was staying with me. She found the body, actually.'

Detective Paul snickered from the comfortable cushions on the sofa where he had plonked himself. 'She'll be able to show you the way,' he said to me, with a sly glance at Thea.

'Is this formal notification?' I asked. 'What time do I have to be there? My wife needs to know when she can expect me back.'

Jessica handed me a card with the name and phone number of a detective superintendent on it. 'You can phone and ask,' she said.

'Who's this?' I asked, showing it to Thea.

She smiled. 'Thank goodness, it's Gladwin in charge. Detective Superintendent Sonia Gladwin. I told you about her. She'll be all right.'

'Actually, you've got the wrong side,' said Jessica. 'Gladwin's not available. It's some bloke called Jones. He's new, and hasn't got his own cards done yet. That's his number, look.'

I turned the card over, to read a neat string of mobile phone numbers, and the name printed in capitals: Detective Superintendent Ralph Jones. West Midlands police. 'What's he like?' I asked Jessica.

'No idea,' she shrugged. 'I'm not with the West Midlands.' She said it with loud emphasis, as if repeating it to a deaf person.

'Sorry. No, of course you're not.'

'But Uncle James is,' said Thea, and then added, 'You know quite a few of the CID people around here, don't you?'

'Not really. I gather Jones is young, keen and friendly. You might meet him for yourselves tomorrow.'

It was past five, and I was aware of the need for a meal and a bed that evening. I had far too much to think about for comfort, and cursed again the fate that had brought Mrs Simmonds to me in the first place. I was floundering in a bog of half-understood facts and growing apprehensions. The police, who I had more or less regarded as my friends up to then, were beginning to feel more and more threatening. From the moment PC Jessica Osborne had spotted the defects on my car, I had been on the wrong side of the law. Now there was the skin-crawling realisation that I was under suspicion for the murder of a council official, and I had no idea what to do about it. It hardly mattered where I lay down for the night, I thought – the chance of actually managing to sleep was vanishingly remote.

'I should go,' I said. 'And find myself a B&B.'

'Oh, no,' said Thea urgently, reminding me of Stephanie. 'Not yet. Jess and Paul will be off soon, and...' she looked out of the window, where the sky was starting to darken, and then checked her watch '...well, it's going to be a long evening,' she finished weakly.

101

'Mum, I'm really sorry we won't be staying. Paul has to be on duty first thing tomorrow. It's my fault – I got the dates mixed up.' Jessica's distress came as a surprise.

She grimaced in an expression of divided loyalties. 'Why don't you just go home? At least you'll have Celia to talk to. You are still friends with Celia, aren't you?'

'More or less. But I won't be able to talk to her. I told you, she's got a new man. They go fell walking or something on Sundays.'

'In Oxfordshire?' Jessica was aiming for light relief, but it fell horribly flat.

'*I* don't know,' snapped Thea. 'Anyway, it's decided now. You're going back, to Manchester and I'm staying here. Drew's going to make his own arrangements, and tomorrow we'll answer questions and try to convince Mr Jones that we had nothing to do with murdering the council man.'

I felt the *we* somewhere in my chest, without giving it any conscious thought.

'Yes. Right,' said Jessica stiffly. 'I'll phone you tomorrow evening, then. I suppose this all means that at least you won't have time to brood.'

It dawned on me that I'd missed something. I looked from face to face, even trying to make some connection with Paul, but gained no enlightenment.

Chapter Seven

In the event, I slept surprisingly well, having left Broad Campden at six-thirty for a small but painfully expensive hotel in nearby Chipping Campden. Thea and I had found it in the phone book, and booked it by going back to the field behind the house and using her phone. She gave me a cup of coffee and a brave smile, and waved me off.

'See you in the morning,' I said. 'Sleep well.'

'You too.'

She had her dog, I told myself, and plenty of practice at being on her own.

My little hotel had a tiny bar, and a modest dining room, so I ate a slow supper and drank two pints of beer with it. I could probably write it all off against tax, I told myself.

The beer helped me to sleep, and I managed over seven hours. I did not dream about Mr Maynard's moist lips or shattered skull. Nor did I dream about Thea Osborne's soft spaniel, which had climbed onto my lap while I drank coffee in Mrs Simmonds' living room. I did dream about Maggs, my trusty assistant, who was gently lecturing me about the state of our cemetery, the need to weed out a patch of thistles in one corner and prepare for a new burial. 'We have to keep people *happy*,' she repeated. 'That's our job.'

I woke with the words still echoing in my head.

103

She was right – even in the face of appalling loss, the reality of death sticking its ugly face above the smooth surface of normal life – my job was to give them consolation. Not quite hope, perhaps, but a sense that this particular dying had been dealt with decently, with due thought and care. I tried to relate these thoughts to Mrs Simmonds and the threat to her last resting place – a place she had chosen so deliberately for herself.

It did make sense, I could see, to suspect me of killing Mr Maynard. He had transgressed my dearest beliefs, trampled on something precious with his pettifogging insistence on property rights. He might have cost me my business, if a lengthy lawsuit over the grave ensued and I lost.

Except, of course, the death of one council official did not in any way guarantee that the whole thing would be abandoned. Some other beastly little bureaucrat would replace him within hours, and the whole thing continue as before. This had not occurred to me until that point.

It did nothing for my state of mind as I ate the cheapest breakfast on the brief menu and made a phone call to my wife.

Almost ignoring the incredible beauty of Chipping Campden's main street, I drove the two or three miles back to Mrs Simmonds' cottage, as arranged with Thea the night before. We would present ourselves at the police incident room in Blockley, taking the initiative, on the grounds that I had to get home. 'They won't like it,' she warned me. 'They like to feel they're in control.'

'Phooey,' I said. 'People turn up to volunteer

104

information all the time.'

'True. So what information are you volunteering?'

'The small fact that I am not their murderer. That I am innocent, blameless and eager to return to my family. Although, actually, they want the pattern from the soles of my shoes, and to have my clothes for forensic analysis. I expect I'll have to drive home naked.'

It was half past nine, and Thea looked as if she had not slept at all. Her dog was droopy, too. 'Bad night?' I enquired.

She sighed. 'I never thought I'd turn into an insomniac. It feels so *stupid,* just lying there, wide awake, just because...' she paused.

'Because a lot's been happening, and you'd be justified in feeling worried or scared?' I suggested.

'No.' She shook her head. 'I'm not scared this time. Funny how irrational fear is – three months ago I was terrified because of a few tracks in the snow. Now we know there's a killer just outside my door, and I'm hardly even thinking about it.'

'So ... what?'

She sighed even more heavily. 'It's the anniversary of my husband's death. Three years ago today. Poor Carl. He should still be here. It was such a ridiculous waste.'

'Ah,' I breathed, thinking, *That explains a lot.* 'Three years, eh? Long enough to move on, short enough to still feel all the pain.' It was, after all, a subject I had some expertise in. 'Same as me and Karen, to a lesser degree. It is at least long enough to get used to a new situation.'

'I suppose that's right. It doesn't hurt like it did at first. It's like a fading photo, the colours have dimmed. It feels less *important* now, which is awful to say. Less jagged and shattering. You think at first that it's all a mistake, that he'll come back. Then you get adjusted, you go on living and the space where he was gets smaller, until you know he wouldn't really fit any more if he *did* come back.' She waved a jerky hand as if scribbling something out. 'No, that's banal. What really kept me awake was wondering how I *should* be feeling. Should I be clinging to the memory, accepting that nobody like him will ever be in my life again – or should I wrap him up and put him away and reinvent myself?'

'Both, I imagine. And some other things as well.'

'We were so foolishly *happy*,' she moaned. 'The perfect couple. At least, that's how it feels now. We hardly ever argued. He was sweet and clever and patient and focused. He had strong opinions – one of those people who sees what needs doing, and makes every effort to do it.' She looked at me, with a little frown. 'Rather like you, I think, with your natural burials. Carl would have *loved* all that.'

I was feeling less and less comfortable in the presence of this Carl-ghost. What was I supposed to say?

'We'd better get moving,' was all I could manage. 'If you're going to be OK, that is?'

'Oh, yes.' She was suddenly brisk. 'It'll be something else to concentrate on. Poor Mrs Simmonds needs a defender.'

'Oh?' I hadn't seen it quite like that. 'Well, I

106

guess you could say that whoever killed Mr Maynard *was* defending her. If it had anything to do with her, of course. Which it probably didn't.'

'It's frustrating, isn't it? Not knowing who might have hated him enough to murder him. What on earth could he have done to warrant that?'

'I really can't imagine it,' I confessed. 'We don't have enough facts to begin to guess.'

'We have to assume we'll understand it eventually. There always is some sort of explanation, if you dig hard enough for it.'

'Usually something rather trivial,' I said. 'In my limited experience.'

'Is it limited, though? I was thinking, in the night, that you and I have something unusual in common.' She didn't give me time to respond before rushing on. 'We both have some sort of need for the big stuff. The larger-than-life events that nearly everybody ignores or forgets. Violence, rage, death, decomposition, loss – all that scary dark side that people look away from.'

This was familiar territory. 'I know,' I said. 'Now, let's get going.'

The incident room had been set up in a hall in Blockley that would have been impossible to find on my own. We took both cars, since I was optimistic that I could make a quick departure for home as soon as the interview was over. Thea led the way, with a sudden right turn down a tiny street, giving me an impression of a town built on crazily uneven land. It seemed to tip and tilt in three directions at once.

A uniformed police constable was sitting just

inside the door, with a small table in front of him. He looked up as we went in, his head cocked sideways. 'How can we help you?' he asked.

'Drew Slocombe,' I said. 'I think you want to question me.'

'Mr Slocombe for interview,' he muttered, with a slight air of reproach. He tapped the keys of a laptop computer in front of him, and nodded. 'Oh yes. DI Basildon will be with you right away.'

The daft sense of self-importance soon evaporated as I scanned the crowded room. A whiteboard was perched on a kind of easel arrangement, and a row of tables ran down one side, each with a computer and officer. A middle-aged couple I recognised waited uncomfortably with typical chunky village hall teacups at their elbows.

'That's Mr and Mrs Watchett,' whispered Thea. 'Mrs Simmonds' friends.'

'Yes,' I said. 'I remember them.'

'And you are, madam?' said the doorkeeper.

'Thea Osborne. I was ... um ... at the scene when the body was found. My daughter is PC Jessica Osborne. I ... well, I thought you might want to interview me as well.'

He scanned his screen and shook his head. 'Doesn't look like it.'

She hesitated, realising how foolish it would look to insist, under the circumstances. 'Oh. Well, that's all right, then.'

'Unless you have information for us that you think will be helpful,' he added.

'No, not really,' she said vaguely. 'I didn't ever meet him – the victim, I mean.'

The officer sighed, with barely concealed impatience. I was reminded of my own emotions when working at the funeral director's, before I set up on my own. We would get 'persistent viewers' – women who had a taste for dead bodies, and would come to the chapel to view remote acquaintances. This policeman seemed to think that Thea was there from morbid curiosity, or an inflated sense of her own usefulness. Her role as mother of a young police officer cut no ice with him at all. 'Don't wait for me,' I told her. 'I'm sure you've got things to do.'

She met my gaze for a second, and I understood what a stupid thing I had just said. She had nothing to do but mourn her dead husband, walk her dog, and sit in an abandoned house for no good reason at all. But neither did she have any reason to wait for me. I had to be somewhere else, the moment I was permitted to make my escape.

Before she could leave the hall, her mobile warbled. Stopping in her tracks, she extracted it from her bag and looked at the screen. With an apologetic glance around the room – which everybody ignored – she put it to her head.

'Um ... yes, hello,' she said in response to an opening remark at the other end. 'That's right ... I have no idea ... well, possibly, I suppose... That's entirely up to you, isn't it?... What do you want me to do, then?' This last after a lengthy silence, during which I shamelessly stood my ground and listened, instead of proceeding to my interview. 'No, not really,' she was saying reluctantly. 'All right, then. I'll see you later. Bye.'

She met my eyes again. 'The sister,' she told me. 'Judith Talbot. She's heard about the trouble over

109

the grave and wants to come and see for herself. She wants me to be here to explain what's been happening.'

'Does she know about all this?' I waved a hand at the police activity.

'It seems not. She did say she was going to contact you as well.'

'And you didn't tell her I was here.'

'No. I thought you might want to keep your head down.'

'Thanks, but I can't really leave it all to you, can I? What time's she due to arrive?'

'Eleven or a bit after.'

'I might as well stay, then. I guess I sort of owe it to her.'

Thea smiled, a much happier smile than the conversation warranted, and a long-forgotten little imp inside my chest turned one of his somersaults – which I had no control over whatsoever.

My interview with DI Basildon was peculiar, to say the least. Conducted at a formica table in the middle of the room, with a detective constable as witness, it felt oddly informal. The young detective made notes on an electronic gadget, which I found disconcerting. The inspector began by clearly informing me that I had made myself freely available to assist with enquiries into the murder of a certain Mr Maynard, and that I was jeopardising none of my rights by giving this assistance. For the first time, I wondered whether I ought to have asked for a solicitor to be present.

'Please tell me in your own words exactly what contact you had with the deceased before his death, from the beginning,' came the first stilted question.

'Well, I suppose you could say it all started when one of your officers came to my home yesterday morning and demanded that I return here to Broad Campden to face a council accusation that the grave I had arranged was a trespass.' I found myself stumbling over the language, trying to maintain an equally formal delivery to that of my interviewer. He watched my face and said nothing. 'I did as I was asked, and met Mr Maynard at the grave. He told me that Mrs Simmonds had not been the rightful owner of that field, and that the grave would have to be moved.'

'And...?' he prompted.

'Well, I argued with him. I thought he was being unduly bureaucratic and unreasonable.'

'Did you threaten him?'

'Of course not. What possible threat could I make against him?'

'How was the matter left?'

'Inconclusive. I assumed I would receive a letter from the council, and we would have to take it from there. I had some idea of checking ownership of the land, and the possibility that Mrs Simmonds had squatters' rights over it. It's a major exercise to move a grave, as you probably know.'

He then requested me to recount every detail of my movements in the thirty or forty minutes between leaving Thea and the others at the cottage, and rejoining them for our walk to the pub. Realising its importance, I put all my concentration into giving a full and frank report, with timings as precise as I could manage. I wished I'd been more familiar with the layout of the village, so as to be able to put names to the various locations. 'I really need to show you on the ground,' I sighed, as I tried to describe everything I'd done. 'I walked across a field, roughly parallel to the Blockley road, then veered left out through a gateway – which was where the body was found – turned left up the road, and then stupidly turned right at the top, instead of left again.'

Basildon tapped his teeth with a pen. 'But the cottage is actually *visible* from that junction,' he protested. 'We checked it this morning.'

'I expect it is,' I agreed. 'But I hadn't seen it from that angle. I just blindly followed Jessica's car, having no idea where we were going to finish up. And when I went out again on foot, I crossed the main street to the footpath, which was what confused me. Coming out a different way, I somehow just assumed it was to my right. Everything looked new to me, and I wasn't concentrating.' I sighed. 'I know it sounds stupid – but why would I lie to you about it?'

He raised both eyebrows at this, as if to say, *Why do you think?*

'Anyway, it can only have added about five minutes to my total time away. I realised quite quickly what I'd done.'

'Mr Slocombe, sir, you walked a total of seven hundred and fifty metres, at a generous estimate. How did that take more than half an hour?'

'I was on the phone. I was admiring the view. I took a wrong turn.'

'Does that happen to you a lot?' asked the detective blandly. 'Taking a wrong turn, I mean.'

112

'Not really. But I was thinking about my wife and things at home. I wasn't paying proper attention.' I still failed to grasp how I was coming across, in this naïve display of incompetence. I was under the impression that the simple truth was all that was required, so I doggedly repeated myself, in the hope that he would believe me.

Basildon raised a decisive hand. 'Thank you, Mr Slocombe. Before we go any further, we'll need to increase the formalities somewhat. I'm going to caution you, and offer you the option of having legal representation. I will need to take a number of samples from you. We will relocate to the police station at Cirencester, and a statement will be prepared for you to sign.'

Good God, what had I said? I wondered. 'What? Now?' I stuttered.

'That's right. We can take you in a car, and bring you back here afterwards. It won't take more than an hour or so.'

'So you're arresting me.'

'Technically, yes. In the sense that you don't have any choice in the matter. But we won't need to keep you in custody, so long as you undertake to keep us informed of your movements.'

'Do you honestly think *I* killed the wretched man?'

He smiled wearily, as if everybody asked the same question. 'That is not the point,' he said. 'We need to understand everything that took place in the hours before he died. You are clearly going to be very helpful in the investigation.'

'OK – I'm already being helpful. Why do you need to arrest me? Doesn't that run the risk of making me hostile? Wouldn't it be better just to let me talk as we are?'

'We need to be able to use whatever you might say as evidence,' he said, and then went straight into the words of the police caution, which I had never expected to hear directed at myself.

Far from feeling hostile, I was bewildered and scared. Crazily, I thought of my expired road tax and bald tyres. I was already on the wrong side of the law, suspected by Jessica Osborne of being feckless and unreliable. What guilty secrets would this man unearth in the course of his questioning? The petty misdemeanours I had committed throughout my life loomed large in my mind. I had fudged my tax returns, plucking figures out of the air with no documentary proof. I had lied to relatives of the dead, in the interests of a quiet funeral. I had kept my children off school, saying they were ill, when we fancied a day out at Lyme Regis or Weston-super-Mare.

But I had not coshed Mr Maynard on the head with a large stone.

Chapter Eight

In the event, the formalities in Cirencester proceeded fairly gently. I was given an oral swab, which was mildly unpleasant physically and much more humiliating than anticipated. My fingerprints were taken, and my shoes whisked off into another room, exposing a small hole in the heel of my sock. My jumper and trousers were bagged up and labelled, and a new clean tracksuit provided in their place. 'We'd like it back at some point,' said DI Basildon. Mercifully, my shoes came back after ten minutes or so. The results of my interview in Blockley were typed up and produced for my signature. I read them through carefully first, and then signed that they were accurate 'As far as they go,' I said to the inspector. 'I want to write in big red capitals – I did not kill Mr Maynard.'

'We are well aware that you have not made a confession,' he said stiffly.

'I would have to be a psychopath to murder him,' I continued. 'I was annoyed with him, and worried about what would happen next, but it's barmy to think that would make me kill him.'

'I can't comment, sir.'

'You can check that I made the phone calls to my wife and colleague.'

'Indeed,' he nodded. 'But you haven't claimed that you spent the entire time speaking on the phone.'

'I've told you the exact truth of what happened.'

'So you were completely startled at the discovery of the body?'

'Of course.'

'We have a suggestion that you seemed quite unsurprised.'

'What? Jessica, I suppose. She didn't even look at me. Her mother and I stayed back, letting her do her job. Thea realised what was happening before I did.'

'You had no idea what was going on?'

'Of course not. How could I?' I tried to recall

my feelings, what I'd been thinking at the time, in vain. I fell silent, helpless to influence the way this man regarded me.

Then I was kept hanging about waiting for a car to take me back to Blockley, feeling increasingly like a wriggling bug on a pin, scrutinised through the implacable lens of the law. Everything I said seemed to increase my guilt in their eyes. My heart rate had sped to a painful level, everything inside me thundering with anxiety. Even my bowels were turbulent. It was all well beyond my control, and this was before I had even begun to consider the implications for my family and business.

'Sorry to keep you waiting,' said a man behind me. He was in uniform, and I had not seen him before. 'We can go now, if you're ready.'

'So I'm no longer under arrest?'

He blinked. 'Haven't they told you that?'

'Not really.'

'You're still under suspicion, as I understand it. That means you're bailed to attend any further interviews or proceedings. You are not at liberty to leave the country.'

'I won't leave the country,' I promised him.

They took me back to my car. Only then did I remember that I was meant to be meeting Mrs Talbot for more questions and probable anger. I was sorely tempted to just leave it, and drive home as quickly as I could. But I had told Thea I'd be there, and I was only ten minutes late, surprisingly. The morning already felt as if it had lasted a couple of days.

She must have been watching for me, and came

116

out of the house as soon as I turned off my engine. 'How did it go?' she asked, as if I'd been sitting an exam. She eyed the tracksuit critically, but didn't laugh.

'It was annihilating,' I said dramatically, having found the word during the drive. 'Completely annihilating.'

'Oh dear. Come and have some coffee. The sister will be here any time. She's even later than you. I've been playing with Mrs Simmonds' coffee machine, so there's plenty, and the power is still on, mercifully. The tracksuit is rather fetching, by the way. Much better than going home naked.'

'I need the loo first,' I said unceremoniously. Nothing in my gut was behaving normally, and there was a certain urgency to my need.

We waited for Judith Talbot in near silence. I could tell that Thea was curious about my experience as an interviewee, but she was deterred from asking by my bemused condition. Also, perhaps, she understood that I had had enough of answering questions for a while.

Before we had time to get restless, the visitors were upon us. They arrived in full force: not only the sister, but her older son and her husband as well. I focused on Charles, thinking he looked different from when he'd come to my Somerset office, a week earlier. A week which felt like a month or more. I looked at him, wondering what he was going to say to me. More than his parents, he looked hostile and accusatory.

'You remember Charles, I suppose,' his mother said, having registered my presence with a flicker of surprise. 'And my husband, Oliver.' The introductions struck me as superfluous, but she made them deliberately, as if it was important. I realised how little I knew about Judith Talbot – what she did for a living, whether she was older or younger than her dead sister, why her two sons were so vastly separated in age. Her hair was dyed a coppery colour and her figure was firmly in control. She seemed fairly intelligent, and more concerned than angry, for which I was duly grateful. Charles was a few years older than me, I guessed, a colourless chap who manifested very little in the way of thought or emotion on our first encounter. It had been Thea who mentioned the nasty divorce he was undergoing.

'Of course. I'm pleased to see you again, although I very much regret the circumstances.' I was automatically slipping into undertaker mode. I hoped I wasn't unctuous or oily – rather, approachable and reassuring. Reliable and friendly. The undertaker's role is to persuade people that although death is a really bad thing to happen, it isn't the end of the world. There are routines and formulas for getting through it, which we ignore at our peril. Even when the burial is in a cardboard coffin in unconsecrated ground, there are still correct procedures to be followed, to ensure due dignity.

'We need to know that the grave won't be disturbed,' she asserted, wasting no time. 'The very idea is horrifying.'

'I agree,' I said. Forcing myself to concentrate, I went on, 'How did you hear there was a problem?'

'Susan Watchett phoned me on Friday evening.

She said she'd been thinking it over, and got more and more uneasy about it all. She took her time to admit it, but after a bit she told me she'd reported it to the council. She just caught them, apparently, before they closed for the weekend.'

Thea gave a strangled gasp at this, which made us all look at her. Her eyes were wide with surprise. 'But she *liked* it. She approved of it. She came here last week with her husband and talked glowingly about the whole natural burial thing.'

'She can be like that – changes her mind from one second to the next. I learnt about fifty years ago that you can't rely on Susan.'

'You've know her that long?' I queried.

'We went to school together, in Chipping Campden. Susan, me, Greta, Helena. We always kept in touch.' A dreamy look crossed her face. 'Sometimes it feels as if you can't escape your childhood – those friendships you make so carelessly when you're eleven stick with you for life. All it takes is a Christmas card every year and the odd letter, and you're in it for the duration.'

'That's nice, though, isn't it?' said Thea.

Oliver Talbot made a sound, suggesting scepticism. 'Susan's brought us a fair bit of trouble over the years,' he said, in a voice I had scarcely heard thus far. He was a Scot, I noted.

'Who's Helena?' asked Thea. I began to feel she was taking curiosity slightly too far. The conversation could go on for hours at this rate, and yet again I felt the demands of my family urging me to hurry it up and get back home.

'Helena Maynard, she is now,' said Judith easily. 'Married to a chap on the council.'

She didn't know. She had not watched local TV news or heard any gossip. It was twenty-four hours since the murder, very nearly, and still there were people who didn't know.

Either that, or she was the best actor on the face of the earth. Stupidly, I kept my gaze on her face, not looking at her son or husband – who might perhaps have been less relaxed at this reference to the new widow. I missed any chance of catching a hint or clue to any knowledge they might have had. Thea, too, lost the opportunity.

'But he's *dead*,' she said, recklessly. 'He was murdered yesterday.'

Judith froze, then threw bewildered glances at her menfolk. 'Excuse me?' she said. 'Who do you mean? Nobody said anything about a murder.'

I squared my shoulders and took a deep breath, hoping that Thea would recognise that I needed her to remain silent. It worked. 'I met him at the grave yesterday morning,' I said. 'About an hour later, he was killed. I've just got back from being questioned by the police about it. Obviously, given the situation, they regard me as being involved.'

The Talbots absorbed this information in three different ways. Charles rubbed his cheeks and chin with a chubby hand, swallowing hard and frowning in apparent confusion. His father coughed and sniffed as if a noxious gas had been squirted at him. As if information so stark and terrible was a physical substance capable of injuring him. And Judith uttered a high hysterical little laugh, her face turning pink and shiny.

'I can't believe it,' she said. 'I really can't believe it.'

After that, there was a period of shocked questions and assertions that followed no logical thread. Charles said nothing, his eyes turned on some urgent inner musings which rendered him deaf to what the rest of us were saying. Gradually, Judith pulled herself back to the original reason for their visit.

'But the grave,' she said. 'What about the grave?'

'We'll have to wait and see,' I replied. 'Nothing has been decided.'

'But it was Helena's husband who complained to you about it – is that right? You met him to talk it over. What did he say, exactly?'

'He said your sister never owned the field, but rented it from the council. She couldn't possibly have believed it was her property, or that she had any right to use it for her burial. He hinted that there might be some financial agreement we could make–'

'Buy it from the council, you mean,' interrupted Oliver Talbot. 'Cheeky wee devil.'

'Oliver!' his wife rebuked him. 'The man's dead. Mind what you say.'

'The village will have a field day over this,' continued her husband, gloomily. 'Our name will be all over the papers. Old Bill Kettles is going to be in seventh heaven, silly old sod. You'd think a body would have told us, all the same. Where's yon Susan when she's needed?'

Susan, I thought, had already done enough damage, by alerting the Talbots to the trouble over the grave. Although they'd have had to know eventually, of course.

'Who's Bill Kettles?' asked Thea.

121

'He was a friend of our mother's. Makes mischief every chance he gets. Greta always liked him, but I couldn't stand the old goat.' Judith was almost back to normal, I noted, marvelling at the resilience of the human spirit.

'Why wasn't he at the funeral?'

Judith smiled smugly. 'Because we didn't tell him when it was going to be. Or where. I made Susan promise not to tell him, and Miriam Ingram likewise.'

I had forgotten the Ingrams. 'Do they live here as well?' I asked. 'The Ingrams, I mean.'

She nodded. 'Practically next door to the Maynards, as it happens.'

'And were you at school with her, too?'

She gave me a narrow look, as if suspecting me of flippancy. 'No, I wasn't. She doesn't come from round here. Graham does, of course – but that's got nothing to do with anything.'

Thea laughed. 'Gosh, I do love the way these connections work, especially in villages like this. Everybody knows everybody, all their secrets, all the old feuds and resentments. So many stories hidden just below the surface.'

Judith was visibly offended. 'Stories?' she repeated. 'These are people's *lives*. They might sound like funny stories to you, but to some of us they're deadly serious.'

Despite her attack on Thea, I was warming a little to Judith Talbot, as she got into her reminiscences. At least she wasn't attacking me for sloppiness over her sister's grave.

'You're quite right,' said Thea apologetically. 'I didn't mean it the way it sounded. And you must be feeling awful about your friend Helena. You'll be wanting to go and see her, won't you?'

Judith Talbot turned pink, all over again. 'Oh!' she gulped. 'Well, not today. No, no. She must be overwhelmed with it all, if it only happened yesterday. She won't want us crowding in on her. I'll send her a card.'

I'd seen it many a time, the instinctive recoil from sudden grief and pain. Most people did it, afraid of saying the wrong thing, of being sobbed on, of entering a realm where naked emotion ruled and normal procedures were abandoned. I didn't blame them – it was genuinely alarming if you weren't used to it.

I definitely needed to take my leave. I told them so. 'But we need to clarify the question of the grave,' I added. 'Why did your family rent the field in the first place, when it's nowhere near the house? How far back does that go?'

Judith rolled her eyes to the ceiling and then looked at her silent son. He reminded me of Detective Paul, withdrawing from the conversation, gazing out of the window, chasing particles in his back teeth. Charles Talbot was abnormally disinterested, given the nature of our business. Two people dead, a disputed grave, a redundant house-sitter who still sat stubbornly in place like Horton hatching the egg – didn't any of it capture his imagination?

'I suppose we can tell them,' his mother said, trying to obtain his agreement. 'What do you think, Charles?'

He shrugged. 'Don't see why not,' he muttered, for all the world like his much younger brother.

Judith took this as permission, ignoring anything her husband might have to say on the matter. 'It's no great mystery. My father had a horse, which needed a paddock. He rented that field a year before he died. That was seventeen years ago. I have no idea what the rent was, or how they paid it. For all I know, it was simply an annual standing order from the bank, and nobody gave it a thought. They probably forgot all about it.'

'But your sister didn't forget it, did she? She arranged for herself to be buried there, after all. And standing orders expire if the account holder dies.' I had had enough of picking my way through the skeletal facts, making little sense of them, and yet it needed to be done. Somehow I felt sure the fact of Mrs Simmonds' grave connected to the killing of Mr Maynard, although it would have been just as likely there were two parallel problems going on, neither of them looking at all good for me.

Thea was frowning, her eyes flickering in deep thought. 'So, when did your mother die?'

'Three years after Dad.'

'Right. And Greta's husband?'

Judith blew out her cheeks. 'Marcus? God, he disappeared *decades* ago. They were only married for five minutes. No need to bring *him* into it.'

'I never even knew him,' offered Charles, from his seat by the window. He looked slowly from me to Thea to his mother. 'Where's all this getting us, anyway? I think we ought to go.'

'Right,' I agreed heartily. 'I don't think there's any more we can do at the moment. The ball's in the council's court now. Once they've recovered from the loss of Mr Maynard, they might pursue it – or they might forget the whole thing. We'll just have to wait and see.'

'But the police were involved, weren't they?' Thea remembered. 'They contacted you in the first place.'

'That's true,' I agreed. 'So?'

'So, it'll be on file, something to be followed up – especially now there's a homicide as well. They're not going to just forget about it.'

We all paused to entertain gloomy thoughts about what was to come. 'Poor old Greta,' said her sister. 'I always thought she was being un-realistic to think she could get away with it. But she would just steamroller her way through, ignoring anything we said to her. It was the same when she joined that dopey community. We all said it could never work out.'

'How long was she there?' asked Thea.

Judith smiled ruefully. 'Six or seven years al-together. I admit it was a lot longer than we ex-pected. She helped to set the whole thing up, from the beginning. But it wasn't all smooth sailing, not by any means. She was always fighting with one or other of the people there, complaining about their dogs or their noisy cars. Just one thing after an-other. They must have been so glad when she finally left.'

'Who lived here, then? Who were the tenants?' Again, I admired Thea's sharp mind, deftly filling in the gaps in the story.

'They were called Andreason, a youngish couple. I met them once or twice, that's all.'

'They didn't come to the funeral,' I observed.

125

'No.' Judith laughed grimly. 'If they had done, it would have been to dance on the grave.'

'Oh?'

'They *hated* her. She threw them out, with minimal notice, when she needed to come back here to live, and they had nowhere else to go. Susan said there was a massive scene, right outside the house, with screaming and shouting, and all kinds of threats.'

'Oh,' I said again, rather wishing that it had been Greta Simmonds who had been murdered rather than the infuriating Mr Maynard, since here was an apparently obvious motive.

'Judy,' said Oliver warningly. 'That's nae quite true, is it? Greta wasn't personally involved, which is how you made it sound. She had an agent handling it all.'

His pedantic delivery plainly annoyed his wife. 'It comes to the same thing,' she insisted.

He held up an admonitory finger. 'And she did give the tenants fair warning. Anybody would have done the same as she did. She hadna any choice once the community people asked her to leave.'

'That community sounds interesting,' suggested Thea, who looked desperate to avert an argument. 'Did you ever go there?' She asked the question of all three Talbots, eyes wide with encouragement.

'I did,' said Judith reluctantly. 'It was one of the first co-housing groups to be set up. They were a weird lot, talking in jargon most of the time. They pooled all their money and bought a big farm. All the barns and sheds were converted into little houses. Heaven knows how they got planning permission for it all, but they did.'

126

'Why wouldn't they?' asked Thea.

'Plenty of reasons. Dense occupancy. Change of use. Adverse effect on the local villages. There were about a dozen families altogether – nearly thirty people.'

'You know something about planning laws, then,' I said, noting her familiarity with the language.

'Doesn't everybody?' she snorted. 'I sometimes think that half our lives are spent wrestling with planners.'

Nothing had been resolved, but neither had I heard anything that made my situation worse, which was a relief in itself.

'This house must be mine now,' said Charles, unexpectedly. He looked around at the walls with new eyes, as if only then understanding his changed status. 'She said she'd leave it to me. I still haven't checked the will, but I can't imagine there'll be any difficulties. I'll get onto an agent tomorrow, with a view to selling it.'

I frowned at him. 'But you're her executor. Surely you saw the will when it was drawn up?'

'No, I didn't. She told me where it was and the name of the solicitor, and said I wouldn't need to do anything until after she died. We both thought that was twenty years away. It just goes to show,' he added vaguely.

'So it's for you to give me my instructions,' Thea realised.

'And pay you,' I said firmly.

He looked cornered for a moment. His mother humiliated him by coming to the rescue. 'Yes, yes. We came with the intention of doing just that.' She began to rummage in her handbag. 'The chequebook's here somewhere.' I had half expected her to launch into an argument with Charles about selling the family house, the one she had grown up in. People were generally rather sentimental about such things.

'Not you, Mother. Me,' said Charles, although making no mirroring effort to produce any means of payment. 'Gosh!' He almost rubbed his hands. 'This is going to put Clare's nose right out of joint. She'll wish she hadn't been in such a rush to sign those divorce papers now.'

His mother sighed. 'Oh, Charles. Sometimes I think you care about nothing but money.'

'Not fair, Mother,' he protested weakly. 'But Auntie Greta knew what she was doing. She could see I was going to need some capital.'

Mrs Talbot looked at me, and then Thea, and rolled her eyes ambiguously. I had the impression that everything there was to be said had already been covered in numerous family discussions. 'You haven't got a chequebook, have you?' She looked at us again. 'He does all his finances on the computer. Says cheques are obsolete.'

'I quite like cheques,' said Thea inconsequentially.

'Well, as for instructions,' said Charles, slightly too loudly, 'it would be helpful if you could stay on just for another couple of days. We need a valuer to come and have a look, for one thing. And meter readers. Plus, if there's any more trouble about the grave, it would be good to have somebody on the spot.'

'We haven't settled anything, have we?' said

Judith, as she stood up and reached for her coat. 'Greta is still dead.'

I blinked at her. Had she hoped that her visit would resurrect her sister? 'Try not to worry about the grave,' I said. 'I don't think they'll make us move it, when it comes to the crunch.'

'Thank you,' she said with a quick smile. 'That is the main thing, I suppose. She can melt away into the ground, just as she wanted to. Pity we'll be selling the old house, though. It holds a lot of happy memories.' I inwardly reproached myself for my premature assessment. She looked round, much as Charles had done. 'But none of the family wants to live here now.'

'Jeremy does,' muttered Charles. 'You always forget about Jeremy.'

Odd, I thought, how late they'd left it to mention their other son, so much younger than his brother, born apparently to a much older mother than normal.

'He liked his aunt, didn't he?' said Thea. 'He said she always sent him some cash for his birthday, and read the stories he'd written.'

'Blimey!' said Judith, raising a general smile. 'You *must* be a good listener! He never tells *anybody* about his stories.'

'I felt sorry for him,' she said simply. 'He seemed rather lonely.'

'They keep trying to convince me he's got Asperger's, or one of those things, but he's just an ordinary teenager, the way I see it. Of course, he's had to cope with his sister–'

'Mum,' said Charles warningly. 'Don't start on that.'

By a friendly, encouraging waggle of her head, Thea managed to elicit slightly more on this new member of the family. 'She's called Carrie,' said Judith. 'She's been ill for a long time. It's been a big strain on us all.'

'How old is she?'

'Nineteen. They were very close when they were little. He followed her everywhere.'

'Poor Jeremy,' murmured Thea.

'Oh, he's fine, really,' asserted the boy's mother. 'He's always done well at school.'

'It's just people he doesn't like,' said Charles, inscrutably. 'All except for Carrie and Auntie Greta, of course. Trust him to choose the misfits in the family.'

After they'd left, Thea and I indulged in a few minutes of debriefing. I edged hesitantly towards the door, little by little, as we talked, knowing I had to leave before the question of lunch arose. If I stayed to eat with her, it would be past two before I left, nearly four when I got home, the weekend almost over, and my conscience twingeing.

'We have to assume that the murder had nothing to do with Mrs Simmonds' grave,' said Thea.

I agreed with her.

'After all, he probably had loads of enemies at work, or people he annoyed with his nit-picking.'

I agreed again.

'I'm going to leave here on Tuesday, and go back home. Witney, I live. It's near Oxford. I've got my own house there.'

I nodded. 'Sounds nice,' I said.

'There'll be a lot of dusting, and weeding, and

130

sorting out to do. There always is after I've been house-sitting somewhere. I have to spend a week just getting back into my life there.'

I was at the door. I opened it, looking out at my car.

'Bye, then,' I said.

Chapter Nine

Monday was almost surreal. I had the threat of being accused of murder hanging over my head, while making every effort to carry on with normal family and business life. After much internal debate, I had opted to say nothing about the murder to either Karen or Maggs. I elaborated extravagantly on the matter of the grave, the ownership of the land, the family involvement, which worked very well as a smokescreen. When asked about Mr Maynard, in his role as council official, I merely said I thought he would present little further difficulty. 'It's mostly resolved now,' I lied. 'Although I might have to go up there one more time, to really make sure it's all going to be OK.'

There had been an awkward moment when I realised I was wearing an unfamiliar tracksuit that even Karen would spot was not part of my wardrobe. I solved it by pulling on an anorak I kept in the car and dashing upstairs the moment I got into the house, shouting that I was desperate for the loo. I quickly changed, and stuffed the alien clothes into a plastic bag.

Maggs had successfully transported Mr Ever-scott in Den's trailer to our tiny mortuary, where he lay on a slate slab, awaiting his cardboard coffin. 'Wednesday,' she told me. 'Better go and get digging.'

We dug our own graves, with a recently-acquired mini digger that I still regarded as more of a toy than a practical tool. We went four feet down, as opposed to the usual six, hoping there would be better aerobic activity, aiding decomposition and releasing nutrients to the soil. Any shallower, and there were risks of wildlife making inroads, with resulting distress to all concerned. Despite Mrs Simmonds' cavalier attitude, the reality was far from acceptable.

'Any mourners?' I asked.

'Two, I think. One from the nursing home, and the granddaughter who's paying for it. She phoned on Saturday, wanting to know the routine. She sounded nice.'

Mr Everscott, unlike Mrs Simmonds, had not paid all expenses in advance. He had wanted to, but his only interested relative had insisted that she would carry the costs. It was one of our strengths, that we would go along with all sorts of different financial arrangements to suit the myriad family patterns that existed.

Arranging an alternative funeral was not straightforward. The mainstream undertakers held most of the cards – they were the default removers of bodies from nursing homes or sudden accidents; they operated streamlined procedures that carried the families along before they quite knew what was happening. We got very few requests

132

after the death had occurred, much to my frustration. Despite advertising and word of mouth, we were not high profile. In the shock and haste that followed a death, even an expected one, far too few people made the effort to track us down and initiate our services in those first hours when the body had to be tidied away, retrieved from hospital or home and taken somewhere cool and competent.

Two mourners sounded forlorn, even to me, who had conducted funerals where nobody came at all. A life ended with scarcely any fanfare implied a person ignored, disliked or forgotten. Mr Everscott was none of these – he had simply lived too long. He had been married, gone to work, joined clubs, had lifelong friends – but, as he had explained to me when I met him, he had outlived it all. Even his two sons had predeceased him, leaving a single grandchild to carry on the line. 'If I'd been a veteran of the Great War, they'd be wheeling me out every November, and giving me a state funeral,' he'd chuckled. 'As it is, I'm just plain Sid Everscott, ninety-three and not at all proud of it.'

His sight had dimmed, his hands and head quivered constantly, but he still maintained a dry wit and a contented outlook. I liked Mr Everscott a lot.

'Poor old chap,' I sighed.

'Could have been worse,' Maggs said.

She was right. The granddaughter, who was well into her forties, turned up that afternoon to finalise the details and commit herself to paying our fees. She was, as Maggs had surmised, a nice woman, who was full of admiration for her grandfather's choice of final resting place. 'He always did have perfect taste,' she smiled. 'And he held on to his atheism to the end. The prospect of a service in church before his burial always infuriated him. This is going to be exactly right for him.'

It warmed me to hear her, and we parted with a handshake that managed to express how much we approved of each other.

But my complacency was short-lived. I was in the house, having just finished lunch, debating with Karen as to which of us would collect the children from school, when the phone rang. It was the same phone in the office and the house, with an extension upstairs. We always answered as if responding to news of a death, and the kids were completely forbidden from ever touching it.

'Mr Slocombe? This is Helena Maynard.' She obviously expected me to grasp instantly who she was and why she might want to speak to me. When I said nothing for a second longer than expected, she added impatiently, 'My husband was murdered on Saturday.'

'Oh! Gosh. I mean, yes, of course. I'm so sorry. What can I do for you?' It was an abysmal performance. I was only glad that Maggs wasn't listening and pulling appalled faces at me.

'I'd like a straight answer to some questions, actually. The police will tell me almost nothing about what happened after Gavin left home on Saturday morning. All I know is that he was brutally murdered by a blow to the head.'

Gavin? That pompous council official had been called *Gavin?* It didn't seem possible. Only as a secondary observation did I note the controlled tone of her voice.

'Well, I'm not sure–' I began, still trying to find my feet.

'He went out to deal with something about a grave – that's all I know. That's the last thing he spoke to me about. Somebody phoned here on Friday evening, and Gavin contacted the police straight away. Then he went out to meet you the next morning. I found your name on the pad by the phone. I had to go to some trouble to trace you.'

Slowly I gathered my wits. This sounded nothing at all like the scores of new widows I had spoken to over the years. This was a brisk and angry woman. 'Yes, I met your husband on Saturday morning to discuss a burial that I conducted on Friday. And then, in the afternoon, I was present soon after the discovery of his body. I don't know what else I can tell you.'

'Nobody will tell me *anything*,' she said bitterly. 'We were married for eighteen years, for God's sake, and now I'm being treated like dirt. Somebody in the village said you were questioned about it. You *must* know what's happening.'

Who in the village, I wondered, had known I was being questioned? I suspected the gossipy Susan Watchett. But my mind was still not properly in gear. The inhabitants of Broad Campden were assembled in a sort of fog in my mind's eye – couples, and old Bill Kettles and the dead Greta Simmonds.

'Do you live in Broad Campden?' I asked, thinking I should already know the answer to

135

that, and remembering Gavin Maynard walking away from his encounter with me, unaware that he was living out his final moments.

'More or less. We're half a mile out, on the road to Draycott. Why?'

'Well, your husband appears to have walked everywhere on Saturday. At least there was no sign of a car when I met him.'

'No, that's right. I needed the car. It *was* a Saturday,' she added defensively, and a picture began to form in my mind: a row between the couple, with him insisting on pursuing the outrage of an illicit grave on council property at the weekend, instead of waiting until Monday. Her telling him he'd have to do it on foot, then. Wondering where he was, taking so long to come home, thinking he must be sulking after their argument, then the gradual realisation that something was wrong – police, stunned disbelief, tears, rage. And maybe guilt at having spoken harshly to him, panic as to the implications – and, surely, grief?

'I'm truly sorry for your loss,' I said, making my voice as firm as I could. It was a tone I had naturally developed in the course of my work: sincere, straightforward, reliable. Nothing smarmy or false, as in the worst caricatures of undertakers. Besides, I really was very sorry that Mr Maynard had been murdered. It affected me personally quite badly.

'Thank you,' she said, her own voice quite steady. 'I suppose you won't be surprised when I say I still can't believe it. At least – I *know* it's true, but it hasn't got through to the heart of me yet. If that makes any sense.'

Finally, she was beginning to sound more

136

human and vulnerable. 'Oh, yes,' I assured her, thinking she was – at least for longer than was usually the case – to be deprived, by the restrictions of a police investigation, of the solace of a funeral, and the distraction of deciding about music and clothes and where to eat afterwards. It would be weeks, at least, before her husband's body was released for disposal. 'Do you have any children?' I asked.

'No,' came a low reply after some seconds. Either there had been a child, or the lack of one caused ongoing pain. I regretted my question. 'There's only me,' she added.

Why had she called me? We were skirting around something that still had to be voiced. She wanted information from me, that much I understood. But what exactly did she need to know?

'Well,' I began, 'I hope they won't keep you waiting too much longer before they tell you everything that happened, and release the body. I know it's horrible having to wait.'

She murmured a wordless hint of acknowledgment that I had understood her complaint. 'It was Greta Simmonds' grave, was it?' she went on. 'That the trouble was about? I heard she'd died, of course, but I never knew ... I mean, nobody seemed to know the details of her funeral. I'd have liked to have been there.'

'You knew her?' Something from the scrambled disclosures made by Judith Talbot rang in my clouded memory.

'Of course.'

'And your husband? He knew her?'

'Yes, yes. She lived here when she was younger,

137

and again for the past year or more. She was always great fun. Gavin met her later, after we were married. She was a *friend*.'

'But...' I was desperately trying to recall every word I'd exchanged with Mr Maynard, 'he never said. Your husband never gave the slightest sign that he knew her.'

'Well, no, he wouldn't, would he? It was official council business. Whether or not he knew the person in the grave would be irrelevant to what he had to say to you.'

'But...' I stammered again, struggling to grasp the complexities. 'Surely...? I mean, it seems strange that he could behave as he did. He said it was a travesty,' I remembered with a surge of bitterness.

She remained quite calm. 'It was, to him. Not just a trespass, but a kind of sacrilege. He was a devout Christian, you see. He thought Greta would be an outcast in the next world, being buried where she was.'

'So it wasn't at all irrelevant,' I said. 'His personal feelings were involved, if not in his words, then in his whole attitude.' A kind of relief went through me. The council man and the outraged Christian had not been kept as separate as all that. Neither was his wife as uninformed as she had first implied. She knew quite a lot about the events that preceded his death, after all.

'Who killed him, Mr Slocombe?' The question burst urgently into my ear. 'That's what I'm asking you. Who killed my Gavin?'

'I have no idea, Mrs Maynard,' I said firmly. 'I have no knowledge of Broad Campden and its residents. I'd never been there before Friday. I had the bad luck to meet him shortly before he died, which brought me to the notice of the police. But I know nothing whatsoever about how or why he was killed. You must believe that.'

'Must I?' she said, suspicion ripening. 'And what about that woman in Greta's house? What's she doing, hanging around, now that Greta's dead? What does she think she'll gain by it?'

'Mrs Simmonds' nephew asked her to stay. He owns the house now. He wants her to supervise the preparations for the sale, which I understand is to happen as soon as possible.'

An unpleasant laugh came down the line. 'Is it, now? Well, he'll have to think again about that, won't he? I happen to know there are several anomalies to do with ownership of that particular property. I think Mr Nephew will find that the Land Registry has a long list of questions for him, before he can even think of selling it.' Before I could ask my next question, the answer came unbidden: 'I should know. I work for the solicitor who handled old Mrs Goodwin's will. That was Greta's mother. There are things about that house which will ruffle a lot of feathers, once they're out in the open. That's what happens, you see, when a property changes hands.'

She wouldn't tell me any more, and I found myself reluctant to persuade her, even though experiencing a strong curiosity. My thoughts had flown to Thea, and the prospect of her being embroiled in disagreements about ownership rights, and access issues. I had known a number of cases where battles over property had raged fiercely, only days after someone had died. It was almost a cliché. Only when payment of the funeral bill was jeopardised did I ever get personally involved, but I had heard many a dreadful tale of what could happen.

Maggs had appeared at my elbow, listening attentively to my end of the conversation and waggling her eyebrows at me. 'Mrs Maynard, I have to go now,' I said. 'I'm sorry I can't be of more help to you, but I'm sure you won't be kept waiting too much longer before being given all the facts you need.'

I'd reverted to my initial stilted delivery, but this time it was deliberate.

'I expect we'll meet one of these days,' she said, as if making a threat, before abruptly replacing the receiver at her end.

'What was all that about?' demanded Maggs. She had no reservations about coming into my house, if she couldn't find me in the office or out in the graveyard. She was, in effect, part of the family. At times she had been the central pillar on which we had all relied. She had earned the right, many times over, to free access anywhere she liked.

I took her outside, one hand on her shoulder, rapidly debating with myself what I should tell her. Already I had kept important information back from Mrs Maynard – who was bound to discover that I was chief suspect in her husband's murder. Similarly, Maggs was sure to get the whole story sooner or later, even if my worst fears were not realised, and I was not forced to stand trial for murder. So I gave her a rapid summary of events, omitting all reference to Thea.

'When did all this happen?' she demanded, with a frown. 'You said there was some trouble over the grave, and that was it. When you didn't mention it this morning, I thought everything was OK.'

'I know, but we were preoccupied with Mr Everscott. The Cotswold thing isn't your problem.'

'Hmm,' she sniffed crossly. 'I thought we were a partnership.'

'Don't give me that. If it comes to me being charged with murder, then you can come and be my character witness. As it is, I'm only under suspicion, and it's quite likely to stay that way.'

'Right. And if you're found guilty I'll have to do everything here on my own, won't I? You'll be banged up for twenty-five years. Do you want me to keep the seat warm for Timmy – or is Stephanie your main heir to the business?'

I gathered my tattered shreds of dignity. 'Listen – don't say a word about this to Karen. It'll only upset her for nothing. I did not kill him, Maggs. I won't be going to prison, unless it's for driving an untaxed car.'

'*And* having bald tyres,' she reminded me. 'In fact, I'd give that top priority for this afternoon. Sounds to me as if you're likely to be ordered back to Sodding Bunkum, or whatever it's called, any time now. I can't pretend I understand all that stuff about stones and gateways, but they're not going to just forget about you, are they?'

'Broad Campden. It's actually a very nice little village.'

'Sounds it,' she said. 'I bet you're thrilled that

you had to go there on Friday.' She gave me a closer look. 'I meant that sarcastically,' she explained. 'You're not supposed to look like that.'

'Like what?'

'Like you're not as totally *un*thrilled as you should be.'

'Maggs, I promise you I have no reason whatsoever for liking Broad Campden, and the things that happened to me there. Now, let's get on, shall we?'

'You're a terrible liar,' she told me cheerfully. 'Well, I'll find it out in the end – you know I always do.'

'Shut up,' I said, wondering whether Karen, too, could see through me, the way Maggs did.

Chapter Ten

To my relief, Karen seemed entirely focused on the children and the state of our bank account that day. I tried to shield her from the depressing facts about our financial situation, but she insisted on knowing the full details, blaming herself for our precarious position. 'That's daft,' I told her, over and over. 'Without your compensation money, we'd be in real trouble.'

'Without my injury, we'd be perfectly all right,' she always countered.

'It wasn't your fault. You're lucky to be alive. The money doesn't matter, sweetheart, compared to that.' I repeated these and other reassurances, on roughly a weekly basis, and had done for the past three years. It never seemed to change: Karen never let it drop. I did my best to imagine what it must be like to have a scar in your head left by a bullet. Her brain had only been grazed, according to the doctors, the bruising and swelling dangerous at first, but soon dispersed. She had been unconscious for a day or so, but when she woke up she knew who everyone was, could remember her whole previous life, and insisted on returning to normal. But there were repercussions that only gradually made themselves manifest. A tremor in her right arm and leg that never went away; poor focus in her right eye; and the permanent scar where hair would no longer grow, along the side of her head. And a kind of low-level lack of coordination that sometimes seemed more psychological than physical. She was still my Karen, still the mother of my children, but strangely changed.

I had devoted the past three years to working out precisely *how* she was different. It occupied a lot of my waking thoughts, and I never gave up trying to revive the person she had been before. But it was like trying to track down the end of the rainbow. When I told myself she was understandably anxious about small, silly things, she would do something reckless, with no thought for the consequences. When I reorganised my working week so as to be available to cope with the children, she would push me aside saying she was perfectly capable of doing it herself. The new Karen was deeply, impossibly unreasonable. The old Karen had been entirely logical and balanced. The difference never got easier to live with.

The only point on which she remained consistent to the point of tedium was money, and how it was her fault we never had enough of it.

I could not tell her about the events of Broad Campden, and Maggs knew better than to mention it in front of her. Karen's reaction could equally well be a relaxed chuckle or a frantic terror that I would spend the rest of my life in prison. Or both. Or something else again. Sometimes I wondered whether that bullet had broken a kind of mainspring inside her head, some regulatory function that no longer worked. So her inner mechanism now ran insanely fast or slow, like a clock in a cartoon, hands whizzing round its face, only to stop abruptly every now and then. The only strategy that worked was to keep life predictable, with routines and habits that helped us all to feel secure. The children mostly colluded with this quite happily. They seemed to understand their mother a lot better than I did. When she was worked up, they simply sat quietly and waited for her to calm down again. She never hit them and seldom directly accused them of causing her flare-ups. If they were too noisy for her, she put her hands over her ears and they quietened down. I worried that they were being unnaturally repressed, but then remembered that most children through the past umpteen centuries had been prevented from making undue noise, at least in the Western world, and it was more or less the human condition by this time.

It was surprising, I sometimes thought, the way we had all adapted. The facts, starkly described, painted a picture of a family badly damaged by a single act of violence. But the reality was that we were still Drew and Karen and Stephanie and Timothy, and we all loved each other and got on with life as we'd constructed it for ourselves. We laughed and played together. We had catch-phrases and silly stories. And there was Maggs, who had always provided a kind of safety net, simply by being her own extraordinary self.

Without Maggs to confide in, I would have stewed much more over the death of Mr Maynard in Broad Campden. Having dumped most of the story on my stalwart colleague, I felt free to get on with the daily round, which although not arduous, did require my attention. The business was not simply burying the free-thinking dead in my field, but maintaining links with the probable sources of these dead. I had a habit of visiting three or four of the nearest nursing homes, making myself plea-sant, reminding them that it was not only perfectly ethical, but actually their duty, to add my name to the possible list of undertakers, when asked by relatives of their inmates. This was akin to the repetition of housework: if I didn't go regularly, my name got dusty and cobwebby in their minds, and they forgot to mention me. In theory, they had little objection to the way I did things. They all liked me and were taken by Maggs, but they seemed to switch into automatic mode, calling the same number they always had – that of the big efficient undertaker who had men on standby right around the clock, and could be there in twenty minutes. Even when the dead person had expressed an interest in a natural burial, this could happen. I couldn't bear to count the number of funerals we'd lost, for no good reason at all.

On Monday afternoon, I went to see Carole Mitchell, matron of a large private nursing home in Wincanton; then I took the car for its new tyres and collected my children from school. I felt complacent at having achieved so much, and ready for the aromatic spaghetti bolognese that Karen was cooking for us. I thrust all thoughts of the Cotswolds from my mind, and was rewarded with some very satisfactory marital sex at the end of the day.

Tuesday dawned fine and sunny, with birds singing outside. My first thoughts were of the children, with only four more days of school before the Easter holidays began. I relished the prospect of relaxed breakfasts and grubby clothes. We could go out as a family, perhaps, taking a picnic, weather permitting. Somehow the whole miserable business of the murdered council man would be resolved, releasing me from suspicion completely, and letting Mrs Simmonds lie where she was in perpetuity. It all seemed obvious in that first hour of the day.

At nine-fifteen the phone rang just as I had sat down in the office and started to plan my day. It was a woman whose husband had just been admitted to the hospice. He wanted to be buried in my field, and would I go with her to his bedside and take down his wishes. 'I don't want to press you,' she said, 'but the truth is, I don't think there's very much time.'

'I could come on Thursday,' I offered, thinking I should give Mr Everscott due attention until

146

then. 'Would that be all right?'

'I suppose so,' she said softly. 'It feels wrong to be in a hurry – and yet...'

'I understand,' I told her. 'But please try not to worry. There isn't really a great deal to decide, when it comes to it, once I know you've chosen my burial ground.'

'But he does want to see you,' she said, more urgently. 'And could you bring some pictures, as well? He wants to be able to ... visualise it.' Her voice thickened. 'He's being fantastically brave.'

'That's good,' I said, sincerely. People who could confront their own demise earned a dozen gold stars in my book.

'Is it?' she said.

'I promise you. So, I'll meet you at St Mildred's at eleven on Thursday, then, Mrs Kalinsky.' I had jotted down the name as soon as she'd intro-duced herself.

'Kaplinsky,' she corrected. 'With a "p".'

'I'm sorry. I've got it now. Thank you for ring-ing.'

When the phone went again, five minutes later, I thought it was the same woman, perhaps changing the time or asking another question. But it was a voice I recognised for its clear sweet tones, even though I had not consciously registered it when face-to-face.

'It's me, Thea Osborne,' she said, with a shade of apology.

'Hello,' I replied, attributing my speeding heart rate to fear that I was in more trouble.

'There's a bit of bother up here, I'm afraid, and

I didn't know who else to speak to. It's a real cheek on my part, I realise that.'

'Not at all. What's the problem?'

'Mr Maynard's wife came here last night, and shouted at me. She's found out about the grave and you – the whole story, really.'

'Yes, I know. She phoned me.'

'Oh ... she never said. Anyway, she's furious with the police, demanding to see his body and start arranging his funeral. They won't let her, of course. The coroner's officer must have told her that.'

'People don't always listen.'

'Right. But there was something odd about her. She didn't seem *upset* enough. I know shock does funny things to people, but she obviously had something on her mind that wasn't just the fact that her husband was dead.'

'I thought that as well,' I recalled. 'She's angry.'

'And scared.'

'Oh?' A crazy thought occurred to me, but I didn't voice it. 'I missed that.'

'Well, that's what I thought. And it could be simply that she's afraid of living on her own, or getting through the coming weeks, with all the paperwork and so forth. The whole business can be frightening for some people. But this struck me as different, somehow.'

She was speaking my lines. *I* was meant to be the expert on the newly bereaved. It made me chuckle silently to myself. 'I'm still not sure where the problem is,' I prompted. In my experience, women very often took forever to come out with the real reason for their sadness or worry. I'd taught myself to be patient about it, but I very much wanted her to get to the point.

'Oh, sorry. Yes. Well, she says I should be very careful what I say to Charles Talbot. That I should not go along with his plans to sell the house, because it could get me into trouble.'

'She told me some of that, as well,' I said. 'She seems to be pretty well acquainted with the planning laws.'

'This isn't *planning*. It's ownership of the house. I don't really get it, but somehow in her mind, this house is linked to her husband's murder. Seems a rather poor motive to me, I must admit.'

'I imagine people have killed in order to get their hands on a very nice Cotswold cottage, once in a while,' I suggested.

'Maybe. But how on earth does Mr Maynard fit into it?'

'I have no idea – but at least it would get me off the hook, wouldn't it?' I brightened at the thought. 'Nobody could accuse me of even knowing about it.'

'Well...' she said carefully, 'they might. They might think Mrs Simmonds told you the whole story. They might think you and Mr Maynard argued about it on Saturday.'

'Well, those things didn't happen, and they would have to provide some sort of evidence, wouldn't they? Evidence that doesn't remotely exist.'

'You don't have to convince *me*,' she laughed. 'I'm just telling you how it might look.'

'Is that what your daughter would say?'

'Never mind her. She's caused enough trouble

149

as it is.'

'Only doing her job,' I protested. 'Don't be so hard on her.'

'Don't panic. It's nothing like as bad as it sounds.' There was a pause, during which I struggled to find something else to say.

'When are you going home, then?' I finally asked.

'Later today, I guess. I don't want to get involved in any more of this, and there's no need for me to be here any longer. I'm dropping the keys with an estate agent in Chipping Campden, and hitting the open road.' She sounded wistful.

'But it's like unfinished business,' I hazarded.

'Precisely. Just drifting off and abandoning it all. Who's going to visit the grave? This is a nice house, with a lot of family history, and they're just disposing of it as fast as they can.'

'Mrs M's right, though,' I said. 'There's no way they can just sell it before the probate stuff's been done. It's not as if Mrs Simmonds *expected* to die when she did. Everybody thought she had decades to go yet.'

'I wonder about that, actually. I have a feeling she knew she didn't have very long. Why would she have arranged her funeral and made sure her will was all up to date otherwise?'

'Peace of mind? Change of circumstances? It went with leaving that commune place.'

She sighed. 'There are so many loose ends. I hate that. It's like losing a book before you've got to the end. I'm always going to wonder what happens next.'

'Don't worry,' I told her, 'it's obviously not the

150

end as far as I'm concerned. I've still got to convince them I didn't kill bloody Mr Maynard.'

She laughed, and I took not the slightest offence.

'Sorry,' she giggled. 'It isn't funny, I know. It must be a really horrible feeling, in fact. But I don't think they seriously suspect you.'

'Hmm,' I said gloomily. 'I wish I could be sure. It would help just to know what the next step is. I've got business here, tomorrow and Thursday, that I can't avoid. It's unsettling to think they might cart me off at any moment, leaving Maggs to do everything.'

'Maggs? Is that your wife?'

'No, my wife's Karen. Maggs is my partner. She's a treasure. You should meet her—' I stopped. What was I saying? I was never going to see Thea Osborne again, never introduce her to the people in my life, never going to get entangled in anything of that sort.

'Well, maybe I will one day,' she said, as if to reassure me. 'And maybe you could keep me posted about what's going on here? I have this insatiable curiosity, you see – I always have to hear the end of the story. Even if it means getting myself into trouble.' Was that a coded message? It gave me a cold shiver, along with the thought, *It wouldn't be you who got into trouble though, would it?* And I wasn't thinking of my situation regarding the police.

'I won't know how to contact you,' I said, disingenuously. Of course I would be able to find her if I really wanted to.

'You could email me. Have you got a pen?'

151

'I don't really do email,' I admitted. 'I leave all that to Maggs.'

'Oh.' She thought I was brushing her off. Perhaps I was. I definitely knew that I ought to, that there was no good reason to maintain contact with her. I could and should just forget her, and the small part she had played in the murder of Gavin Maynard.

'Give me your phone number,' I said.

Not a lot more happened that day. Maggs kept saying I should phone the police in Gloucestershire and demand to know where I stood. 'Take the initiative,' she urged. 'Don't just sit and stew about what they might do next. It isn't fair.'

'Maybe they'll just forget all about me,' I said, with crazy optimism. 'If they find who did it, they'll just file me away as a red herring.'

'Under "R", I suppose,' she quipped. 'And they'll keep your DNA and fingerprints on their computer for a million years. Doesn't that worry you?'

'A bit,' I admitted. 'For the principle of the thing. Isn't there some ruling that says they have to destroy it?'

'I think they're still contesting it,' she said vaguely. 'I'll ask Den.'

'Meanwhile,' I persisted, 'I think I'll just take it a day at a time, and assume they'll adopt a reasonable view. If they want to question me again, they'll have to come here to do it. I can't be forever driving up there and back, now, can I?'

She rolled her eyes and lapsed into silence for half an hour, while I marked Mr Everscott's grave on our detailed plans of the burial ground, and checked his meagre paperwork. One good thing about a burial was that there was no need for the cremation papers signed by two doctors. Another good thing was that we could be relaxed about the timing, instead of obsessively watching the clock. Ten or twelve other good things regularly occurred to me as well, even after years of operating my environmentally benign business. A shame, then, that the great majority of the population still unthinkingly signed up for cremations in all their stark and sterile glory.

I thought, too, about Thea, wondering whether she had reached home yet, whether *I* ever would actually phone her, whether we would meet again. I thought a bit about other women – my wife, Mrs Maynard, Judith Talbot – the things they had said and their feelings towards me.

It was a day for phone calls. Just as I was sitting down with Karen to enjoy the scrambled eggs she had prepared, it rang again. I answered, expecting something unpleasant, which is what I got.

'Mr Slocombe? It's Daphne from the school. I'm afraid Stephanie has had a bit of an accident.'

A bit of an accident meant deep coma, shattered spinal column, acid across the eyes, in common English parlance. 'Where is she?' I choked, all the breath gone out of me.

'She's right here beside me. She banged her head, half an hour ago, and we've been watching her for any worrying signs. She seems fine, but is rather upset. Could you speak to her for me?'

'Daddy? Hello,' came the voice of my daughter, far more faintly than it should have done.

'Steph? What happened to you, sweetheart?'

'Harvey Johnson pushed me,' she said. 'My head's got a big lump on it and it hurts.'

'You poor thing. Has Mrs Foster put something on it for you?'

'Cream. It *hurts*. It's like a little man thumping me inside my head.'

'I'll come and get you, right away. We can go to the hospital and they can see if everything's all right.' I had caught Karen's eye and held it, from the first words, and she seemed to have ceased breathing completely. She did none of the stupid silent mouthings that people always did in films. She simply waited trustingly, knowing I would do as much or more than was necessary. Where Stephanie was concerned, nobody doubted that I could pick up Everest and shift it half a mile to the east.

'Thank you,' said my little girl.

I reported the facts to Karen, while pulling on my jacket and taking a final mouthful of egg. 'I'll let you know what they say,' I promised needlessly. 'But it might be a while.'

'What about Timmy?' she reminded me quietly.

I froze. It was just past one o'clock. I was unlikely to be able to get back from the hospital in time to collect him at three-fifteen. 'Um...' I said.

Karen exhaled. 'I'll ask Irene to take him to hers for a bit.' The reproach was gentle, scarcely there at all, but I felt it just the same. I had forgotten my other child completely, ready to drive off with our only car, leaving him stranded

154

at school.

'OK,' I said. 'Anyway, we might not be long. I might be back.'

'Yes, you might,' she agreed. 'They put children to the front of the queue. And it should be quiet in the middle of a Tuesday. It doesn't sound too serious. Did she black out at all?'

'I don't know.'

'If she had, the school would have called an ambulance. She'll be fine, Drew. You know she will.' Tears stood in her eyes, belying her words. More than anything, she was distressed at this reminder of the fragility of life. It could all veer off to the edge of the cliff at any moment, and there was nothing you could do about it. She was being immensely brave, in her own quiet way, reassuring me, calming me down, acknowledging that Stephanie was the most precious person in my life at that time.

Stephanie and I had spent a great deal of time together in her early years. Karen had gone back to teaching, and I took on the childcare in a fashion so cavalier that, when I looked back on it, I couldn't understand how it had worked so well. My little girl had played contentedly in a corner of my office, ridden in the back of my car, watched calmly as the newly bereaved choked out their wishes for a funeral. She had been parked on strangers at times, hustled into her clothes, rushed through skimpy meals, to suit the needs of my fledgling business – and remained serene throughout. Now seven, she remembered nothing of that period, but I retained my admiration and gratitude for the way she had made it so easy for me.

At the hospital, nobody showed any particular concern. The young female doctor shone a torch into Stephanie's eyes, and palpated her neck, and asked her a few questions. Steph conscientiously cooperated, and was deemed unharmed and in no danger. Nobody said, *Children bang their heads all the time, you know,* but it hung in the air anyway. I prattled excessively, assuring everyone that we did not make a habit of panicking, that I had never rushed a child to casualty before, that it was the level of pain that had alarmed me.

'No harm done,' said the pretty doctor with a smile. 'It's what we're here for.'

It was a line often used by undertakers – one that always worked well. I smiled back, and ushered my daughter out to the car.

'That wasn't too bad, was it?' I said, as we left the overpriced car park.

'I knew I was all right,' she said. 'What about Timmy?'

Like me, she had only belatedly thought of her brother.

'Irene's fetching him, I think.'

'Irene won't be there today, because Jacey's got a cough. She's away.'

'Oh. Well, one of the other mums, then. Colette or Jenny or someone.'

'Mm.'

I refrained from worrying. Whilst not really part of the school mums' social circle, Karen knew their names and phone numbers. If all else failed, she would get the school to sort it out. One of the teachers could drive Tim the two miles home. In

156

the olden days, the kid would have walked it without a second thought. Recently, there had been a more focused attempt to prevent everybody from using their cars, with a thing called a 'walking bus' taking the nearer ones on foot. They all wore fluorescent jackets and marched two-by-two in a painfully regimented fashion. It made me cringe to see it, but I was forced to admit that it was an improvement on using motor vehicles for trips of a few hundred yards.

By four-fifteen we were all reunited, Stephanie's head sporting an angry lump that was already purple with smudges of blue at the edges. Timmy was playing up, angry without quite understanding why. I tried to be patient with him, letting him talk about his short stay at Colette's house, where the twin girls had forced him to eat cake with marzipan on it, even though it was horrible. 'Never mind, Tim,' I consoled him. 'You're home now.'

'It was an emergency,' said Stephanie, nodding earnestly at her little brother. 'That's why you had to go to that other house.'

'Mrs Harris said it was annoying, not knowing who was taking me.'

I glanced at Karen, imagining the scene. Home time at the primary school was a laborious drawn-out process, whereby every child in every class was carefully liberated in turn, the teacher clutching the shoulders of each child until its parent was identified standing on the pavement outside. If someone was missing, the child had to wait. It meant teachers having to recognise two or three faces for each pupil. Mrs Harris clearly found the whole procedure as stupid as I did, her patience worn thin after a day in the company of twenty-two five-year-olds. The surprising part was that she stuck to it so religiously, week after week, term after term. It caused delays and traffic jams and quite a lot of bad temper, but still nobody dared to permit a child to leave the building without clear evidence of a responsible adult five yards away to receive it. Even I, in my late thirties, had almost forgotten there had ever been a time when things were different – when schoolchildren strolled along streets or across fields, or down quiet path-ways unsupervised, and arrived home without ever having encountered the word 'safety'. Now, the parting shot after many lessons or excursions was 'Be safe!' – an injunction that encapsulated society's attitude all too comprehensively.

Karen smiled back at me a bit vaguely, content that everything was back to normal – that she had done what was necessary to come through the small crisis without mishap. She knew, I pre-sumed, that it had actually been me who did everything – all that had been required of her was to make one or two phone calls. But this was to miss the point. She had not fallen apart, or lost the plot, or withdrawn into some safe, quiet corner. She had *functioned*, and still, after three years, we both knew this could never be fully taken for granted.

I had almost forgotten the unfinished business in Broad Campden, the continuing threat hanging over me of being charged with murdering Gavin Maynard, of being remanded in some distant police cell, unable to fulfil my duties to family or work. As Tuesday drifted uneventfully to a close, I found myself hoping that it was all being settled without me, that DI Basildon had solved his case and deleted me from his database, seeing no need to let me know. Did the police go to the bother of telling suspects that they were off the hook, as part of their routine? I doubted it. We were probably meant to keep an eye on the local press, and draw our own conclusions. I found myself feeling glad I had not burdened Karen with the full story. She knew nothing of the council official's death, and only a few scraps of the complexities of Mrs Simmonds' family and property. Even Maggs had been given an edited account.

There was only one woman who shared the full story with me, who understood my position and sympathised with it. And it was beginning to look as if I would never see or speak to that woman again.

Chapter Eleven

Mr Everscott's funeral was the big event of that Wednesday. Even with only two mourners, and with everything well in hand, Maggs and I were fully absorbed in the preparations. We seldom had more than one burial a week, which meant that every one was important. This is not to say that every funeral isn't important to much larger and busier undertakers, but there can be a certain conveyor-belt mentality if there are five or six cremations in a single day, as is not unusual. We were at the other end of the spectrum. We fiddled with the cardboard coffin, sealing down the lid and checking the weight. Lowering it into the grave was a challenge when there were only the two of us to do it. Maggs was almost as strong as me, and we had a good system worked out, but even so, it could easily become undignified if we weren't careful.

There was to be no service, as such. I would read some words, agreed with Mr Everscott in advance, and the granddaughter had expressed a wish to say something, even though there would be so few of us to hear her. 'I'll be doing it for myself,' she said. 'If you can understand that.'

I did, of course.

Two o'clock was the planned time for proceedings to begin. At one-fifteen, the telephone rang, and I answered it from the office. A small part of my mind formed the thought that it would be the school again, with Stephanie complaining of a blinding headache or double vision.

But instead – and I found my lack of surprise an indication of how all along this was what I had been expecting – it was the Gloucestershire Police.

'Mr Slocombe – I'm afraid we need you here again as soon as possible. We have a new development.'

'I can't,' I said flatly. 'I'm conducting a funeral in half an hour.'

'How long will that take?'

'Forty-five minutes,' I lied, multiplying by at least three.

'So you could be here by five quite easily,' he asserted.

No, I shouted inwardly. There wasn't enough fuel in the car, I had no wish to spend another night in the Cotswolds, and the subtle humiliation that went with police questioning was to be resisted as far as humanly possible. 'It would be extremely inconvenient. Can't you send somebody to talk to me here?'

It seemed to surprise him, whoever he was. 'Well ... just hold on a moment.'

Surely, I thought, people were normally questioned in their own homes? It was a stratagem to find out more about them, seeing how they lived. If it came to a choice between that and being dragged yet again to Sodding Hampton or whatever Maggs had called it, I chose the former. But even that was far from inviting. Karen and the children would want to know what it was all about. The uncertainty on the part of the officer made me think I was in no very serious trouble, at least. If they believed they'd found evidence of my guilt, they'd have sent a car to collect me. Wouldn't they? My friendship with Den Cooper, one-time police officer, had taught me that theory and practice seldom coincided. There were always constraints or distractions: issues about the weather or bank holidays, maverick individuals who broke the rules for the sake of it, and sheer clumsy incompetence, all leading to a reality that bore little resemblance to the slick operations we all watched on the TV.

The man came back. 'We could leave it until tomorrow,' he offered.

This was very strange. 'And then what?' I queried.

'Then you come up here to answer some questions.'

'Where, exactly?'

'Cirencester.'

'And it has to be there, does it? Not here?'

'Definitely.'

'And you can't come to collect me?'

'Normally, sir, that would be the procedure. But just at present we have nobody available. There are trains, I believe.'

His sarcasm went over my head, my mind racing down other lines. They wanted to confront me with tyre tracks, or shoe impressions, or a picture of my fingerprints on the dead man's neck, or a witness picking me out of a line-up to say I was seen bashing the hapless Gavin with a rock.

I gave in. 'All right. I expect I can be there by about eleven. How long will your questioning take?'

'I suggest you bring a toothbrush,' he said, with a very inappropriate little laugh.

I had to lie to Karen. And then I had to ask Maggs to do much the same. I could not bring myself to disclose to my wife the embarrassing fact that I was involved in a murder enquiry. Three years had elapsed since any of us had brushed against the violence and brutality of deliberate killing, but that wasn't long enough to eradicate the trauma of it all. All it had done was lull us into a false sense of security. We had all three somehow forgotten that such things could happen. We had lost the ability to deal with it, the thick skin, the black humour, since Karen herself had almost died at the hands of another person. I remembered the startled little lurch that had happened inside me when Thea Osborne had said, 'At least she wasn't murdered,' when speaking of Greta Simmonds. Perhaps, I thought wildly, Thea had somehow triggered the subsequent events. The word ought never to be uttered lightly. The imps and demons that lurked invisibly around us must have heard her and decided to do something about it.

'I've got to go back to Broad Campden again,' I told Karen, after the burial of Mr Everscott had taken place.

'What on earth for?' she demanded, unusually animated by her annoyance.

'Oh, just more nonsense to do with the new grave. It's completely my own fault, for not checking ownership of the land properly. They're talking about exhuming the body, now, and I have to try to prevent that.'

'Why didn't you sort it out once and for all, at the weekend?'

'The important people weren't around. I did my best. Don't be cross, Kaz.' I only called her *Kaz* when I was wheedling. She didn't really like it as much as she had ten years earlier.

'So we're back to the school problem again. Honestly, Drew, we've got to get another car. This just gets more and more ridiculous.' We had had two cars until one of them catastrophically failed its MOT, and the finances prevented either its repair or replacement.

'I know,' I said meekly. 'I'll go on the train.'

163

Maggs was every bit as confrontational when I told her the situation. 'You still aren't telling Karen what's going on?'

'I daren't. I don't know how she'll take it.'

'That's daft. When will you be back?'

'They didn't say.'

She looked at me narrowly. 'Have you really told me the whole thing?' she probed.

'I've told you most of it,' I promised. After all, the only detail I'd omitted was the existence of Thea. At that moment, I understood that I was more afraid of the conclusions Maggs might come to than anything my wife would think. There were definitely too many women in my life, I thought next, all of them expecting unreasonably good behaviour at all times.

'You didn't kill him, did you?' Maggs had the nerve to ask. 'He does sound terribly annoying.'

'Don't be stupid,' I snapped. 'That isn't funny.' It was not only unfunny, it was rather frightening. She made it sound very nearly possible.

'Sorry.' She held up her hands in surrender. 'How long do you *think* it'll be?'

'There's rules about it. Something about twenty-eight days.'

'That's for terrorists, stupid. It's only twenty-four hours for normal criminals.'

'That's a relief. See you on Friday, then. Or Saturday – when you won't be here, so it'll be Monday.'

'And what if we get a removal?' she said innocently.

'I'm not taking the car. Karen can't manage without it. Maybe Den would go with you?'

'Drew, that isn't very fair, is it? He'll do it once in a while, but you can't expect him to drop everything when he's not part of the business.'

'Once in a while is all I'm asking. When was the last time – eh? Well over a year ago, when I took my family on holiday for one week. You've just had a fortnight in the sunshine.'

'Yeah, yeah,' she shrugged. 'Just don't take us for granted, right?'

'As if I would.'

Her attitude only increased my stress. She hadn't seen what it was like to be interviewed by a detective inspector. Even being reprimanded by a young female constable was bad enough. 'At least the car's legal now,' I said. A new thought occurred. 'I wonder if PC Jessica told the Cirencester people about that? Would it make me a likely suspect, the fact that I didn't keep my car in order? Put me in a category with members of street gangs and hopeless reoffenders?'

She grinned. 'Instead of the fantastically upright model citizen that you really are?'

'Precisely. Don't they know who I am? An undertaker, for heaven's sake. How much more respectable can a person get?'

'Alternative undertakers don't count. Especially if they drive untaxed cars with bald tyres. Why don't they come and fetch you, anyway, if it's so important?'

'You might well ask. Something to do with pressure of work and nobody being available. Budget cuts, in other words. I've a mind to just sit tight and see what happens. They'd have to come for me then, wouldn't they?'

'Try it – I dare you,' she challenged.

I didn't, of course. Nobody in their right mind alienated the police like that. I had promised to get there, and somehow I would. By Thursday morning – another windy day, reflecting my swirling thoughts – we had checked train time-tables and found that I could just about manage to get to Cirencester, changing twice and taking several hours.

'You need someone to give you a lift at least part of the way,' Karen concluded. 'Call the police and see if they can fetch you from somewhere along the way. And ask them when you'll be able to come home again.'

It was a good suggestion, and I carried it out early that day. The person who answered the phone had no idea who I was or what I was asking, but finally passed me to someone who did. 'We can make no firm commitments about when you'll be released,' he said pompously. 'But perhaps you could speak to Mrs Osborne. She's due here this morning, as well.'

'Thea? What on earth for? She's not a suspect as well, is she?' Too late I remembered Karen at my elbow. I still hadn't said anything about Thea to my wife, nor about anybody being a suspect for anything.

'I can make no comment on that – but since the two of you are coming here, it just occurred to me that you might share a car.'

'But she's in Oxford and I'm in Somerset. How could that possibly work?'

I could hear his shrug. 'We're expecting you at

166

eleven, Mr Slocombe.'

'And what happens if I can't manage it? Will you come and collect me? That would solve a lot of problems.' The craziness of the situation hit me all over again. Whenever had such agonising over logistics featured so large in a murder enquiry?

'We would have to, sir, but there would be no requirement for us to take you home again. And the inconvenience would be considerable.'

Just as Maggs and I had worked out for ourselves. I heaved a noisy sigh. 'I'll try to contact Mrs Osborne, then.' It seemed a further bizarre twist that he should try to throw us together in this way. Didn't the police generally endeavour to keep their witnesses apart?

'Who's Thea?' asked Karen, as any wife would, having overheard the conversation. 'And what did you mean about her being a suspect? A suspect for what?'

'She's the dead woman's house-sitter,' I said casually. 'She was at the funeral. The police are raising a whole lot of difficulties about the grave, and now they think there's been some sort of deliberate misdemeanour on my part. They suspect me of ignoring the rules. But I can't understand why the police would want to question Thea. She lives in Oxford.' My insides were spasming with the guilty risks I was taking by telling such lies to my wife. It was all the worse because she so readily believed me.

'So she's hardly likely to come all the way down here, is she? Is that what they were suggesting? It would take *hours*.'

'Right. Though I suppose I could at least get a

167

train to Bath or somewhere and meet her there.' I looked at her, reading her face, trying to convey my sense of floundering in something that normal people would find a mere trivial detail. 'Why is this so difficult?'

'Maybe because you're making it so,' she suggested shrewdly.

I frowned. 'Am I? What do you mean?'

But she had turned away from me, so I could only see the side of her face. She was pale, and listless, already dealing with my imminent absence and the responsibilities she would have to shoulder. 'I don't want you to go,' she muttered. 'I don't feel well, if you must know.'

She would never lie about it. If she said she felt ill, then she genuinely did. The iron fist clutching my guts took a tighter hold. 'Kaz,' I begged her. 'I would stay here if I could – you know I would. But too much depends on it. If we get embroiled in a serious legal battle, we could lose everything. I have to convince them I acted in good faith, and I can only do that face-to-face. I thought about just letting it go along without me, but I daren't risk it. Honestly, love, there really isn't any choice.'

'OK,' she said. 'I'll cope. Just get back as soon as you can.'

Chapter Twelve

The plan worked almost too well. I phoned Thea on the number she'd given me, and she confirmed that she too had to return to the Cotswolds, for reasons she did not entirely understand. She would normally just buzz along the A40, but she could easily come down through Cirencester to Bath, and be there by ten. She gave the impression of having a map of the whole area in her head, rattling off road numbers, while I struggled to visualise her route. 'It sounds terribly out of your way,' I protested feebly.

'It is a bit, but I really don't mind. I'll come and meet you at the station, then, shall I?'

'If you're sure. The traffic in Bath can be horrendous. I never go there if I can avoid it.'

'Well, if I'm late, just hang about where I can see you.'

'OK. I'll have to go now. Karen's taking me to Castle Cary. It's all rather a rush.'

'The whole thing is completely ridiculous,' said Thea, with absolute conviction. 'I don't know why we're humouring them. If they want us, they damn well ought to come and fetch us.'

'Yes,' I said briefly, wanting to articulate some more of my thoughts, but aware of Karen rushing the children into their coats, ten minutes earlier than usual. Luckily, the school was open for a breakfast club, and we could drop them at any

169

time after eight.

I caught the train, along with hundreds of commuters, letting myself be jostled aside by more experienced travellers. I found myself without a seat, standing with two other men in the area by a door. Nobody spoke and the time passed slowly. Less than an hour, and it seemed like a whole day.

I was twenty minutes early for Thea, but waited obediently at the front of the station, watching every car as it swung off the road to drop or collect a traveller. The city of Bath was not a favourite of mine, despite the history and beauty. I could see some of the fine old buildings from where I stood, with a hill rising behind the busy streets. Traffic hummed on every side, and I was left with an impression of a tired old town no longer fit for purpose. At least the Cotswold villages offered peace and quiet, whereas here the demands of the motor car seemed to have created a sort of perpetual low-lying bad temper that was almost tangible.

As I stood there, my thoughts slowly calmed, the demands of family and business behind me. There was nothing more I could do to make life easier for Karen or Maggs. They had the car, and each other. I was stepping into a different world, with new things to think about, such as exactly why the police wanted to speak to me again, and whether one of the people I had met at the weekend was the actual killer of Gavin Maynard.

I had not previously noticed Thea's car, so had no idea what to watch out for. Something small and environmentally responsible, I assumed. She had not struck me as a person interested in conspicuous consumption.

The first thing I saw was her spaniel, sitting on the seat in a red Fiesta that I expected to occupy myself. Its black and white head with the long flapping ears bobbed excitedly as the car turned into the station forecourt. As I stepped towards them, the dog reared up, scrabbling at the window in a frenzy of welcome, as if I was a long-lost master, pined over for years, and suddenly miraculously restored. I smiled, in spite of the silliness of the thing.

Thea leant over to restrain the animal, beckoning me to get in. I could hardly see her for the impossible ears and flailing paws. With an impressively powerful heave, she tossed the dog over her shoulder onto the back seat, and beckoned at me again. I opened the door cautiously, half expecting Hepzibah to escape into the traffic of Bath the moment I gave her the chance. Behind us a car horn tooted.

'Hurry up,' Thea encouraged me. 'Sling your bag in the back with Hepzie.'

In seconds we were away. She threaded the car back into the stream of traffic and headed in a direction I supposed must be north.

'This is very kind of you,' I said. 'It sounds pathetic, but we were really stuck.'

'Anyone would have been,' she sympathised. 'The police are behaving very oddly. I have no idea what they think they're doing.'

I remembered that she was already acquainted with members of the local police force, and therefore presumed some sort of special treatment. 'I can't imagine what they want with you,

171

anyway,' I said.

'No. I'm very insignificant. I never even met the wretched Mr Maynard.'

'But you were almost the first to see his body.' I thought it through again, from the beginning, greatly facilitated by the atmosphere inside the car. The spaniel had settled down, and Thea drove reliably, with no sudden jerks or alarming manoeuvres. 'Those other people – the bird-watching couple and the two women in the car – are they relevant, do you think?'

'Unlikely. Although you never know. It isn't always sheer bad luck when somebody finds a body. Especially one that's only been dead a few minutes. I imagine they've all been thoroughly questioned by now. But the most important thing has to be that the police have persuaded themselves that there's a connection between Mrs Simmonds and Mr Maynard.'

'Which is where I come in,' I said glumly. 'I'm the missing link.'

'But I can't understand it. I mean ... I get that the council don't like the grave being where it is. But Mr Maynard was only doing his job. He wasn't *personally* involved. So it seems a bit mean to murder him just because of his position in the council.'

'But he *was* personally involved,' I said slowly. 'Very much so. He called it a travesty. His wife said he had strong religious beliefs, which implies he thinks my whole operation is blasphemous. That's certainly the way he came over.'

'So he was killed by an atheist. Is that you, then?'

I laughed. And then I remembered where we

were going. 'That's probably what the police are thinking. It must look beautifully neat to them – a nice simple fight over the theological implications of burying somebody in an unconsecrated field. They want you to give a character analysis of the woman in the grave, plus adding your impressions of me, and maybe the Talbots.'

'Could be. But they need evidence. And they won't get it, will they?'

'I got the impression they'd found something, when they phoned yesterday.' My skin began to prickle with a fresh wave of anxiety. 'After all, I had recently met him. One of my hairs could just possibly have got onto his jacket.'

'Did they take samples from you, for comparison?'

'I'm afraid so.' I had suppressed the memory of the faintly disgusting procedure by which they scraped the inside of my cheek. It reminded me unpleasantly of Saddam Hussein undergoing the same humiliation.

'They'll keep it on record for twenty years,' she told me. 'Doesn't that make you furious?'

'It might, when I stop to think about it. Maybe it'll just be a very effective deterrent against my committing any crime during that time.'

She turned her head quickly, to check my expression. We had scarcely looked at each other at all since I had got into the car. Real drivers, as opposed to those in films, only remove their gaze from the road ahead for the briefest half-second at a time.

'You're not serious,' she accused. 'You sound like my daughter, saying that.'

'Well, I can see both sides. And I don't think it is twenty years, is it? I thought it was less than that.'

She snorted. 'It shouldn't be twenty *minutes*. It's an outrage.'

Her energetic indignation was a delight. 'And you sound like my partner, Maggs,' I said. 'Although she's got a lot more mellow lately, she's still very *certain* about everything. And she had a lot to say about the song and dance she and her husband had when they tried to get back into the country from Syria last week.'

'Syria?'

'They were there on holiday. I've hardly had a chance to ask her about it, yet, but I gather they had a fantastic time.'

'I'd like to meet her,' said Thea simply. I tried to envisage such an encounter, and concluded that they would probably like each other enormously.

'She's a one-off,' I said fondly. 'There's nobody in the world like Maggs.'

For a moment I interpreted Thea's silence as some sort of offence – praising one woman to another was not always a good idea, after all. But a glance at her face revealed no sign of displeasure. Behind us, the dog was curled contentedly, as if riding in the car was her natural condition.

'Is your mother still alive?' she asked suddenly. 'And your father?'

'Mother, yes, father, no. He died ten years ago. My mother's only sixty-eight. She's always very busy.'

'Sisters?'

'One. Married, no kids. Is this some sort of rehearsal?'

'Pardon?'

'For my police interrogation.'

She huffed out a little laugh. 'Oh, sorry. I just wanted to put you in context. You strike me as a man surrounded by women, so I was just checking. Did I sound rude?'

'No, not at all. But it was rather a sudden change of subject.'

'Was it? It seemed quite logical to me.'

'So tell me about your parents and siblings. Incidentally, you're more or less right about being surrounded by women. But I do have a son.' I thought about Timmy for a moment, with the usual niggle of self-reproach. 'I'm afraid I favour his sister, though. Isn't that a wicked thing to admit?'

'Honest,' she said. 'I have a mother, but no father, as of a few months ago. Two sisters and a brother. I'm third in the family. We're all quite close. Eight nephews and nieces – and the daughter you've already met.'

'Eight! That's a clan. A tribe. Your mother must feel a proper matriarch.'

'She doesn't, really. I don't think she feels very connected to any of them. My big sister has three boys and my little sister has five.'

'Five boys?'

'No, no. Two boys and three girls. She just kept popping them out, but it looks as if she's stopped now.'

'So you're still in mourning for your father.' It was a statement, based on firm personal expertise. 'Right after your husband. That must be hard.'

'Not right after. There were nearly three years

175

between them. But yes, it did bring it back, and I took it very personally, both times. They were too young, especially Carl.'

'But it's made you stronger,' I observed.

'Has it? I'm certainly different. If "stronger" means not being easily scared, then yes. I don't feel I have very much left to lose, which is quite a powerful way to be. Except, in my last house-sit, I lost my nerve big time. I spent a week feeling sheer terror. It was all very cosmic – I was scared of being abandoned, losing my grip. It took all my energy just to want to stay alive. Gladwin saved me. And the rabbits.'

'Rabbits?'

'It's a long story. And sad.'

We were already in the Cotswolds, I noticed. The distinctive stone houses and tip-tilted land had begun to appear on all sides. 'Do you always do your house-sitting in this area?' I asked her.

'Actually, yes. It began more or less by accident, but then I decided it would be fun to really get to know the place. The history is fantastic, once you start delving into it. Like Broad Campden, in fact.'

'Really?' All I had noticed was a big flamboyant hedge and a funny little church.

'It was the absolute heart of the Arts and Crafts Movement a century ago.' She said it with a flourish, as if revealing something amazing.

'What's the Arts and Crafts Movement?' I asked humbly. 'Sorry to show my ignorance.' I ransacked my memory for some link, some piece of information buried deep, but found nothing.

'William Morris? You've heard of him.'

'Wallpaper,' I managed. 'My mother raves about it. Big flowers all over it.'

'Yes, well, there was a lot more than that. It was a whole philosophy. Everything should be hand-made and beautiful. I'd have thought you'd be in sympathy with all that. It's like your coffins.'

'Sounds great,' I agreed.

'We might be getting back to something of that way of thinking, with consumerism falling out of favour.'

'I doubt it,' I said. 'Nobody recognises quality any more. My grandfather was a joiner. He made wonderful things. But we're never going to get back to anything like that.'

'Undertakers used to be craftsmen, didn't they? I remember seeing photos of them, with the lovely handmade coffins. And they did all sorts of other things as well.'

'Traditionally, yes, they've usually been builders. I did meet one, when I was working in the main-stream, who could make incredible furniture; he did it as a hobby. I'd forgotten until now. He was young, too. The youngest proprietor in the busi-ness, for a bit.'

'There you are, then.'

'I'm not arguing with you,' I protested mildly. 'But I just can't see society going back to some idyllic way of life, where everything's made by hand. There are too many of us, for a start. And everybody has such high expectations, wanting so many possessions but paying so little for them.'

'That'll soon change,' she said darkly. 'It's going to have to.'

'Well, I just hope it includes natural burials,' I

said. 'Business really isn't very good just now.'

'There's a taboo,' she said. 'See what's happened to poor Mrs Simmonds.'

'Right,' I sighed, remembering again the way Mr Maynard had spat out his favourite word – *travesty*. 'And that brings us back to what we should really be talking about.'

'Murder,' she said miserably.

'Yes. And to be precise, whether there's a connection between Mrs Simmonds and the unfortunate Gavin.'

'Gavin? Is that his name?'

'I'm afraid so. I'm getting used to it now. At first I'd've put him down as a Dennis or a Malcolm, but I suppose he's a bit young for either of them.'

'But you can't help feeling that a Gavin ought not to be murdered,' she said, putting her finger on the exact feeling I'd experienced. 'Nor a Malcolm or Dennis, come to that. But Bill or Shane or Jackson – they live much more dangerously.'

'Stop it,' I begged, trying to stifle my laughter. 'This is awful.'

'Childish,' she admitted.

'Silly.'

'Unworthy. What would my daughter say?'

'I can't bear to think. And Maggs would be almost as bad.'

She took a deep breath, and changed to a lower gear as we approached the lights at Stow-on-the-Wold. 'We're avoiding the issue,' she said. 'Not that anyone could blame us.'

'Connections. We're wondering about connections.'

'And we can't possibly draw any conclusions

178

from the little we know. All the same, it might be interesting to go over it together. Pool our resources. Let's suppose that somebody killed Mr Maynard because of his attitude towards Mrs Simmonds' grave.'

'Which was hostile. So the killer would have been sympathetic. And that brings it back to me. This is not a promising avenue.'

'Plenty of other people must have approved of her choice of funeral.'

'Oh? Who? The Watchetts come to mind first, and I can't help feeling they were only pretending to be enthusiastic. But at least they knew Mr Maynard. They definitely ought to be on the list.'

'The Talbots,' she said succinctly.

I shook my head. 'They didn't know him, they weren't here when he was killed, and all they care about is getting the house.'

'Even the young one? He's a shifty character, if ever I saw one.'

'Honestly, Thea – he's just a typical teenager. You're clutching at straws.'

'Did you know,' she began after a short pause, 'that there's a theory that Jack the Ripper was actually a philanthropist? He wanted to get the East End cleaned up, so he did those gory murders as a way of drawing attention to the conditions there. I often think about that – after all, the victims were all prostitutes, and in those days, they'd have seemed subhuman to almost everybody. Sacrificial lambs. Easy to reconcile with a person's conscience.'

'Ri ... i ... ight,' I said slowly. 'And your point is?'

'Could it be that the murderer of Mr M wanted

179

to highlight the scandal of natural burial – that they actually agreed with him, and wanted to make it a public issue?'

I groaned. 'Poor old Gavin, in that case! Rather a high price to pay to get his opinion heard, don't you think? Besides, that sort of abstract motive isn't very convincing. You do need to be really angry or really insane to bash someone hard enough to kill them. It's not like pushing a forceful argument. Anyway, I still don't see any indication that there's a connection. He was a council official in charge of– Hang on...' I stopped myself as a realisation dawned. 'No, he wasn't in charge of planning, was he? He was Parks and Recreation, which is different altogether. A much more lowly post, for a start. A ragbag of issues ranging from leisure centres to canal towpaths. The responsibility for burials must have arisen because it didn't really fit in any other department.'

'Um...' she said, vaguely. 'I think we're almost there. Do we want to rehearse our stories for the police?'

I looked around. 'Where are we going? I thought we were supposed to go to the police station in Cirencester. That's definitely what the chap said on the phone yesterday.'

'God, no, that's not what they told me. If we are, then we're about twenty miles in the wrong direction. They want us in Blockley again, close to the scene of the crime.'

'I hope you're right,' I said doubtfully. 'He was pretty clear about it.'

'I'm always right,' she breezed. 'They changed their minds. It happens all the time.'

Chapter Thirteen

And of course, I need never have doubted her. The detective inspector was waiting for us, smiling tightly, shadows under his eyes. The investigation appeared to have grown more pressured since the weekend, days passing with little progress, I surmised. Money being spent on a multitude of forensic tests, teams of officers asking repetitive lists of questions and not a lot to show for it. The people of Blockley were no doubt growing restless at the usurpation of their hall, and the increased traffic as police came and went.

When Thea and I were ushered in, it seemed like a different place. Several more whiteboards had been introduced, and a whole lot more computers. Partitions had been erected, to give better levels of privacy for interviewing. Most of the tables sported piles of paper and plain-card folders. A nice-looking woman police officer was stationed near the door, to welcome in potential witnesses, who might be moved to contribute their ideas or fleeting sightings of something suspicious. The murder of Gavin Maynard had evidently risen higher up some mysterious scale of importance with every passing day.

I needed to assess my own place in this investigative network. I had obviously featured fairly prominently at the outset, my apparent shelving in the meantime perhaps a figment of my own wishful thinking. The fact that I had been brought back suggested a return to basics, a going-back-to-the-beginning that very probably indicated an enquiry that had hit a brick wall. I could guess at the general direction of thinking, but had no way of knowing what actual evidence had been gathered, or what it might imply. The whole business of evidence was confusing to me, anyway. I had never liked the Sherlock Holmes stories, where wild deductions so often seemed to follow from a tiny flake of paint or mud. To my secret shame, I tended to feel that it was not playing fair, that the villain sometimes deserved to escape, such had been his care to cover his tracks. Walking backwards through snow, for example, seemed so clever that it earned a Get Out of Jail Free card.

I found myself in a partitioned box in one corner of the hall that felt remarkably like being in a small isolated room. DI Basildon was cordial, but well short of friendly. My heart rate increased as I envisaged the interrogation to follow. I had nothing to hide – I was perfectly innocent, and yet I felt I had to engage all my mental faculties and enter into a gruelling bout of jousting that had appallingly high stakes. Innocent people had been charged and convicted of murder many times before. It could happen to me, if I had left a hair on the dead man's wrist. That would confirm the evidence of my footprints near his body. A jury might well arrive at the conclusion that it must have been me who killed him. In a strenuous effort to be objective, I tried to imagine myself on just such a jury – what would I believe? Unless the counsel for the defence came up with a plausible alternative explanation, my goose was very likely cooked.

I wanted to trust this man, this detective who surely only wanted to uncover the truth, but my body wouldn't let me. My hands were literally shaking as I took the chair he indicated and waited for the questions to begin. There was a small tape recorder on the table between us, and a different colourless young detective constable sitting next to the inspector was nonchalantly introduced to me. He said not one word throughout the entire interview.

When it came, quite early in the conversation, the implied accusation was laughably easy to counter. 'You have changed the front tyres on your car in the past few days,' the DI said, in a neutral tone. 'Could you tell me why?'

'Because the old ones were illegal. Ask Constable Jessica Osborne – she pulled me up about them on Friday.'

'Excuse me?' He blinked in momentary confusion. 'Osborne, did you say?'

'Yes – you remember her. She was first on the scene on Saturday. Her mother is Mrs Simmonds' house-sitter.' *Keep up,* I wanted to tell him.

'So where are the old tyres?'

'I have no idea. Probably at the garage I went to for the new ones. It's in Shepton Mallet.' I had a vision of police being shown a large stack of bald tyres and invited to sift through them. 'I suppose they melt them down for something, don't they?'

'It's not important,' he decided, apparently sharing the same vision. 'We can check with Ms Osborne.'

'That's right,' I endorsed, wondering whether he meant Jessica or Thea.

'More relevant to our enquiries is Mrs Simmonds' will. I assume you are familiar with its contents?'

'Relating to her choice of funeral? Well, yes. That is, she wrote it all out for me, and left it at my office, to be carried out when she died. Some people do put it all in their will, at the same time – my name and address and so forth.' I was rapidly relaxing – this wasn't nearly as bad as I'd anticipated.

But then he hit me. Not physically, but metaphorical hitting can be very startling. 'No, not that,' he said. 'The part I'm talking about is where she leaves you her house here in Broad Campden.'

'*What?*'

He was obviously joking, teasing me with a piece of unfunny police humour. I had always been an easy target for that sort of thing. The young constable beside him threw a glance at his superior, as if also gauging the sincerity of his words. I smiled warily. 'You're joking,' I said.

'Not at all. Although your reaction is rather similar to that of Mrs Simmonds' sister and nephew when they heard the news. They had already embarked on preparations to sell the house, in full confidence that it had been left to them.'

'Ergghh,' I said, in an attempt to express sorrow on behalf of the disappointed family.

'You can see, Mr Slocombe, I'm sure, that this makes for rather a bad impression.'

I merely stared at him, trying to understand what I had been told. Why would the stupid

184

woman do such a thing? I had only been aver-
agely nice to her: agreeing to conduct her funeral
according to her wishes; putting safeguards in
place to cover the eventuality of my going out of
business; noting down the exact location of her
field and the name of her executor. It had been a
bit more work than usual, but nothing outside
my comfort zone.

What was this detective trying to say? Any
implications had yet to occur to me, although in a
dim sort of way I knew that people who inherited
surprising largesse were often under suspicion. 'I
didn't force her to do it,' I blustered. 'I had no
idea it was in her mind. Besides – she wasn't expecting to die so soon. She ought to have lived
another twenty years.'

He steepled his fingers and pushed out his lips.
'Not so, according to her medical history.'

My own fingers had begun quivering again.
'Really?' I bleated.

'She was diabetic, and had been a lifelong
smoker. The occlusion she died from was technically unforeseen, but she was far from in robust
health. Her blood pressure was in the top five
percentile and she had high cholesterol.'

'But she wouldn't have *known* that, would she?'
I almost begged.

'Oh, she knew. She went for regular health
checks, and was given the full story, no holds
barred.'

My head began to clear, as if the sun had burnt
off some of the fog. 'But this isn't evidence, is it?'
I said. 'It doesn't *prove* anything.' Even I, with my
slender grasp of the convolutions of the law,

could see that much. For almost the first time, I caught the eye of the junior, whose sole role, I presumed, was to witness the proceedings. He held my gaze without a flicker of emotion.

'It puts you under further suspicion – and I have to say we were already treating you with special interest.'

'Oh dear,' I said.

'Mr Slocombe, I put it to you that you deliberately killed Mr Gavin Maynard on Saturday, March 17th.'

'I ought to have a solicitor, then,' I realised worriedly. 'Aren't you supposed to provide me with one?'

'Only if you request it. I did inform you of your rights, on Sunday, if you recall.'

'Did you? I must have thought it wouldn't be necessary.' I rubbed my face with both hands. 'How long have you known about this will?'

'Let's see now – what's today? Thursday, I think. Well, then, it must have been Tuesday, latish. You were right about one thing – the Simmonds lady kept an awful lot of paper. We took a little while to track down her last will and testament.'

For the first time I thought of Thea. Had she been present for the search? Had she known all along what they had found, and refrained from telling me? 'Was Thea there?' I asked, before hearing how foolish a question it sounded.

'Excuse me?' This phrase had always irritated me, used in this context. It sat oddly on the lips of a bluff Midlands detective, when I mainly associated it with American teenagers.

'Mrs Osborne, the house-sitter. Was she there

186

when you searched Mrs Simmonds' papers?'

'What difference does that make? As it happens, no she wasn't. She'd gone back home by then.'

'Why did you want her here again, then?'

He pushed out his lips again, disapprovingly. 'No comment,' he said. 'I'm the one asking the questions, remember?'

He had evidently forgotten it himself for a moment. I glimpsed some light ahead. He wasn't behaving as if he had a murderer in front of him, despite his plain warning that he was actively seeking evidence against me.

'I don't want a solicitor,' I decided. 'Why should I? I did not kill Mr Maynard. That's the key fact here. I met him a few hours before he died. I shook hands with him. We walked close together. It was very windy. You might find one of my hairs on him – but I didn't kill him. I was at the pub with Thea and her daughter. And Detective Paul. I mean Paul something ... Middleman. You know who I mean,' I finished irritably.

He doggedly went back over the same old ground we had covered days earlier. 'You were gone, all on your own, for nearly half an hour at very much the exact time the killing took place. You knew the deceased was working against you over the matter of the grave. And now we discover that you have inherited a very nice cottage in a very desirable village, making it very much in your interest to eradicate the potential unpleasantness and bad feeling over your unorthodox burial of the former owner of that cottage.' It was a long speech, clumsily constructed, but clear enough.

'But how exactly do you connect his death with

my inheriting the house?' The phrase *inheriting the house* echoed in my head and generated the first small spark of excitement. I had a house! It must be worth half a million, easily, even in a stagnant market.

'Think about it,' he advised me.

I thought, in vain. At the edge of my thoughts were the mysterious remarks made by Mrs Maynard concerning rightful ownership of the property, cautioning me not to raise any hopes. This recollection only served to muddle the DI's suggested logic even further. 'I still can't see it,' I said. 'Plus, you won't find my fingerprints on that stone, either.'

He emitted a small sigh of disappointment, as if he had hoped I wouldn't say that. 'We think there is more to Mrs Simmonds' choice of burial place than meets the eye,' he revealed. 'We think you and she both knew she had no legal claim to the land, and that you deliberately conspired to use it, for reasons we have yet to discover. This was so important to her that she rewarded you for your assistance, rewarded you very handsomely, in fact, with a valuable house. Unfortunately for you, Mr Maynard from the council got wind of it only hours after the burial had taken place, and threatened to have the body exhumed and buried elsewhere. This threat jeopardised your inheritance, so you killed him to protect it.'

'How? How on earth could he jeopardise my inheritance?'

Again, a flicker of disappointment. 'Because, Mr Slocombe, the bequest is conditional. You only inherit the house if you agree to live in it as your main residence, and ensure perpetual protection of the grave by turning the field into an alternative burial ground.' He was quoting from notes on a sheet of paper in front of him. It took me a few seconds to translate it into an idea I could understand.

'But that's impossible,' I concluded. 'We'd never get permission, for a start. And surely that kind of proviso isn't legal?'

He pursed his lips. 'Not for me to say. Sounds feasible to me, on the face of it.'

I started to think seriously about it. The field was a quarter of a mile from the nearest dwelling, at least. It was the right sort of size – two or three acres. It was well screened by trees. It could just possibly work, given the goodwill of the locals and my own expertise. But the Talbots would not like it, not one little bit. I shuddered to think of how much the Talbots would dislike the proposal.

'In any case, I don't want to live in the Cotswolds,' I concluded. 'I'd have to move my family here, and they can't be disrupted like that.' *Goodbye inheritance*, I realised wistfully. I'd known it was too good to be true, all along.

'Think about it,' he said again, but more nastily. 'That's if you haven't done so already. I am far from convinced that this is all news to you.'

'You credit me with more acting skill than I possess,' I objected.

He gave me a long look. 'I wonder,' he said.

I struggled to straighten my tangled thoughts. As police interviews went, this one seemed quite unusual. The revelations had obliterated most of my original expectations, leaving me less afraid, but much more stunned than I'd anticipated. 'We need to understand why she did it,' I concluded. 'There must have been a reason.'

'We?' he repeated, eyebrows raised at my instinctive assumption that he and I were essentially on the same side. It had been an unintentional slip, but I had the feeling it hadn't done me any harm at all.

I pressed my point. 'Yes – we both need to work out what's been going on. We both want to know who killed Mr Maynard and why. I can understand why you thought it could have been me, but you've got no evidence against me, and I assure you, there isn't any to find, other than the accidental fact of my walking along the same path as Mr Maynard presumably did, a little while later. Better to make use of me in your efforts to find the real murderer, don't you think?'

It was a boyish attempt to convert him, which was obviously doomed to fail. His eyebrows rose higher, and a cynical little smile played on his lips. 'Sir, we do not employ amateur detectives in this police force. I'm afraid you're going rather too fast for me. Nothing you've said has persuaded me to remove you from our list of suspects. In fact, I believe the next step will be to formally charge you with suspicion of having committed the unlawful killing of Mr Gavin Maynard.'

The abrupt switch of tone and mood was disorienting. 'What?' I croaked again.

He cleared his throat and intoned the formal charge again. Then he stood up and said something about bail conditions. My head was ringing so loudly that I missed the exact words. I felt a very long way from home, caught in a trap that had somehow been laid for me, perhaps by Greta Simmonds herself. But alongside all that there was an echo, a repeating word from something I had just said myself. *Accidental,* it was. I had said it was an accident, a coincidence, that my path had crossed with that of the dead man. I frowned at DI Basildon.

'Hold on...' I began. 'I just thought of something.'

'Sorry.' He shook his head. 'This interview is now concluded, at...' he glanced at his watch, 'eleven-twenty-seven a.m.' He stood up, and the young man next to him did likewise.

'Are you going to keep me here?' I asked, looking round half expecting to see a cage waiting for me.

'No, sir,' he said loudly. 'You will be released on bail, but at least for the next day or two, we would like you to remain here in Gloucestershire.'

This last comment, rerunning the events of the weekend, had probably been intended to upset me, but in fact it fitted well with what I wanted. After almost a week, I understood that the village of Broad Campden was part of my destiny. I had done my best to ignore it, but it had finally forced itself onto my attention. If nothing else, I was at least momentarily the putative owner of property there.

'Right,' I nodded. 'Bail.' Then I remembered that bail meant money. In effect it was like putting yourself in hock – you paid for your freedom, but if you absconded they kept the cash. 'How much?'

He smiled jadedly. 'You don't have to pay

anything these days,' he told me. 'Just give us an assurance that you won't run off anywhere.'

'Goodness me,' I said, with genuine surprise. 'Do people really stick to promises like that?'

'Sometimes.' The smile became more sincere. 'I have a feeling that you'll be one of the obedient ones.'

The compliment did nothing to improve my mood. It probably wasn't even a compliment anyway.

'So where do I sign?' I asked, confident that there would be plenty of paperwork associated with this bizarre system.

He laughed unfeelingly, and ushered me out of the makeshift room and across the hall to another partitioned corner. There he indicated with a little dance of hand and head movements that the silent constable should take custody of me, and see to the mundane business of letting me go. I was escorted to a woman at a desk with a computer on it, and made to listen to a lot of jargon about bail conditions. She managed to inject considerable gravitas into it, and I nodded submissively at the injunctions she laid on me.

Behind me a shadow fell across the doorway, but I did not turn around. I finished giving my assurances to the woman, and stood wondering what I ought to do next.

'How much did you have to pay?' came a familiar voice.

She had been waiting quietly, a small figure in clean respectable clothes, looking as if she might have come to offer some sort of professional service to the police.

'They don't accept money any more, apparently,' I said. 'All you have to do is promise not to abscond.'

'Amazing,' she said, her eyes widening. 'They must lose half their suspects that way.'

'That's what I thought,' I said.

We left the building together as if it were the most natural thing in the world.

Chapter Fourteen

It turned out that we were both thirsty and also quite hungry. Breakfast had been hours ago, and the sun had come out.

'We could leave the car at the cottage and walk to the Baker's Arms,' she suggested. 'Clear our heads.'

'Where's the dog?'

'She's been in the car all this time, poor thing. She'll come with us to the pub, of course.'

Which, of course, she did, even though we had to sit outside again. We had left the car locked up and sitting outside the house I still thought of as belonging to Greta Simmonds. Then we walked slowly along the village street with me resisting the temptation to recount the salient points of my interview with DI Basildon until we were somewhere more settled. Instead we talked about Jessica and Paul, and the same walk we had done on Saturday, unaware of poor dead Gavin Maynard awaiting discovery in a gateway. It did not occur to me to ask Thea about her own interview, which I assumed had been brief and insignificant. I was much too full of my own gruelling experience.

We arrived just as the pub door was opening. Thea marched straight through the bar, uttering a subdued rant about the way pubs had become so restrictive, when they all used to admit dogs without raising an eyebrow in the past. 'We should just plonk ourselves down by the fire, without asking permission,' she stormed. 'They probably wouldn't have the nerve to say anything if we didn't make the mistake of asking permission.'

I laughed. 'Never ask permission – that's my motto, as well,' I said. 'Especially where councils are concerned.'

She cocked her head, and I explained about the rules about alternative burials – or rather, the lack of them. 'It's only a matter of time before they pass a new law,' I sighed. 'But at the moment, it's remarkably unregulated.'

'Unlike the rest of life in this country,' she scowled. 'Whatever happened to personal privacy?'

It wasn't a subject I had given much thought to. Where I lived, there were very few CCTV cameras, and I couldn't say I felt especially under surveillance. 'Mmm,' I said carefully.

'You wait,' she warned me. 'Now you've come to the attention of the police, they'll be able to trawl through every phone call you've made in the past year, every time you drove along a motorway, every transaction you've made with plastic, every email you've sent – and a whole lot more. Doesn't it make your flesh crawl?'

She was almost shouting. I leant back in my chair. 'Whoa!' I begged. 'I agree that's terrible – but they won't find anything incriminating. They'll just be wasting a lot of expensive time.'

'You agree it's terrible?' she pressed me. 'Do you really?'

The fog was back, my brain fumbling about for a few clear thoughts. 'You make it sound totally unacceptable,' I began. 'And in theory it is, of course. But I don't personally feel that it matters very much. I suppose I still trust the authorities to use it for the right reasons,' I concluded, feeling pathetic.

'Aha!' she pounced, holding up a finger. 'There you have it. We might be able to trust them *now*, but governments change, often very suddenly, and we have all that mechanism in place for a full-blown fascist state. They know *everything* about us. It's all stored on databases – how we vote, who we speak to, what we read, what we buy.'

I took a deep breath, her passion like a small storm in front of me. Why had I never even thought about this stuff? All I could dredge up from my torpid mind was a few thrillers I'd read, where fugitives had to outwit the state authorities in various clever ways. And I had watched *Spooks* with no great involvement in the way cameras and computers could track every move a person made. It just made for a good story.

'I suppose that's right,' I said, even more pathetically than before.

She relaxed slightly. 'I'm sorry,' she said. 'I don't know when I got so het up about it, but it's been a gradual process over the past year or two.

The more you're sensitised to it, the more ghastly it all starts to look. I feel like a real Cassandra at times – but I know I'm right. It's all crept up on us, with so many reassurances and promises, we've just let it take over. When something like today happens, I just have to explode.'

'So what did the police ask you?' It wasn't such a change of subject as it sounded. I was worried that she'd exploded all over one of the police officers, as well.

She winced exaggeratedly. 'Oh, they wanted to know how well acquainted with you I was, basically. I think they're intrigued by my part in all this, being Jessica's mother and so forth. Plus, I imagine they've got a whole database just for me, after what's happened over the past couple of years. I do tend to turn up in all the wrong places.'

'Weren't they embarrassed at the way they fobbed you off on Sunday?'

'Not so's you'd notice. Of course, now they have woken up to my part in it all, I'd really rather they left me alone.'

It was a confusing answer, delivered in a wry, almost bitter, tone. 'You said to me, at Mrs Simmonds' funeral, "At least she wasn't murdered". It struck me as funny at the time. Now I find it a bit scary.'

She smiled. 'I know. It was idiotic of me to say that – but I have been involved in a few murders, one way and another. And so have you, I gather?'

I conceded that it was something we shared. 'Not for a while now, though,' I added. 'I thought I was going to have a nice quiet life for the next fifty years.'

'How old are you?' she asked, with startling directness.

'Thirty-seven and three-quarters.'

'I'm forty-four,' she said, solemnly.

This echo of the playground seemed to mark some kind of stage in our friendship. It made no difference to anything – how could our ages matter, after all? But it was a deliberate mutual disclosure of a personal detail, freely and honestly made, and it brought a little bubble of fresh air with it.

'So what happens now?' I wondered. 'I'm stuck here with no car, required to stay within earshot of DI Basildon, probably followed at a discreet distance, in case I incriminate myself.'

'There's only one option,' she said robustly.

'Oh?'

'We find out who really did kill Mr Maynard.'

'Oh, yes,' I said. 'Why didn't I think of that?' I frowned into my pint glass. 'And how do you suggest we do it?'

'I have no idea,' she said.

We were still giggling when the sound of raised voices from inside the pub alerted us to something going on. Two men were arguing vociferously, it seemed, the noise they made jarring on the quiet respectable village pub. I doubted they had much trouble, even on Friday nights, with drunken yobs and their graceless girlfriends. On a Thursday lunchtime it had to be dramatically unusual.

'What's going on?' wondered Thea superfluously.

One of the voices had an accent I had heard in

the last few days, exaggerated by the evident anger behind it. 'That's Oliver Talbot!' I said. 'I'd better go and see.' In my mind, Mr Talbot was a client, somebody I had provided a service for. Whatever might have happened subsequently to put me and him on an antagonistic footing, I still felt an instinctive loyalty to him.

I hurried to the back door and peered in. Two men were standing in classic aggressive postures, jaws thrust forward, eyes bulging. Oliver Talbot was almost unrecognisable from the quiet detached husband I had hitherto known. He held a glass beer tankard in one hand, the contents slopping as he brandished it at the other man. He, too, I had met before, but it took me a few moments to fix a name to him. Ingram! This was the male half of the Ingram couple, who had been at Mrs Simmonds' funeral, briefly introduced to me, but paying little part in any of the proceedings. I forgot his first name, but recalled his wife was Miriam Ingram, a name I had repeated to myself as worthy of attention for its pleasing rhyme. I had intended to share it with Maggs at some point.

'What the bloody hell d'ye mean by it?' Talbot was snarling. 'Just ye tell me that, and make it quick.'

The barmaid was a slender colourless creature, cringing nervously under the shelf of wine glasses. Where was Barbara Windsor when you needed her, I wondered? She would never have stood for such a breach of the rules.

Ingram was not to be intimidated. Both hands clenched, he stood his ground. 'I mean what I

198

say,' he shouted. 'Don't you bully me. I'll say it again, for the world to hear.' He raised his head, as if addressing a large crowd. 'Your family never did right by Greta. Nor by your own children. Always Charles, and never the other two. We all saw it, time and time again. Greta knew she was sick, we all knew it around here, but you never came near. Thinking you'd get the house for that son of yours, after he'd driven his poor wife half crazy. It's true, every word of it, and it's time somebody told it to you straight.'

I sensed Thea at my shoulder, but did not turn around. From my very limited experience, I fancied there was no real danger of violence. Two middle-aged men, with perhaps a pint or two of beer inside them, might bluster and shout, but they were very unlikely to actually hit solid living flesh. Except, I remembered, somebody had done just that, only a few days earlier, when Gavin Maynard was killed. I watched more closely, hoping to detect the crazed expression of a violent murderer in one or other of these men.

'Just mind yer own bloody business,' Oliver Talbot growled, already subsiding. 'You mind what you say about things you dinna understand. I could have ye for slander.' He looked round at the other people in the bar. They totalled five, including me, Thea and the barmaid. The other two were a young couple with rucksacks who were plainly every bit as terrified as the barmaid was. Oliver recognised me with obvious shock. I spread my hands to indicate that I was there by sheer unlucky accident, and had no comment to make on what I'd heard.

Ingram was left with his dignity likewise in tatters. 'Well, you look to your family for a change,' he grumbled. 'There's plenty that's wrong at home, without you interfering in matters you'd be better leaving alone. Helena Maynard is none of your business, and she wants nothing to do with you. You made a big mistake creeping back here, trying to bully her the way you did. She's in no fit state to talk to you, and you should know that.'

'And what's it to you?'

'She's a friend, always has been. She's been looking to me for protection – and I've no intention of letting her down.' His voice was rising again, and the fists danced in front of his chest.

'All right, all right.' The Scotsman was backing away, the tankard slammed down on the bar. 'I get it.' He attempted a sly grin, the innuendo so grotesque that in Ingram's place I might have wanted to hit him myself. 'I'm to stay clear of Helena, because she's your property. Now I have it.'

I braced, waiting for the punch to land, but instead, Ingram merely sneered and turned away. 'You don't deserve that family, you bastard,' he said loudly. 'Every one of them's too good for you, and that includes your bloody Charles.'

Carefully, I steered Thea back out to our garden table. 'Phew!' she said melodramatically, when we were sitting down again. 'That was exciting.'

'Did you see Talbot's face when he saw me?' I mused. 'He was horrified.'

'Didn't want you to see him behaving so badly. Loss of self-respect,' she nodded. 'That was what defused the whole thing. Lucky you were there.'

'And you. He wouldn't want you thinking badly

of him, either.'

'Phooey. I'm just a house-sitter. He doesn't care what I think.'

'But what was it all about? Ingram must have said something awful about the Talbot family. And Mrs Maynard – where does she fit in?'

'It sounded as if Mr Talbot came back here, wanting to pick her brains about the mystery of the deeds or mortgage or whatever it is she knows about Mrs Simmonds' house. You can see why it would matter to him, if he thought she could straighten it out. And Mr Ingram's her self-appointed defender, for whatever reason, and took umbrage at her being questioned in her fragile condition.'

The summary was clear, complete and rather amusing. I smiled cheerfully. 'You'd make a brilliant barrister,' I said. 'Cutting right to the heart of things.'

'I thought barristers specialised in obfuscation, actually,' she demurred.

I smiled again. 'Maybe they do. Anyway, it did look as if they'd both touched raw nerves. Talbot's a lousy father, and Ingram's got inappropriate designs on Mrs Maynard.'

Thea's eyes widened. 'And if he's been carrying on with her, he might well not be too upset if her husband got himself bumped off.'

Carrying on? Bumped off? If not Enid Blyton, then something not much more sophisticated was directing her vocabulary. I suddenly wanted her to be a lot more serious. The whole thing mattered very much more than her attitude acknowledged. This was a woman who had just been passionately

201

denouncing the surveillance society, after all. Surely the deliberate killing of one human being by another warranted at least as much mature consideration as that?

She saw my expression, and quickly sobered. 'Sorry,' she said. 'That sounded flippant, didn't it? But it wasn't meant to. I mean ... it's not a light thing to accuse a man of murder, even if he isn't here to hear me. That must be why I lapsed into Biggles-speak.'

I was thoroughly disarmed. 'Right,' I said. 'So what do we do now?'

'We'll have to think about that,' she said. 'But first we need another drink.'

Chapter Fifteen

It was a very weird feeling, being under police suspicion and yet free to roam the country lanes of Gloucestershire as much as I liked. Even more strange was being allowed to remain in the company of Thea Osborne. Somehow I would expect us to be kept separate, with injunctions slapped onto us to stay at least a mile apart. Did the police not realise what dynamite she was? Not only her passionate adherence to the cause of civil rights, but her past record for interfering in murder investigations might have alerted them. Over the course of that Thursday afternoon, she treated me to detailed descriptions of the experiences she had had as a house-sitter and girlfriend of a senior police detective, and I began to learn what sort of person she was.

'I think it's mainly nosiness,' she admitted. 'Curiosity about the things people do, and why.'

'Sounds more like a sort of commitment,' I corrected her slowly. 'You can't just walk by on the other side and leave it to somebody else.'

'That's true, I suppose. But there's no *virtue* in it. I can be pretty nasty at times, actually.'

'So can anybody. It's not human to be sweetness and light the whole time.'

She shook her head. 'I won't forgive myself for the way I was with Phil, when he hurt his back in Temple Guiting. Poor man – it wasn't his fault at all, and I gave him hell for it. And I can be horribly abrupt with my mother, as well.'

I resisted the natural urge to reassure her. Perhaps she had been unkind to the boyfriend. So what? Looking at her, and remembering what I'd experienced of her in the past few days, I knew she was essentially decent and straight. This confession of her faults made me uneasy, venturing onto territory that was just a bit too personal. Besides – I had a confession of my own as yet unmade. I had said nothing to her about my inheritance of Mrs Simmonds' house, persuading myself that there had been no opportunity. First her rant about the state of the nation, then the fight between the men in the bar. Now was the moment, but I couldn't bring myself to voice it. It was too starkly suggestive of my guilt; it raised suspicions even in my own mind, which was crazy, but true. Gavin Maynard had threatened to scupper a promising potential business, and

203

wouldn't anyone be tempted to silence him for ever, in those circumstances? I had often seen the awkward embarrassment that new legacies could produce in people – the sense of undeserved largesse that changed a whole range of delicate interpersonal balances. Now I was feeling it for myself. At some irrational level I was ashamed of the inheritance, worried that I had inadvertently given Greta Simmonds grounds to regard me as a rightful heir in more senses than one.

So instead I invited Thea to carry on describing some of her earlier house-sitting adventures. She readily complied, treating me to anecdotes that were exciting, funny, and sometimes almost incredible. Cold Aston, Duntisbourne Abbots, Blockley – she reeled off the names of villages, most of which I had never heard before. The stories were all very different, and she had worked out plausible reasons why each killing had taken place where and when it had, but the fact remained that she had found herself in the centre of some dangerous and unpleasant events.

Finally, light dawned. 'I get it,' I announced. 'The police have deliberately let us loose in the hope that we will solve this case for them. They know what you're capable of and they think you'll do it again.'

'That would mean they don't really believe you're guilty,' she demurred.

'Maybe they don't. Maybe it's all part of a devilishly clever plot.'

'Too clever,' she said. 'And it isn't the way they work. They're probably just waiting for you to make a wrong move.'

'Well, I won't,' I said. 'And don't think I've forgotten that I owe you for driving me about, and being so nice about everything.'

She shrugged disarmingly. 'Think nothing of it,' she said.

This pleasantly prolonged conversation took place as once again we walked the village environs with the dog. We turned sharply left, past the locked Quaker meeting house and onto a footpath that led to Chipping Campden. The sun had come out and the wind had finally dropped, but it was not at all warm. I could feel my nose turning red with cold and wished I had thought to bring a scarf with me. When my mobile tinkled in my pocket, it brought a startling reminder of the wider world when it turned out to be a very upsetting phone call from Maggs. She had tried several times already, only to find my phone unreachable. 'Does the name Kaplinsky ring any bells?' she began in a deceptively sweet voice.

It took me a moment, and then – 'Oh, my God! It's Thursday, isn't it? I said I'd meet her at the hospice. I forgot all about it. Ohh!' I grabbed a handful of my hair and pulled it hard.

'You didn't write it down,' she accused. 'I could easily have gone.'

It was the stuff of nightmares, guilt the most crippling of emotions. 'Can't you go now?' I begged.

'She doesn't want me. She doesn't want either of us. She's been completely let down.'

It was the ultimate sin to be unreliable if you were an undertaker. There are no second chances. At least with a wedding that goes horribly wrong, you can do it again. Mr Kaplinsky could die at any moment, without having his last wishes recorded. 'Ohh,' I wailed again. 'I'll phone her.'

'Leave it until tomorrow,' Maggs ordered me. 'She's too angry now to want to listen to you. So am I, actually.'

The loss of Maggs's respect was not to be contemplated. 'I can't tell you how sorry I am. It's this bloody business here, sent everything else out of my head.'

'I realise that, Drew. But you can't afford to just forget your obligations. Too many livelihoods depend on it.'

She often addressed me as if she were a school-mistress and I a disappointing pupil, but there was generally a jokey edge to it. Not this time. Miserably, I apologised again, and ended the call.

Thea had heard it all. 'Problems?' she asked gently.

I told her the whole story. 'It's unforgivable,' I concluded. 'That poor woman.'

'Well, it's not beyond salvation,' she judged. 'He can still have the funeral he wants. You missed an appointment, that's all. Phone tomorrow and tell them you'll reduce the costs and give them the sunniest spot in your burial ground. That should mollify them.'

I stared at her, my heart lifting. How was it possible to assuage my self-disgust so quickly? 'Thank you,' I said. 'I feel better already.'

She smiled girlishly. 'It's what I'm good at,' she admitted. 'Putting things into perspective.'

'Well, it's a great gift,' I said, somehow feeling she'd helped me to get away with something –

206

that I had escaped punishment that was due to me. She spent a few minutes reminding me about her past encounters with murder, as if to show me how serious life could get. Not that she said anything that really outweighed my transgression, but at least it was a distraction.

Then I began to worry about where I would spend the night. 'Technically, I suppose I could claim the right to stay in Mrs Simmonds' house,' I said, without thinking.

She looked at me, eyes wide. 'Say that again.'

'The police told me this morning. She left it to me in her will,' I muttered. 'But I don't expect I'll get it, and I can hardly pretend it's actually mine for ages yet. What about you? Are you going back to Witney?'

'Wait!' she held up a hand. 'Don't let's change the subject. This is a serious development. Why on earth didn't you tell me right away?'

I tried not to wriggle or look sheepish, with not much success. 'I didn't know what you'd think.'

'I think,' she said thoughtfully, 'that it would be a great motive for the Talbots to murder you, but I can't see how it links to Mr Maynard. Except there's something we still haven't grasped about *Mrs* M and ownership of the house. Something she knows about, that wouldn't be good news for the Talbot family.' She lifted her chin triumphantly. 'I know! Greta must have told her she was leaving the house to you. That'll be it. And she'll have told Gavin, and he'll have thought it was the worst idea he'd ever heard and gone out of his way to prevent it.'

'And so I had to kill him to protect my inheritance,' I supplied. 'Right. That's what everybody's going to think.'

'So we have to prove them wrong,' she asserted stoutly.

Speaking to Maggs had activated my conscience to a painful extent. I had deserted my post as undertaker, husband and father. I was having a pleasant time in the thoroughly gorgeous Cots-wolds, with a very nice woman. I might be in trouble with the police, but for the moment, it felt as if I was playing hookey while other people shouldered my rightful responsibilities.

'I don't see how we can,' I said. 'And for the moment I need to settle the question of where to sleep.'

'I should go home, I suppose,' she said, without enthusiasm. The dog, forever at her side, gave her a slow wag, as if expressing an opinion on the matter – though I couldn't tell where its prefer-ence lay. 'But then you'd be stranded. I brought you here – by rights I should take you back again.'

'Not at all,' I assured her. 'I can get a bus or train or something. Besides, we don't know when I'll be allowed to go. I have to check in with the police again tomorrow. Actually, they probably want to know where I'm staying tonight. I'm out on bail, remember. I'm surprised they didn't put one of those electronic tag things on me.'

We had turned round after my phone call, and were walking down the uneventful street of Broad Campden, and it was approaching half past three in the afternoon. The gardens were full of cheerful daffodils and little blue things. Almost no traffic passed by.

Thea didn't respond to my comment about tagging. Instead, she directed my attention to our surroundings, pointing out footpaths that ran in various directions, to Chipping Campden one way and Blockley another. I asked a bit more about the Arts and Crafts business and she rattled off some stories about artists and others who had lived in the village a century ago. Only slowly did I begin to wonder whether she was merely keeping me company out of pity for my situation, thinking I'd be hopelessly bored on my own. If so, she was right – I would. But I could hardly expect her to give up days of her own life simply to entertain me.

Nonetheless, she appeared perfectly happy to remain at my side. 'Mrs Maynard would be a useful person to speak to,' she mused. 'But we can hardly just walk up to her front door and demand an interview.'

'We don't even know where she lives.'

'We could find out.'

I stared at her. 'No,' I said at last. 'It wouldn't be right. Besides, she hates me. She more or less said so when she phoned me on Monday.'

'I expect she was just in shock. You know as well as I do – better, if anything – that you can't judge people by what they say in a moment of crisis.'

'That's true,' I conceded. 'And she did mellow at bit, as we talked. But I still don't think we can just descend on her unannounced.'

Thea sighed impatiently. 'I've done it before and it usually works out all right. She'd probably welcome a friendly visit, if we said we'd come to pay our respects.'

'But I'm the chief suspect for her husband's murder. How can I possibly face her?'

'How would she know that?'

'I imagine everyone knows by now. My reputation is in tatters.'

'All the more reason to do your best to clear your name.'

'I agree. But I can't face Mrs Maynard. I'm sorry, but there are limits. What in the world should I say to her?'

'Well, all right. But I think it would be fine, when it came to it.'

I stood my ground. 'No, Thea, it would not. Especially as she's probably got a houseful of friends and neighbours already commiserating with her. That would make it even worse. Besides, she's already angry. I might set her off on a full-blown tantrum.'

'You said that before. You think she really is angry? Not upset?'

'You saw her for yourself.' I had forgotten until then that Mrs Maynard had visited Thea. 'What did you think?'

She thought about it. 'Well, she was frustrated at being stalled by the police. I got the impression she felt sidelined, as if she expected to be consulted more. And she doesn't approve of me.'

I grimaced. 'Ditto. When she phoned she seemed to find your presence in the village unsettling. She knows a lot about the legality of the house, because she works for the solicitor who looked after Greta's mother's affairs.' I was dredging up as much detail as I could from the phone call. Monday felt a very long time ago.

'Yes – so she probably did know you'd inherited the house. She probably typed up the will that had it in.'

I thought hard. 'You know, I think she must have done. She made some sharp little remark about 'Mr Nephew', meaning Charles, implying she knew something about the future of the house. That was quite witty, in a way, the Mr Nephew comment.'

'Do the widows of freshly murdered men often crack jokes?' Thea asked sharply. 'I know I didn't, when my husband died.'

'Sometimes,' I told her. 'It's the shock. It makes some people say terribly inappropriate things. You should hear them at the funerals.'

'Hmm. Well, she strikes me as a hard woman, from what I've seen of her.'

'I'm starting to think she's got some crucial information,' I said. 'She could be a direct link in the whole story. She might even know who killed Gavin.'

'She might even have done it herself,' said Thea. 'After all, it usually is the spouse.'

I humoured her, rather against my better judgement. 'Perhaps she thought she'd get the house, on the grounds of her long friendship with Greta. But when Gavin let Greta know how much he disapproved of her plans for her burial, she changed her mind and left it to me. Which infuriated his wife so much that she murdered him.'

'But it would be just as likely to make *him* want to kill *you*. Besides, he obviously had no idea of Greta's plans for her burial. If he had, he'd have

211

told her the field wasn't hers in the first place, and she would have to think again.'

'And Judith or Charles Talbot would be the aggrieved parties, whichever scenario you take. They should really have murdered me, as well. Heavens, I'm lucky to be alive.'

'Maybe they will yet, now they know you're getting the house. It is a nice house,' she added inconsequentially. We were approaching it, as we spoke, having meandered some distance past it, heading east, and then turned back when the road became narrower and steeper and less appealing altogether.

'Can we go and have another look at it?' I said on an impulse. 'Just so I can dream for a few minutes. I'm certain it never will be mine. The conditions are impossible.'

'OK,' she concurred. 'But it's getting rather chilly, and it'll be dark before long.'

It was four o'clock, and I knew I would have to find somewhere to sleep very soon. The prospect of returning to the Chipping Campden hotel for a long lonely evening and potentially sleepless night was more grim every time I contemplated it.

'Just for a minute,' I promised her.

I hadn't properly taken in the house on my earlier visit. I'd been far too engaged with the people to notice room sizes or furniture, or the immaculate thatched roof. I was even momentarily puzzled as to how to find it.

'Down here,' said Thea, turning into a small street on the right.

'Oh yes.' My confusion of Saturday came back to me. The place was perfectly straightforward on the map, but there were odd turnings and a closed-in feeling, which meant you couldn't see anything further ahead than a few yards in some places. The house was on our right, bigger than I remembered. I looked up at it. 'How many bedrooms are there?'

'Four, although one is very tiny. The thatch is nice, isn't it?'

'Gorgeous. And this little garden must be wonderful in summer. Look at all the roses, and laburnum.'

'Ceanothus, wisteria, clematis, peonies – she certainly liked a lot of colour,' Thea observed knowledgeably. For the first time in hours, I thought of Karen and how she loved a garden.

'I suppose it'll sit empty now for ages, while everyone wrangles over it,' I said wistfully.

'It should by rights stay in the family, don't you think?'

'Except none of them wants it.'

'The boy does. Jeremy. Nobody listened to him, but he loves it here. There's a room which is more or less his. He'd been coming here a lot since Mrs Simmonds came back from her commune thingy.'

'Ah yes – the co-housing people. None of whom came to her funeral, even though it's only been a year and a bit since she left them.'

'I suppose because she left them in a huff – it sounds as if she fell out with them in a big way.'

I thought about it, again ransacking my poor brain for anything Mrs Simmonds might have said about them when she came to my office. 'I have got the address,' I said. 'She was living there when I met her.'

'They'd be easy to find, anyway. I don't suppose there are many places that call themselves co-housing communities in Somerset. I could look them up on the Internet.'

Which made me wonder exactly where Thea intended to stay the night. She'd surely have to head back home before much longer. Somehow I didn't feel able to ask her, despite the apparent opening she'd given me already.

'You know what,' she said, as if reading my thoughts, 'I think I could get in here quite easily, and we could use it as free accommodation tonight. You don't want to spend money on a hotel again, and I'm in no rush to get back. I've got all I need in the car.' She looked at the long-suffering dog that had trailed after us on our meanderings around the village for the past two hours or so. 'I've even got my new Blackberry.'

When I worked out how long we'd been walking, I immediately felt tired. And thirsty. But much more strongly, I felt apprehension. 'The neighbours will see us, and tell somebody,' I objected. 'We'd be trespassing.'

'They know I've been here. They'll just assume the family want me to stay on. I don't think they'll want to get involved, anyway. They're too rich and busy to bother with what's going on here. It's amazing, you know, how these villages operate nowadays. A lot of the properties are second homes, for one thing, so they're empty most of the time. The rest are people who've moved here from somewhere else, and haven't established a proper sense of community. It's the same everywhere – except Blockley. They do

214

seem to do a lot of social stuff in Blockley.'

'And what will they think about me?'

'They won't think anything.'

'But ... but ... there's been a *murder* half a mile away. They'll be acutely aware of anything unusual or suspicious. Won't they be scared, as well?'

She shook her head firmly. 'I doubt it. Anyway, I'm not unusual or suspicious. I'm ordinary and familiar, and I've got a dog. Trust me, nobody will take the slightest notice of us.'

'So how do we get in? Didn't you have to give the key to someone?' The idea was making me more and more nervous, not only because it was almost certainly illegal. 'If anybody finds out, we'll be in real trouble.'

'I don't see why. We won't do any damage. We can just act dumb if anybody comes.'

'The key?' I prompted.

'There's a spare one in a flowerpot round the back. I shouldn't think anybody knows about it.'

I sighed with slight relief. At least she wasn't proposing to break in. But I did not understand exactly why she was making the suggestion in the first place. The idea that she wanted somewhere quiet and private to be alone with me was dismissed as soon as it occurred – she had given no indication of any such notion, and my experience with women was that they seldom regarded me in that sort of light. Karen had been special in that respect, right from the start.

Thea effortlessly unlocked the front door and ushered me into the house. She reached for the light switch to illuminate the murky hallway, but nothing happened. 'Drat!' she exclaimed. 'I forgot about the electric being turned off.'

No hot water, no light, no telly, no heating. The list grew longer as I contemplated the lack of power. 'That's that, then,' I said, trying to hide the gladness in my voice.

'Don't be such a wuss,' she said. 'There's bound to be some candles.'

'It'll be cold.'

'Not especially. It's an old house with thick walls. I've hardly used any heating since I've been here.'

She was too much for me and I gave in. At least I was indoors, not spending any money, and had a well-charged mobile phone in my pocket, even if I had to walk up a hill before it would work. Things could be worse.

'I'm going to pop over to Chipping Campden before the shops close, and get some food, OK? No need for you to come. Look after Hepzie, will you?'

She had left her car outside the cottage while we had walked around the village for most of the afternoon. The spaniel and I looked at each other. 'All right,' I said. 'So long as she doesn't make a fuss.'

'She won't. She takes to everybody. She has a very independent spirit for a dog.'

And so it proved. In the thirty-five minutes that Thea was gone, the animal had jumped onto the old leather sofa next to me, and snuggled warmly against my leg. We were both tired, it seemed, and I leant back my head and let everything drift for a bit. A cup of tea would have been perfect,

216

but I supposed we'd have to drink water and nothing more, unless there was some sort of paraffin stove tucked away somewhere.

Thea returned carrying armloads of shopping. She dumped it in the kitchen, and went out again, returning with our luggage. A tapestry bag, a bulging white plastic carrier bag, my own little holdall and a rucksack all dangled from her at odd angles. She let it all drop onto the floor in front of me. 'Dog food with dish, dog blanket, overnight stuff for me and plenty of food from a nice little old-fashioned shop I found,' she enumerated. 'What have you got?'

I had forgotten all about my own packing. 'Toothbrush, pyjamas and a clean shirt,' I reported. 'Come on – there's more than that in here.'

'A book. Socks. Phone charger. Camera.'

'Camera?'

'I thought it might come in useful. I meant to bring it on Friday, to get a picture of the grave for my records, and forgot.'

'Doesn't your phone take photos?'

'If it does, I don't know how to work it. I've never been very good with gadgets,' I confessed. 'Maggs does all that sort of thing.'

'For somebody only thirty-seven and three-quarters, you're quite old-fashioned,' she commented. 'You'll be telling me next you don't know how to create a website.'

'A what?' I said.

'Very funny.'

She was right, of course. I was a genuine unapologetic technophobe. It went with my line of work, my entire take on life and society, in a mud-

217

dled kind of way. I liked the outdoors, personal contact, long considered conversations. Texting and emailing and superficial connections, such as existed on Facebook and the like, struck me as almost dangerously inhuman. Before taking the job with the funeral director, I had been a nurse. I had touched a lot of suffering flesh, looked into many frightened and pleading eyes and understood, right down to my bones, the stark need everyone had for a real live connection. The wholesale plunge into remote, detached communications via small hand-held machines appalled me as much as closed-circuit cameras did Thea. I just didn't rant about it the way she did.

'Just like Carl,' added Thea, after a pause. 'He didn't like machines, either.'

I made no response to that. If she was telling me that I was her kind of man, then I should quite definitely not be staying alone in a house with her for a long March night.

Chapter Sixteen

Our first task was to find candles and create some light. The sun would be setting in less than an hour, and the windows of the house were small. Already there were deep shadows spreading out from the corners of the room. Thea knew where to look, and before long we had set up three light sources, although she ordained that we ought not to use them until we had to.

218

For food, she laid out a quiche that looked handmade, coleslaw, Pringles crisps, two apples and a bottle of red wine. 'That should keep us going,' she said. 'We won't have it yet, though – just some water from the tap.'

It was sufficiently like a camping holiday from my youth to make me feel boyish and irresponsible. I readily forgot why I was there, what was likely to happen next and what Maggs was going to say to me when I eventually returned home. My immediate thoughts were on the evening and night ahead, and the dawning understanding that I was alone in a house with a very beautiful, witty, clever, kind woman. I resisted all thinking along such lines quite firmly, without even pausing to argue with myself. There was no argument to be had. Subject closed. Think about other things.

I was still very worried about the legality of what we were doing. 'People will see the candle-light,' I said. 'And wonder what's going on.'

'No, they won't. And if they do, they'll just accept it. Honestly, Drew, you worry too much, for no reason. Now then, there's a stack of board games in the back room. Would you like to play Scrabble? I warn you, I'm fantastically good at it.' A surprising look of pain crossed her face. 'I used it to distract me when Carl died. It passed an enormous lot of time.'

'Who did you play with?'

'People on the computer. There are clubs. You can play with anybody, all around the world.'

'Blimey,' I said. 'Fancy that. Actually, I'm not very keen on Scrabble, if that's OK. I don't mind canasta or gin rummy. I used to play those with my granny.'

'Thanks very much,' she giggled, ruining my subconscious hope that I could somehow pretend to myself that it was in fact my grandmother here in the house with me. 'But I don't think there are any playing cards.'

'We should talk more about Mr Maynard,' I said, with some hesitation. 'That's the important thing.'

'Haven't we said it all already?'

'We need a plan for tomorrow,' I insisted. 'Pity about your computer we could have looked up that co-housing place.'

'Oh, we still can,' she chirped. 'I've brought my splendid new gadget with me this time. Jessica gave it me for Christmas.' She waved a shiny black thing at me that obviously had a thousand useful functions.

'But there's no signal here.' I knew only too well the truth of this, since all my troubles had arisen because of it.

'There is if you're with Vodafone, which this thing is. I've been practising with it. It really is amazing. I've completely fallen in love with it.'

'Jessica will be impressed.'

'Won't she!' she said smugly. She got Google running in moments, and searched for the place where Mrs Simmonds had lived. 'This must be it,' she said, reading out the details. I recognised the name of the village.

'Yes,' I agreed. 'That'll be it.'

'They've got an open day, this weekend, for prospective members. "All welcome. Come and see for yourselves how we live. Organic lunches served. Talks and discussions." Sounds as if they're expanding.'

'It must be weird, in a commune,' I mused. 'Endless meetings about what kind of light bulbs to use. No wonder poor old Greta couldn't stand it.'

'Did she say that? Maybe *they* couldn't stand *her*. Maybe they threw her out.'

'It's odd that she kept this house. You'd think she'd have needed the money to buy into the co-housing group. I would assume they have to contribute quite a bit for their living quarters. She didn't have a job, did she?'

'No, but she had the rent from this, and maybe some money from her parents. She could have borrowed against the value of this place, as well. Banks were lending to anyone with property at the time she went there.'

I peered at the computer screen over her shoulder. There were pictures – a big house and a collection of converted farm buildings, with happy smiling people interspersed here and there. 'Looks too good to be true,' I remarked.

'We could go,' she cried. 'We could go to the open day on Saturday.'

Objections crowded into my head. The police wouldn't allow it. It was much too far to drive. We'd be spotted as impostors. 'Could we?' I said weakly.

'We could leave early, spend the day there, and be back in time for supper.'

Were we planning to take up permanent residence here in Broad Campden, then? Was she envisaging three, four, five nights here together?

221

It was like a dream, or a fairytale. Or stark-raving lunacy.

'Um...' I said. 'I don't think... I mean, I have to get home. I can't just abandon everything for days on end. If the police don't come up with something definite by tomorrow afternoon, they'll either have to let me go home, or charge me with something.'

'Aren't you already charged with something? They wouldn't bail you otherwise, would they?'

I shook my head, to try to clear my thoughts. 'They did charge me, yes. But I don't think they can actually insist I stay close by. It's only for their convenience. I really will have to go home tomorrow.'

'OK. But we can still go to the commune on Saturday. I can meet you there. It can't be far from where you live.'

'No,' I agreed, feeling strangely unhappy. 'It's about twenty-five miles.'

'What's the matter?' she asked.

'Lots of things. This is not an ideal situation to be in. I keep wondering where I went wrong.'

'Waste of time,' she said airily. 'What you should be doing is working out what to do next. Take control. Make things happen.' She reached for the wine bottle, which we'd opened but not yet started, and poured out two large glasses full. 'Here,' she invited. 'This'll make you feel better.'

I sipped it warily. 'Doing what you say, I'll only get myself into worse trouble.' I sounded useless, even to myself.

'How much worse can it get?' She gave me a teasing smile, her head tilted sideways, making me think of Stephanie.

'According to you, the police can make their forensic findings fit their theory that I'm the murderer, and I can end up serving thirty years in prison. Isn't that bad enough?'

'I didn't quite say that.'

'You implied it. And it's probably true. If I hadn't been such an idiot as to get lost after I'd made those phone calls, I'd be perfectly all right. As it is, it looks exactly as if I saw Mr Maynard, followed him into that bit of woodland and bashed him with a stone. It would only take five minutes, and then I went back to you and had lunch as if nothing had happened.'

'They have to find evidence that you did that.' She looked doubtful, as if the full force of this hypothesis had only just struck her.

'If they look hard enough, they'll find it. I *did* walk that way. I *had* argued with the bloody man. Your daughter can testify to that.' I was too polite to remind Thea that it was her Jessica who had originally marked me out as the likely killer.

'Well, I can testify that you looked perfectly normal when you got back here. Only slightly out of breath and not a bit bloodstained. I already told them that, actually.'

'Thanks.'

'Anyway, it's time for our supper now, and we can light one or two candles. It's nearly seven o'clock. I can't see a thing.'

Night had fallen gradually, and although our eyes had adjusted to the fading light, there was no way we could see to find anything, or cross the room without collisions with furniture. Thea lit two candles and we ate our little meal, finishing the wine rather quickly, still discussing the murder and the people of Broad Campden.

It was probably about half past seven when we fell silent, and I found myself watching her face in the flickering, flattering light. My irrepressible body was misbehaving worse than ever and I felt a growing panic about how we were going to get through a whole night without something outrageous happening. I summoned the faces of my wife and children, my inevitable shame and fear at what I had done, the horror of being found out, as I surely would be. Besides, I assured myself, Thea herself would have far more sense than to let such a thing happen. She knew the situation, she would feel sisterly solidarity with Karen. There wasn't really any danger at all.

But somehow our eyes had become locked together, and I found myself sinking into the brown depths of her gaze. The normal controls were weakening, my mind no more than a quiet little voice nagging somewhere in the distance. But Thea's controls were evidently stouter than mine. She pulled back and blinked, severing the eye contact. I was still giving instinct too much rein, when I was saved.

Like a sudden bucket of cold water, or the outraged voice of God, someone started loudly knocking on the front door.

Chapter Seventeen

I got up and started across the room to answer it, before Thea hissed at me. 'No! Let me. You're not supposed to be here, remember. Go in the kitchen, quick.'

Stumblingly, I obeyed her, hiding in the dark, but listening intently for whatever was to follow. Why was I not supposed to be there, all of a sudden? Who did she think she was protecting me from?

'Oh ...hello!' Thea's voice was as warm and friendly as always. 'You scared me, banging like that.'

'What are you *doing* here?' came a woman's voice. 'You ought to be gone by now. Shouldn't she, Frank?'

A confirmatory rumble indicated Frank's proximity. I began to guess who they must be, but was no nearer knowing whether it would be safe to reveal my presence. I opted to listen for a while longer.

'Oh, it's all right,' said Thea easily. 'I'm not doing any harm.'

'That is not the point,' said the woman sternly. 'You're trespassing. Why have you got candles burning? I'll tell you why – because the power's been turned off. And *that* means the house is supposed to be empty. Doesn't it, Frank?'

'We just thought–' Frank began, with a hint of

apology for his aggressive wife.

'With everything that's been going on here this week, I should think you'd have more sense than to hang around where you're not wanted. This house has caused nothing but trouble for everybody – ever since old Mr Goodwin died, and that must be twenty years or more.'

'It was seventeen according to Judith,' Thea said, with an apologetic smile. 'Sorry – I'm just showing that I've been keeping up.'

The woman shook her head impatiently. 'What difference does it make? It's a long time, that's all I'm saying, with all kinds of drama and crisis going on. Those awful tenants, for one thing, and now this. You're only going to make it worse, you know.'

'Make what worse?' asked Thea calmly.

'*Everything,*' insisted the woman. I had managed to work out that our visitors were the Watchetts, Frank and Susan, long-time residents of the village, friends of Greta Simmonds and very annoying busybodies.

'Poor Judith – hasn't she got enough on her plate without her house being squatted?' Mrs Watchett continued. I could imagine her wagging a finger at Thea as she advanced into the house. Her voice did seem to be coming closer. 'You're a squatter, young lady, and that's illegal.'

Thea said nothing.

'And the boy, poor little Jeremy. Hasn't he been upset enough already? He *doted* on his Auntie Greta, loved this house. If Charles sells it, his heart will be broken. Won't it, Frank?'

'Susie,' rumbled Frank. 'I really don't think–'

'Not to mention Helena Maynard, poor thing.'

226

'How on earth does my being here affect *her?*' Thea spoke more sharply, finally fighting back.

'It's all connected,' said Susan obscurely. 'After all, she and Greta were lifelong friends. She might have expected – well, she's got other things to think about now. But take my word for it, she won't like you intruding like this, any more than the rest of us do. And parading around all afternoon with that undertaker, for everyone to see. What *did you* think you were doing? What are people supposed to think? I wouldn't have been surprised to find him here as well.'

Silently, I shrank back against the wall. Unfortunately, my movement must have attracted the notice of the spaniel, which came trotting into the kitchen, tail wagging. She jumped up against my legs, making little squeaks. I tried to push her away, but she had suddenly decided I was her biggest chum and we had to play a game together.

'What's that dog doing?' The suspicious question came not from Susan, but her hitherto monosyllabic husband. 'I think there's somebody in there.' And before I could move, he was in the room with me, the faint candlelight from the living room quite enough to reveal my presence.

'Aha!' he cried, like somebody in a stage melodrama. 'Got you!'

It was all desperately embarrassing. I emerged with as much dignity as I could summon, keeping my chin up and saying nothing. 'Lurking in the dark,' said Frank scornfully. 'Guilt written all over him.'

Was it possible that they knew I was the main

suspect in the murder investigation? Would that black cloud follow me everywhere I went for evermore?

'I was hoping to save Thea from embarrassment,' I said.

'Oh yes, I'm sure,' sneered Susan Watchett. 'Well, this is a fine thing, I must say.'

'It really isn't any of your business.' Thea was cool on the outside, but I could tell she was angry. 'I think you should go now. You don't have the right to march in here and make accusations.'

'Oh, don't I? Even when you're breaking the law, and trespassing in my friend's house?'

'It's my house, as it happens,' I said recklessly. 'Mrs Simmonds left it to me.'

It worked beautifully. Her jaw sagged, her eyes bulged, and her hands met in a loose fist resting against her chest. 'Surely she never did that?' she gasped. 'The stupid woman!'

Frank laid a cautious hand on her shoulder. 'Come on, Suse. We should go. I *did* say...' The man never seemed to complete a sentence.

Susan glared at me, her mind clearly functioning well. 'You cunning devil! No wonder Gavin was onto you. No wonder you had to murder the poor man. Well I hope they lock you up for life, that's what. It would damn well serve you right.'

It was highly unpleasant. In the gloomy light of the candle, her face was sinister, with shadows across her cheek and a reflected glow in her eyes. She looked like a very enraged avenging angel. I tried not to cower.

'Does Judith know about this? That she and Charles don't get the house? I bet she's furious, if so.'

'I haven't seen her, but I'm sure she's been told. Charles is the executor.' For some reason this last detail was important to me. It also brought me a pang of guilt towards the rightful heir of the cottage. I felt doubly wretched. 'It came as a total shock to me. I had absolutely no idea.' I remember Oliver Talbot's confrontation with Graham Ingram, in which there had been no sign at all that they knew this latest twist in the tale. The sight of me would surely have elicited a more agitated response from Oliver, if he'd known. 'I don't think Mr Talbot has heard about it, at least.'

'And Helena,' Susan Watchett pursued. 'What about *Helena?*'

'What about her?' demanded Thea.

'She ... well, she always liked this place. She might have thought– I mean, she could be thinking she might buy it.'

'Susan, for the Lord's sake,' bleated Frank. 'Be careful what you're saying.'

But there was no stopping the enraged woman. 'I think you planned the whole thing, seducing poor Greta into thinking she could make use of you for her daft notions.'

'That's ridiculous,' said Thea sturdily. 'Now, if you'd just go and leave us, we can all get on with our own business.'

I was rather sorry she'd spoken when she did. It had felt as if we might be getting somewhere, straightening out some of the muddled connections between Greta Simmonds and Gavin Maynard. But it was too late. The Watchetts departed, oozing self-righteousness. Their thoughts about us

229

were all too vividly portrayed in the set of their shoulders and twist of their lips.

'Oh, God,' I said, when they'd gone. 'That was horrible.'

'Yes, but useful.'

'I suppose so. That bit at the end, Mrs Simmonds using me for her ambitions.'

'She didn't say that,' argued Thea mildly. 'She said *you* used Mrs Simmonds.'

'Well, I didn't.'

She went to sit on the sofa, the dog jumping onto her lap. I remained where I was.

'That wasn't the important bit. They confirmed that Mr Maynard had some beef about you. *Gavin was onto* you, she said.'

'Well, yes – but that isn't a surprise. He didn't like the way I buried his friend. That's what he was shouting about when I met him. Nothing else. Besides, it was all mere speculation on Mrs Watchett's part. She was just jumping to conclusions – exactly as I knew people would when they heard about the will.'

'Mm.' She wasn't really listening to me. Fondling the dog's ears, she stared into space. 'At the very least, it confirms what we were thinking.'

'None of this gets us any further,' I objected impatiently. 'It's all about Mrs Simmonds, not Mr Maynard.'

'Right,' she agreed equably. 'But I think one leads to the other. I just can't quite see how.'

The candles were burning low, but it was still well short of nine o'clock. I could yet go and find myself a hotel, even if it meant walking to Chipping Campden in the dark. The accusations of trespass and squatting had unnerved me. The police were sure to discover where I'd been, and add further transgressions to my file. I was shaken and shamed. 'I ought to go,' I said.

'What do you mean? Don't be daft. You can't leave me here on my own. I'd be awake all night wondering who else was going to turn up and shout at me.'

'Don't give me that. You're the one who copes with people, much better than me. I can't see that anything much bothers you, Mrs Osborne.'

'Just don't call me feisty,' she smiled. 'Then I really would have to throw you out.'

We were, thankfully, back to an earlier humour: bantering, familiar, our minds meshing together quite effortlessly. I sighed.

'Look,' she went on, 'I have to say this, even if it makes me seem a fool.' Her voice was jerky, some of the sweetness missing. 'I know something might have happened before the Watchetts turned up. Probably it wouldn't, though. Probably we've got more sense. We're grown up enough to work out what the consequences might be. And they wouldn't be very nice, especially for you. Do you understand what I'm saying?'

It was new territory for me. I had almost never had anything remotely like this conversation before. At least, not for a long time. There *had* been a woman named Genevieve Slater, several years ago – but I had retained my virtue, if not my dignity, in my dealings with her.

'Yes,' I said. 'Thank you.'

We managed to sleep chastely in two separate

231

bedrooms. Knowing that there were people outside very much aware of our presence made it easier to behave properly. It was all too likely that the news would spread so widely that even my wife could get to hear about it. I therefore had to be able to look her in the eye, cross my heart and swear that Thea and I never even touched each other. Except that Karen was most unlikely to ask for such an assurance. She trusted me so completely that the thought might very well never enter her head. Maggs, however, would be less naïve. Maggs, often the custodian of my morals, had seen me looking softly at other women, once or twice, and dragged me back onto the path of righteousness. Maggs might still be capable of mentioning Genevieve in the reproachful knowing way she had, reminding me that I could be weak and easily led, just like any other man, if the circumstances were right. Maggs would look into my soul and see the truth.

Thea and I admitted to each other that we had half expected a dawn raid from the police, with the front door being battered down at half past five. Instead, we drank water and ate some oversweet muffins for breakfast and debated inconclusively what we ought to do next.

'I guess we are trespassing, technically,' she admitted. 'It all looks a bit more wrong of us this morning.'

'I can't imagine how I let you talk me into it.'

'The thing is, I've already been here for nearly a fortnight, so it feels sort of normal.'

'And we did *know* Mrs Simmonds,' I contributed. 'In the circumstances, I really don't think she would have minded.'

'Right.'

'If she had minded, maybe her ghost would have appeared to tell us so.'

'You don't believe in ghosts, do you?' She looked at me with something like concern, as if I had confessed to a worrying medical condition.

'Do you want the long or the short answer?'

'Long, obviously.'

'Well, I believe that some people have seen some things that were manifestations of some kind. Traces left by a very violent or traumatic event – like echoes of a very loud noise. But I have never personally had anything remotely like a ghostly experience – and in my job, you'd expect that if anyone would be haunted, it'd be me.'

She opened her mouth to reply, but I went on, 'Except, of course, that by the time the dead people reach me, the trauma's all over and done with. I've never had one sit up and talk to me, the way they do in *Six Feet Under* – which I love, by the way. I can't honestly bring myself to believe that dead people suffering terrible remorse or rage or frustration revisit to patrol the place where the event happened. But just possibly they do leave a shimmer in the air, which a few very sensitive individuals can detect. Is that all right?'

'You took the words right out of my mouth.'

I gave myself a shake. 'I must phone home,' I said. 'It's the last day of term. The kids'll be excited.'

'Easter's next weekend,' she remembered. 'That was when Mrs Simmonds was due to come home – Good Friday.'

The death of Mrs S seemed a long, long time ago. She had been visiting the co-housing place when she died. I had collected her body from the hospital at Yeovil where they had done the post-mortem. 'She was staying there quite a long time, then?'

'Actually, I think only one night, before going on to London for a few days, then Paris on the Eurostar. She was very excited about it, going to the theatre and museums and all that.'

'Expensive. She must have had quite a bit of money.' I remembered the way she had so readily paid in advance for her funeral. 'Where did she get it from?'

'No idea. Maybe she had a good pension plan.'

'What was her profession, do you know?'

'I think she was some sort of civil servant,' said Thea vaguely. 'They get good pensions, don't they?'

I shrugged my ignorance. 'We haven't given her very much thought, have we?'

'I have. Don't forget I had all day Monday here waiting for the surveyor – who never showed up, by the way. I spent most of it thinking about her.'

'So she got to the commune, and died that very first night. It must have been a big shock for them.'

'You really believe she died of natural causes, do you?'

I did not like the gleam in her eye, the eagerness for further complications and mysteries to solve. 'I do,' I said, with full emphasis. And then, as some sort of consolation, I added, 'And I'm thinking maybe I do rather like your idea of going there tomorrow, after all. It would fill in the picture. If we can manage it, of course.' Anxiety flooded through me. 'I really ought to be at home all week-end.'

Before she could prevail on me, there came another knock on the door. A polite restrained knock, unlike the thunderous banging of the night before.

Chapter Eighteen

It was DI Basildon himself, looking fresh and smelling of aftershave. 'Good morning, Mr Slo-combe, Mrs Osborne,' he greeted us with alarm-ing cordiality. 'We had a call to say you were here.'

'Well, I couldn't really afford a hotel,' I said defensively.

'None of my business,' he continued amiably. 'Although I understand there is considerable uncertainty over your right to be here.'

'It was you who told me the house was mine,' I accused.

'True. And under the circumstances, I have to take some of the responsibility, I realise that. But you certainly haven't had time to take formal possession of the property, have you?'

He was impossibly civil. It was like being hyp-notised by a black mamba.

'So why are you here?' Thea demanded im-patiently.

'Simply to say that we do not anticipate any need to question you further today, which means you don't have to hang around here if you need to be somewhere else. But please keep your phone switched on, and be ready to return at short notice.'

'I can't promise that,' I protested. 'You know what a hassle it was for me to get here yesterday. I need to know precisely what my position is. You've already lost me a customer.'

His shrug was the merest flicker of a muscle, but it was no less annoying for that. 'I'm afraid a murder investigation overrides almost everything else,' he said with an air of infuriating self-importance. What power the man possessed, to interrupt and distort normal life.

'You could have sent a constable round to tell us that,' Thea said. 'Why come yourself?'

'I felt like a walk. It's a fine morning – although they say it'll rain later on.'

'It's an awfully long walk from Cirencester,' she flashed. 'Why don't you admit you wanted to check that we really had spent the night here together?' Her confrontational levels were escalating by the minute, and I did nothing to reduce them. It was a delight to watch her in action.

'It's none of my business,' he said again, even more cheerfully.

'That's right. But you'll be quite happy to spread the gossip, all the same. I know your sort. I've been around policemen for most of my adult life.'

'Ah yes – your brother-in-law,' he said, with a look of triumph at her obvious shock. 'Although I wouldn't have taken him for a gossipmonger.'

'Not him, but his colleagues. He used to tell us about it.'

'Mrs Osborne, I have rather belatedly come to the conclusion that you are a force to be reckoned with. I was slow to grasp just how helpful you can be, until yesterday. Do you think we could have another talk sometime soon?'

She moved closer to my side, as if to protect me. 'I don't get it,' she said. 'You think I can help, when a man I've just spent the night with is your prime suspect?'

'God, Thea!' I squawked. 'Don't say it like that.' I faced the detective. 'Nothing happened. We slept in separate rooms.'

'More fool you,' he said with a manly shrug that did nothing for my confused conscience. 'Well, must get on. Do keep us informed of your movements, Mr Slocombe, but please consider yourself free to travel anywhere within the UK.'

'Thank you,' I said, as sarcastically as I could manage.

'Do you think they'll tell Mrs Talbot we've been here?' I asked, trying not to sound apprehensive.

We'd spent a final half-hour in the house, putting everything back as it should be and gathering our meagre possessions.

'Probably. At least, somebody will. Susan Watchett, most likely.'

'How do you feel about that?' It was not a question I asked often. Undertakers could enquire into preferences about hymns, and whether or not the deceased should be buried wearing his watch, but direct feelings were best left aside when arranging a funeral. I did, of course, take due notice of my wife's emotions, but in recent

237

years, they had been noteworthy mainly by their absence.

'A bit embarrassed,' Thea admitted. 'Mostly by what Basildon said just now.'

'Good, because so do I.'

'We won't do it again,' she promised.

'Right.'

'And maybe Mrs Talbot won't catch us, if we go now.'

A flicker of rebellion stirred my soul. 'What business is it of hers?' I demanded. 'She has no more rights over the house than I have.'

'Attaboy!' she crowed. 'But I do think we'd be wise to avoid any more confrontations. If you're ready, we'd better get going.'

'Where?'

'Anywhere.'

I gave her a look, making it as stern as I could manage. It helped that she was several inches shorter than me, even though I was by no means tall. 'I have no intention of simply driving aimlessly around England, trying to avoid an irate sister,' I said. 'I have responsibilities.'

She returned the look. 'That's where we differ,' she observed. 'I have none at all, except for my dog.'

'So that's why you do the house-sitting. Now it makes sense. Your daughter said it was because you were running away from memories of your husband.' Even after I said it, I felt no compunction at revealing what had surely been a confidence. I was not sufficiently fond of Jessica to protect her sensibilities. It was, however, riskily personal, and I held my breath in the seconds before she answered.

'Good God – is that what she said?'

'Something of the sort.'

She looked away, her eyes unfocused, stroking her sharp little chin thoughtfully. 'She's partly right, I guess. I don't like being by myself in the cottage. It drags me back to the past, which is never very healthy. Carl and I were perfectly happy. I'm not hung up or agonised about things we never said, or acts of cruelty we can never put right. But I turn into a different person when I'm at home. I was complacent, I dare say, and a bit dull. I didn't do very much with my time. I've never had ambitions worth mentioning, but I kept up with the news and read books and went to films. I did various little jobs that left me plenty of spare time for being a wife and mother. Very old-fashioned sort of life, it was. I slip back into it if I'm not careful.'

'Sounds fine to me.'

'It doesn't keep me engaged with *people*, though. That first house-sit I did, in Duntisbourne Abbots – when I was self-harming, as the jargon calls it, and playing Scrabble on the Internet, and smothering the dog with far too much affection – a nice young man got himself murdered, I was suddenly switched into something real. I had incredibly real conversations with people. I could see their hurt, as if I had magic spectacles. I immersed myself in trying to work out why the murder had happened, going out and accosting people. I was braver than I'd ever been in my life. It saved me, I think, looking back now. I had no idea at the time, but bit by bit, I came out of the tunnel and threw myself into other people's trouble.'

It was a heartfelt speech, and I could see she was working it out as she went along. It felt fresh and vigorous, as if she had never uttered quite these thoughts before. I was being handed something precious and was well aware of the privilege.

'But now you're going to drive me to a railway station, and then you'll go home to Witney,' I said firmly.

She looked as if I'd dashed cold water in her face. 'Will I?' she said.

'Of course.'

'But tomorrow I'll come to Somerset and collect you and we'll go to the co-housing open day.'

'Oh.' I had already forgotten about that. 'Is that what we agreed? Is tomorrow Saturday already?' It didn't seem possible.

'Absolutely.'

'But that's far too much driving. It's crazy. Think of your carbon footprint.'

'Bother my carbon footprint. I like driving, and it's not so far, really. As I said, I've got nothing else to do.'

We drove off, towards Moreton-in-Marsh, where Thea thought I might get a train, and we got there just as one was leaving. It was an hour before the next, so we sat in the little café and drank coffee for a bit. I phoned Karen to ask, somewhat diffidently, whether she could meet me at Castle Cary. She agreed quite placidly, asking no questions. I couldn't shake off a feeling that she didn't much care where I was. The contrast with Thea, whose whole attention was on me and my predicament, was stark. Any man would have warmed to it and made the most of it.

'The police were playing with me,' I said, with some bitterness. 'There was never any need to stay here overnight. It could all have been done over the phone.'

'That would be far too easy,' she suggested.

'Perhaps they have some secret plan, using me as a pawn, or bait or something.'

She smiled. 'Shame it's not Gladwin in charge. She might be up for a bit of double-dealing. As it is, I don't get the feeling Basildon's very subtle.'

'The main question has to be – do they genuinely believe I killed the stupid man?'

'You fit the facts,' she shrugged. 'They'll be tempted to keep you top of the list.'

'But will they carry on investigating? Will they look for anybody else?'

'Depends how pushed they are. You can't rely on it. They've had nearly a week to sift through all the various lines of enquiry, and I get the impression there's nothing remotely interesting, apart from you and that grave. But they're stuck because they've got to find hard evidence, before they take it to the CPS. They won't have much forensic material, with it being outdoors and the wind and everything.'

'What do you mean? They wouldn't have any whatever the weather – if I didn't do it, how could there be evidence?'

'Because you were with him. You might have touched him. We've been over all that.' She spoke patiently, but I could see she thought it an unnecessary repetition.

'They've got the murder weapon. Surely whoever used it would leave flakes of skin or sweat or something on it?'

'In theory, I imagine so. The reality doesn't always work out according to the textbook.'

'Is it right, what Paul said? That a single blow wouldn't produce any blood on the weapon? It sounds a bit odd.'

'I have no idea. I guess if you kind of swung it at him, and then off again right away, there wouldn't be time for the bleeding to start before the rock had bounced off. I mean, there always *does* seem to be blood on the weapon.' She shook her head. 'I don't know. And I hope we're not going to test it.'

I niggled at it for a few more minutes, trying to visualise the moment of impact. 'Heads do bleed profusely,' I said.

'True. There was plenty of blood on the grass to prove it.'

'And maybe on the clothes of the real murderer.'

She nodded non-committally. I knew I was going over old ground, talking for the sake of it, with a faint hope that some amazing insight would arise, if I went over it enough times.

The next train arrived punctually, and I clutched my expensive ticket.

'Will you be all right?' asked Thea.

'I'll be fine,' I said. 'You've done far too much for me already.'

'I'll see you tomorrow, then,' she said, as the train approached.

'I don't know,' I prevaricated. 'It won't be easy. What am I going to tell Karen?'

242

'The whole truth, of course. Why not?'

A certain turbulence inside me suggested that it was not going to be as simple as she liked to think. For a start, I had no intention of telling Karen that I was out on police bail, having been identified as prime suspect in a murder. 'I might say I'm going to meet a client,' I suggested. 'That would save her a lot of worry.'

'Up to you,' said Thea tightly. 'Entirely up to you.'

It was not up to me, and we both knew it. Thea was in charge. She had dictated the timetable for the Saturday, whereby she arrived at my door at ten, and drove me off to the co-housing place, forcing me to explain to my wife just who this woman was. I left it until first thing on Saturday before breaking it to Karen that I was abandoning her yet again. The story about a client wanting to arrange a funeral fell apart before it could be voiced. If Karen had been incurious enough to accept it, Maggs never would. And even if Maggs was not actually present, Karen might mention it to her, and in no time I'd be embroiled in two conflicting accounts of where I had been and who I had been with.

'It's to do with the trouble in the Cotswolds,' I said carefully. 'The police think I had something to do with a murder up there, and I need to go and see some people, to try to sort it all out. Thea Osborne is helping me. She knows everybody involved, and can smooth the way.' It wasn't the whole truth, but it was near enough.

'Oh, yes,' said Karen, with disconcerting mildness. 'What time will you be home?'

It was, after all, the first day of the Easter holidays. The kids were excited and noisy. It was a rerun of the previous weekend, and I felt badly about it. 'No later than four,' I said. 'Probably quite a bit sooner than that.'

'OK.'

'Kaz – are you all right?' I gave her a searching look. Her skin was a bad colour, and a groove had settled between her eyes. 'Have you got a headache?'

'A bit,' she admitted. 'But no worse than yesterday. I hardly notice it. It's fine, Drew. You go off and help the police, or whatever.'

I came within a whisker of calling Thea to abort the whole exercise. Karen's indifference was much more worrying than outright objections would have been. It was as if she only dimly understood the situation, and found the effort of grasping it too great. 'I wish I didn't have to go,' I said. 'I'd much rather be here with you.'

She met my eyes with a dazed expression. 'I'll be all right,' she said. 'I'm perfectly happy to pootle about with the kids. We'll have fun. What's the problem?'

Viewed like that, she was right. I almost envied her the lazy day with the two most delightful children in the world. Even if they spent hours in front of DVDs, it would be cosy and contented and undemanding.

'No problem,' I agreed breezily. 'You'll have a lovely day and I'll be getting myself into trouble and annoying people.'

'See you later,' she said, turning away from me.

It worked just as Thea and I had planned. I knew the way, more or less, and we arrived in time for a welcoming mug of coffee in a big kitchen. About ten people had turned up for the open day – which was two more than expected, because Thea and I had neglected to give advance notice.

'It doesn't matter,' laughed a large fair woman, unconvincingly. 'We can always squeeze you in.'

It turned out that a buffet lunch was to be provided, as well as a series of talks by current residents. Everyone assumed that Thea and I were a couple, and we were whisked from the kitchen to a breezy field of polytunnels and fruit bushes, then to another field containing free-range pigs, then another with geese and a pond, and eventually to the communal sitting room for a question-and-answer session before lunch. Everything was riddled with jargon words that I barely even tried to understand: *intention* was one. It apparently meant a shared interest which brought the group together in the first place. In the case of this particular community, it was self-sufficient food production, which seemed harmless enough to me. I was even mildly persuaded that the whole enterprise was virtuous and reasonable and should be applauded.

'We must ask them about Mrs S,' Thea hissed at me, as we toured the fields. 'That's what we came for.'

'Easier said than done,' I hissed back.

'We need to split up and talk to as many people as we can. Funnily enough, there's a man here who I know vaguely. I met him two years ago, on

245

my first house-sit. He might be useful. It's weird seeing him again. I had no idea he was thinking of moving.'

And then we caught sight, simultaneously, of a figure that was familiar to us both.

Chapter Nineteen

'It's that boy, Mrs Simmonds' nephew, what's-his-name – Jeremy!'

'So it is,' I agreed, impressed that she had remembered his name. 'What on earth is he doing here?'

'Maybe he belongs here.'

'Without his mother? He's not old enough, surely?'

'Maybe he comes to help out in the holidays. Or just for today.'

'We don't really want him to see us, do we?' I said, slowly turning my back on the boy and hoping Thea would do the same.

'He won't remember us,' she said. 'Boys that age don't even look at grown-ups.'

'I think he might remember me,' I argued softly. 'He watched quite closely while I was burying his beloved aunt. And I had to show him how to carry the coffin. I think he might remember that.'

'You could be right,' she conceded. 'But we are out of context here. He's probably not interested in visitors.'

I was speechless with nerves. It seemed that

whatever I did, I was fated to be caught out, and reported.

Jeremy had been emerging from a shed, carrying a spade, and within a couple of minutes was digging strenuously in a weedy patch of ground that seemed to be destined for a new vegetable plot. He gave the impression of resenting the group touring the premises, conveniently averting his gaze from everything but the ground in front of him.

We were quite soon escorted to another field, containing geese and other poultry, with lavish overnight accommodation in clean new coops and runs. By day they roamed free, and the man in charge – Roger, his name was – explained at length about the virtues of geese, but also the necessity of firmly confining them. 'They'd eat every morsel of our lovely young veg otherwise,' he chuckled.

One or two people asked questions, while I felt increasingly uneasy. Thea and I had introduced ourselves as Sarah and Tom, having decided in the car that we couldn't possibly give our real names. We were there as spies and intruders, which was a lot more fun for Thea than it was for me. I lived a mere twenty-five miles away. I ran a serious risk of being recognised by somebody, although I had to admit that it was unlikely that my precise identity would be spotted. Even though these people were in the same general 'alternative' world as Karen and I were, I knew I hadn't performed a funeral for anybody from the community, apart from Greta Simmonds. Nobody had come to her Cotswold burial – which in itself was a reason for Thea's insistence that we give them a look.

Lunch was predictably hearty, with plentiful vegetables, home-made bread and no meat. 'Don't you eat the geese?' I asked Roger, who was sitting next to me.

'We will do,' he nodded, 'but not until the winter.'

'So vegetarianism isn't a requirement for living here?'

'Not at all. We don't have *requirements*, as such. I thought Melanie had explained that.' Melanie had given us a fifteen-minute spiel when we arrived, but since so much of it had been in strange jargon, I hadn't listened very well.

'But there are rules,' I persisted, thinking I should justify my mendacious presence by trying to work out what went wrong for Mrs Simmonds. 'How could there not be?'

'It's more subtle than that,' he said patiently. 'We aim to fit together without any coercion. Disagreements are resolved with discussion and proper process. The pressures are kept to a minimum, and since everyone is here quite willingly, with a clear understanding of how it all works, we have a very successful record for minimising conflict.'

'There must be a few exceptions,' I said. 'There always is – it's human nature.'

'Of course,' he conceded, with a nervous look around the table. A red-haired woman caught his eye and smiled, but I didn't think she had heard what we were saying. Conversation was buzzing quite well, and I saw that Thea, on my other side, was chatting animatedly with a bearded man in his late sixties who I had already clocked as being the most interesting person we had encountered all day. It must be her old chum from the Cotswolds, I realised, pausing to speculate about the coincidence of meeting him again. I listened hard to catch some of their conversation, suddenly aware that he would know her as Thea Osborne and might upset things if he questioned why she was there as Sarah.

He was talking quietly, but I caught something about missing his garden, but having to face up to his own nature, which was not suited to living alone. Thea was obviously very interested, smiling at him encouragingly, and ignoring everyone else at the table.

'So what do you do when someone rocks the boat?' I turned back to Roger, remembering my reason for being there.

'Well, we all do our utmost to identify the underlying difficulties and address them.'

'You sound like a politician,' I said irritably. 'Surely it's often a matter of personality, and you can't change that.'

'No, it's a matter of learnt behaviour, which certainly can be changed.' He sighed. 'Almost always.'

'Have you ever thrown anybody out?'

'Not in those terms, but one or two people have left when it became clear that resolution was unfeasible.'

'Why do you all talk like that?' I demanded. 'Do you all work in management, or something? Or social services? I would have thought with all these spades and animals around, you'd be much more down to earth.'

He blinked mildly at me, making me feel I'd been rather rude. 'How else could I have said it?'

'Well, I would have said something like – there have been people we can't get along with, so they've left. Doesn't that cover it?'

'Maybe,' he said doubtfully. I had a vivid image of their interminable conflict resolution sessions, where emotions were all reduced to long words and convoluted sentences. Nobody would ever shout or cry or throw anything. My brief acquaintance with Greta Simmonds had suggested a woman who might well enjoy throwing things once in a while.

I had to take the plunge. Why else had we come? 'I did know somebody who was here,' I ventured. 'In fact, she died recently, I think. Greta, her name was. She was a distant friend of my aunt, or something. She seemed a nice woman, but I gather she didn't stay here very long?'

His eyes bulged, and a piece of bread went down the wrong way. His violent coughing shook the whole table. If it was a diversionary tactic, he certainly went the whole hog. But when he finally cleared his windpipe, I reminded him of my question.

'Greta was a very difficult person,' he croaked. 'Hypercritical – if that isn't too jargonistic a term for you.' It seemed I had finally managed to locate a nerve to touch. 'Her motives for coming here turned out to be at odds with our intention. I mean, she didn't have the same ethos as the rest of us. She found it difficult to commit to joining in the work. Her visitors behaved as if they were at a hotel. Most of them, anyhow,' he amended. I thought of Jeremy, but couldn't find a safe way of mentioning him. It seemed at least possible that nobody knew he was Greta Simmonds' nephew, and it would be crass of me to give him away.

'I see,' I said. 'As I say, I hardly knew her, but I gather she kept on a house somewhere, so she wasn't homeless when she left here.'

'That was a large part of the problem,' Roger disclosed. 'Everyone else sold their previous pro-perties in order to invest in part-ownership here. That's how it works. Greta displayed real lack of commitment by retaining her former home.'

'So she didn't put any money in here?'

'Oh, yes. She put in quite a lot. That was another thing – she presented as a wealthy person, which jarred with several of the others. Quite a lot of people here are on benefits,' he explained severely, as if this conferred a special sanctity.

'Gosh! She must have been well heeled,' I exclaimed.

'Well, yes. I believe she managed to make some rather astute investments in the 1990s, and cashed them in just at the right time. Of course, she only had one of the smallest units, being on her own. Two bedrooms. And she had the rent from the house in the Cotswolds, to cover all her living expenses. She was very independent. Generous, too. She often said she had no wish to die with a large bank balance left unspent.'

'But nobody liked her.'

'I wouldn't say that. We were sorry when she died. She was here for six years, after all. We regarded her as a fixture for most of that time.'

But you didn't go to her funeral, I noted silently,

251

even though she died during a visit to her old comrades at the community. I waited for this significant detail to be divulged, but it never came.

The main course concluded, we were presented with a large dish of preserved fruit – plums, gooseberries, raspberries, strawberries, all in syrup and coated with home-made yoghurt. I hadn't noticed any cows. 'Where do you get your milk?' I asked, realising a change of subject was called for.

'A farm half a mile away. The last dairy farm in the whole area. They make their own ice cream, and sell milk to local shops. As Melanie said, we do our best to source everything locally.'

'Of course,' I sighed.

'Are you seriously interested in joining us?' he asked, with quite understandable scepticism.

'Oh ... well...' I stumbled, 'it's actually more Sarah's idea than mine.' The small betrayal quickly backfired.

'Obviously, *both* partners have to be equally committed,' he said sternly.

'Obviously. Which is why we came for a proper look. To be frank, I'm not convinced it's for me. I mean ... it seems to be more suited to single people who would otherwise be living lonely, isolated lives. I can see it would be great for them. I'm impressed by the way you can be separate in your own little unit, but with friends and familiar faces just outside the door. Like a village.'

'Right,' he said doubtfully. 'Although there's a lot more to it than that.'

'I suppose it's the ideological aspect that I would have trouble with.' It was true, despite my whole existence being founded on the 'ideology'

252

of natural burial. At least that was a service that extended outwards to the wider society. This co-housing malarkey struck me as pretty inward-looking.

We had another little tour of the buildings after lunch. The heating system ran on wood, which shocked me. Roger explained about carbon capture and offsetting and sustainable management, but I continued to feel it was wrong. Anything that sent smoke into the sky – including cremation of dead bodies – was surely undesirable in the current climate. His spiel felt like rationalisation to me. 'Where do you get the wood?' I asked.

He waved an arm at a sizeable clump of trees a few fields away. 'There are no trucks bringing it in,' he assured the whole group. 'No fossil fuels involved.'

'So you plant a new tree every time you cut one down?' I persisted. 'But even then, you'll run out long before the new ones have grown big enough to burn, won't you?'

'We're looking into solar and wind,' he said stiffly. 'This is just an interim phase.'

'Oh,' I said, wondering if anybody present found that plausible.

I had no chance to speak to Thea until we were ushered back to the big sitting room where we were to discuss our thoughts about what we'd seen, in the final session of the day. She and I managed to hang back and exchange a few observations. 'They're a bit barmy,' I ventured. 'Don't you think?'

'It feels dreadfully unnatural,' she agreed. 'Sort of forced. Of course, they're on display today, so

253

they're bound to be self-conscious. Did I hear you talking about Mrs Simmonds at lunch?'

'That's right. She wasn't sufficiently committed, apparently. Sounds as if there was a real fatwa against her.'

'They didn't *kill* her, did they?'

'Not directly, as far as I can tell. But they might have stressed her out enough for her artery to blow, or whatever it did. I wish we knew why she'd come back. It must have been pretty nasty for the people here to have her die on them.'

'You'd think it would leave some sort of trace,' she said. 'It was only a fortnight ago, after all. They ought to be still talking about it.'

'Not to prospective joiners. They'd be scared it would put people off.'

She shook her head. 'They've got a waiting list a mile long. They think the whole world wants to come and join them. The point of today is for them to weed out the unsuitables.'

'Like us.'

'Exactly.'

'So they're not talking about it because they want to forget it.'

'Which makes you wonder why young Jeremy's here.'

'He's probably gone home by now,' I said.

'How?'

'He's got a bike. I had the impression he cycles long distances, but I must admit this is going rather far. His parents live the other side of Oxford somewhere.'

'He seems so young to be roaming across England on his own.'

'You think so? I'd have said he was seventeen. He looks pretty independent to me. And it's the Easter holidays. Maybe they've given him some work for a few weeks. Casual labour.'

We all settled into saggy sofas and beanbags and window seats and waited for Melanie to do her stuff. We had a minute or two of 'centring', where everybody sat silently and gathered their thoughts. I had never been asked to do that in my life before, but I had to admit it was useful. I listened to other people's breathing, and thought about the turbulence of the world outside, and how appealing many people would find this little enclave, with its own social organisation and well-intentioned members.

Then we went round the room, each person saying something about their impressions. Some of them had been before, and were well into the process of signing up as soon as a vacancy occurred. Others had wandered in on a whim, which was the line Thea and I had decided to take. She spoke before me, acting the part of Sarah with obvious relish.

'Tom and I have only been together for a couple of years,' she began. 'We have properties we can sell, so money wouldn't be a problem. We both have children who wouldn't want to be here full-time, but obviously would visit quite a lot. I really like the farming, and would be more than happy to take a share of the work. I have worked with animals before.'

Melanie held up a hand and stopped her. 'Sarah,' she said with gentle reproach, 'we covered most of that stuff this morning. This isn't a job

255

interview. What I'd like now is your *feelings*. Can you imagine yourself living in this community? What level of commitment do you think you feel at this moment?'

'Well, to be really honest, I don't think it would work. I think the pressures would outweigh the benefits where Tom and I are concerned. I notice you have a lot of unattached women here.' She threw me a possessive look. 'I'm afraid that would worry me.'

Melanie inhaled, and her curly hair quivered. 'Well, thank you, Sarah, for being so honest. You have identified an issue that must, of course, be considered.' She managed to convey that she thought it unlikely that I'd be poached by any predatory females, but stranger things had happened.

Then it was my turn, and I saved everybody's time by quickly confessing to a palpable lack of commitment. 'I suppose we're just not ready for something like this,' I concluded. 'But I am very grateful for the chance to get a closer look at what it would involve. You've all been very open and generous with your time.'

Melanie blossomed under this easy praise. 'Thank you, Tom. That's very kind of you.'

I glanced at my watch, finding it to be past three o'clock. 'We do have to go quite soon,' I said. 'If that's OK.'

'Please don't let us keep you. We've almost finished, anyway.' Melanie swept the room, where another six people were waiting to have their say, and smiled tightly. 'Are you planning to hear the others, or will you be leaving now?' she asked sweetly.

I cocked an eyebrow at Thea and she began to flex her legs, preparatory to freeing herself from the beanbag that clasped her in its depths. 'We'd better go now, I think,' she said. 'Sorry, everybody.'

At the door, we both turned back. 'Good luck,' said Thea to the room in general. 'And thank you. It was extremely interesting.'

Outside, we stifled giggles and somehow managed to be holding hands when we got back to her car. 'Oops – we're still being Tom and Sarah,' I said, feeling hot. 'Better get back to reality.'

'I knew it was you – I recognised the car,' came a voice close by. Looking round, I finally located Jeremy Talbot standing between two woodpiles at the edge of the parking area. 'What are you doing here?'

His accusing stare was locked onto Thea, as if he cared nothing for me and my part in his family's trouble.

'Oh!' she said. 'Hello, Jeremy. What a coincidence!'

'Not really,' he disagreed. 'You've obviously come because of Auntie Greta – but why were you doing the tour with the wannabes? If she told you anything about this place, she'd have warned you to keep clear.' He spoke in a low voice, looking round for anybody likely to overhear. Thea and I moved closer to him, the sense of a conspiracy quite irresistible.

'You don't like it? So why are you working for them?'

He smiled a bitter smile. 'For a start, it's the last place my mum would think to look for me. And it's easy money. They pay over the odds because

257

they feel bad about my auntie. I don't stay here. I've got a place a couple of miles away.' He looked at Thea's car again. 'Your wing mirror's cracked,' he observed.

It was an uncanny echo of Thea's daughter and her criticisms of my car. I snorted, wondering what it was about their generation that made it so satisfying to examine cars for defects. Finally he gave me a proper look. 'You,' he said. 'I didn't believe it when I saw you this morning. What's your game?'

'Much the same as yours, I imagine.'

'What – hiding from my mother?'

'No – checking out precisely what they had against your Auntie Greta.'

He gave me a look, full of suspicion and intelligence and bravado. 'Why would you care about that?'

I groped helplessly for an answer, unable to explain it properly even to myself. It had to do, of course, with my situation regarding the police investigation, which I felt unable to explain to Jeremy – but there was also more to it than that. 'I'm not sure, really. We saw there was an open day and it seemed too good a chance to miss.'

'And you two – is something going on, then?' The directness of the question sent my stomach into alarmed spasms.

'Of course not,' I snarled. 'Mind your own business.'

'Jeremy,' Thea tried again. 'We really haven't any proper excuse for being here. It's exactly as Drew said – we wanted to see for ourselves where Mrs Simmonds had been living. And when she actu-

258

ally died here, it...' she tailed off, no better able to give an account of herself than I had been. 'We just followed our gut feeling,' she finished feebly.

'They killed her,' he said flatly. 'When she came back to see them, being all friendly and nice, they rounded on her and killed her, like dogs.'

We both stared at him wordlessly for a bit. Then I found my voice. 'Were you here?' I asked him.

'For a bit. She and I were going to Paris for three days, and then on to Berlin and Moscow. We had the tickets and everything. It was cheap, because I was young and she was a pensioner, and it's out of season. Anyway, she had plenty of money.'

'Oh, gosh – how awful for you!' Thea's sympathy was genuine. She even reached out a hand to the boy, but he avoided it with a neat backward step.

'I went home to pack my stuff, and fixed up to meet her at St Pancras. Nobody told me she was dead, so I waited, and she never showed and I missed the train. Can you see what a fool that made me feel?' He was flushed with pain and rage and perhaps guilt.

'Didn't you phone her?'

'She never had a mobile, and I never thought to call here. I thought she'd changed her mind. I was in a major strop with her.'

'So when did you find out?'

'My mum called me the next day. She didn't know about our holiday.'

'Weren't you supposed to be at school?' Thea demanded. 'What was your aunt thinking of, taking you off in term time?'

'It was only a couple of weeks early,' he

shrugged. 'And it's college, not school. And I hate the fucking place, if you must know. What chance do I have of a decent job, whatever they say?'

'You look as if you can work well enough when you want to,' she observed. 'We saw you digging, earlier on.'

'They don't count that as *work*, though, do they? No exams and stuff for digging. That's only fit for Romanians and Latvians now.'

He could be a gravedigger, I thought with some irony. There was still money to be made if you were prepared to travel to several different church-yards at short notice. Probably not enough to live on, though, even if it was cash in hand and little risk of the taxman finding out, provided the undertakers played along. Which most of them didn't any more, unfortunately.

We all seemed to be drifting off the main subject. For a moment, I couldn't even recall what that was. Right – Mrs Simmonds and her funeral. 'You came to the burial,' I said. 'With your family. You looked quite together then. What's all this about avoiding your mum?'

He gave me a look that seemed to contain a sort of yearning, as if needing me to understand something, but unable to voice it directly. 'Yeah,' he nodded. 'The funeral was good. Just what she'd have wanted.'

'I hope so.'

'Jeremy,' Thea said gently. 'You didn't really mean the people here killed your aunt, did you?'

'I meant they stressed her out. She wanted to set things straight – tie up the loose ends, was what she said. But it ended up in a fight, though

260

they'd never admit it.'

'Was she ill?' Thea asked.

He nodded, his face clouded with misery. 'Yeah. She never said it right out, y'know, but she dropped little hints about it.' He sniffed and said nothing more for a minute, before squaring his shoulders and facing us full on. 'And now I need a bit of space, OK. I've got stuff I need to think about.' It struck me that his relatives had been planning to sell his aunt's house without consulting him. Perhaps, I thought wildly, I could let him stay in it as my tenant, if I really did gain ownership of it. He could even run the cemetery for me, if that ever materialised. Suddenly it all looked neat and almost predestined. I gave him a beaming smile that seemed to startle him.

'Do you know the Watchetts?' Thea asked him, surprising us both.

He shook his head. 'Not really. Seen them once or twice.' His features hardened. 'None of the others came, did they? The tenants, and old Mr Kettles. Her neighbours. They all stayed away.'

'I don't think they knew about it,' I told him. 'Your mother wanted it to be kept very discreet.'

'Yeah,' he sneered. 'A lot of good it did her.'

'Oh?'

'She thought she and Charles between them could just take over the deeds of the house, and sell it in a few weeks and pocket the cash.' His mouth twisted. 'I knew that wasn't going to happen. Not that she cares a fuck what I think.'

'How did you know?'

He gave me another complicated look. 'I knew she'd left it to you. She told me not to be upset about it. Said you were a good bloke.'

I remembered, for the first time in hours, that I was under suspicion of murder, and therefore not at all a good bloke in society's eyes. 'Thanks,' I said. 'I liked her, as well.'

'Yeah ... well, at least she got the grave as she wanted it. Good old Auntie Greta.'

'We must go,' I realised with a sudden panic. 'I said I'd be home by four.'

'Quarter to, now,' said Jeremy, consulting his mobile. 'You won't make it.' It was some seconds before it dawned on me that this meant he knew where I lived. Understandable, since I'd performed his aunt's funeral, but still quite a surprise. I hadn't expected him to take that much notice.

'Well, we can do our best. Thanks, Jeremy, for talking to us,' said Thea, coming over all brisk. 'We'll see you again, maybe.'

'Can I take your phone number?' I asked, on a whim. 'Just in case.'

'Just in case what?'

'Oh ... well, we might want to keep in touch, don't you think? We both liked Auntie Greta, and want what she wanted, don't we?'

'OK then. Give me yours and I'll put it in.' With relief I handed over my phone and watched his rapid thumb add his number to my meagre list of names.

'However did we manage before mobile phones?' breathed Thea. 'Now, come on. We'll be in trouble with your wife.'

It was a careless comment, not meant unkindly at all, but it gave me a little pang.

Chapter Twenty

Karen was not remotely reproachful when I walked in at half past four. She gave me a sunny smile and poured out a big mug of tea. 'Nice day?' she asked.

I had resisted any temptation to invite Thea in, despite knowing she would probably be glad of a drink before her long drive home. My head was full of impressions, questions, tentative connections and the perpetual dread of what the police might decide to do to me next. Peaceful Repose burial ground was well down the list of my priorities, and my neglected family only a notch or two higher.

'Not bad,' I said. 'Did anybody phone?'

'Not a soul. It's been blissfully quiet. The kids have been brilliant, making Easter cards and stuff. Timmy's got religion. He won the Head Teacher's Merit for telling the Easter story at school. He seems to have got the Gospel of St Matthew off by heart.' She chatted brightly, the perfect happy housewife, and almost had me convinced that everything was utterly normal.

I winced at the reference to religion in the children's school. Karen hadn't been surprised at all by it, having worked for years as a teacher, but somehow it came as quite a shock to me to discover the casual use of prayers and mangled Bible stories and grace before meals. I had assumed that institutionalised religion had somehow withered away, but it appeared to be staging a strenuous revival, with a lot more than I ever had in my own early years.

'I suppose he'll grow out of it,' I said.

'He'll do as he sees fit,' she said pertly, and I registered that this was my old Karen speaking – the wife who had had opinions and stood her ground in an argument.

'I just wish they'd go easy on the brainwashing,' I replied, eager to seize the moment.

'Don't be daft,' said Karen.

It was a topic we couldn't agree on. I could never work out whether it was my experience as an undertaker, or something prior and deeper, which made me so sceptical. I understood quite well that 'Abide With Me' and the standard funeral service were consoling to almost everybody. The ritual had been carefully constructed, and stood the test of time. As far as I could see, it had almost nothing to do with the basic tenets of Christianity, where mankind had somehow been 'redeemed' because a man was tortured to death on a crucifix. There seemed to be a glaring logical gap between all that and the visceral human need to cling to some hope that death didn't instantly obliterate who and what they had once been. Personally, I was content to have my molecules continue as dandelions or honeybees or even a lump of stone – but I could appreciate that this view might change as I approached my final days.

'Well, you know what I think,' I said, wearying suddenly of the topic.

Karen asked me nothing about my day, as I sank

unresistingly into the easy jumble of family life. I took charge of the evening meal, cooking sausages in a casserole with our own onions, stored over the winter, in a sauce made from our own tomatoes – also bottled in the summer and stored. That co-housing crowd couldn't have taught me anything about growing vegetables. Originally Karen's department, I had taken it over after her injury, and made it my own. I liked to think that my poor showing as a money-earner was balanced out by the cash I saved on food.

Before bed, I watched a film with the children, squashed uncomfortably into our big armchair with them both on top of me. I put them to bed, reading a long chapter from *The House at Pooh Corner,* and helping them plan the coming week of their school holiday.

Life went on, regardless. If I was convicted of murder and given a twenty- or thirty-year prison sentence, life would go on. My children would be outcasts, my wife reduced to a shadow by the shame and stress, but Maggs and Den would come to the rescue – even my mother might show hidden strengths in such a crisis. I would find a niche for myself in the prison garden, and get through it somehow. I sat with Karen in our living room, passively accepting my fate, for well over an hour, before I heard Thea Osborne's voice in the distance, telling me not to be such a wimp. Where was my passion, my sense of justice, my self-belief? How could I even for a moment contemplate wrongful imprisonment, without a massive rise in blood pressure and an iron determination to see that right prevailed?

OK, I sighed inwardly. *OK*. That wasn't going to happen. We would find whoever had killed Mr Maynard, and clear my name in the process.

Sunday dawned invitingly, with sunny skies and singing birds. I had nothing planned, other than a vague promise to the children that we could go out somewhere. Karen suggested we drive to Cadbury and climb the ancient ramparts and pretend we were back in the Dark Ages. She had a thing about Cadbury, which Stephanie shared, whereas Timmy and I could see nothing but long grass and occasional sheep. But I made no objection, and having phoned Maggs to tell her where I would be if she needed me, we set off in the middle of the morning.

It was a good enough day, all in all. Karen made sandwiches and drinks, and we had a somewhat chilly picnic on the side of the old hill fort, observed by two squirrels. The children ran free and invented stories about knights and dragons and witches which seemed to fully occupy them for hours.

'Imagine if we'd only had one,' said Karen, as we sat watching them. 'How terrible that would be.'

I couldn't imagine it. Karen was an only child, and having drifted away from her original family in recent years, she insisted that siblings would have improved her life in numerous ways. They would have given her more reason to stay in touch, for one thing. I knew she was obliquely arguing Timmy's case to me, anxious because I demonstrated less love for him than for his sister. Watching him, his lean little body recovering

266

from falls and bumps with typical male bravado, I felt my heart swell a little. 'He's amazing,' I said feebly. 'We're twice blessed, having both of them. It's the ultimate miracle.'

'Don't overdo it,' she said, just as I was beginning to believe my own words. 'They're just children. Anybody can produce children.'

'Not as good as these,' I insisted, earning a contented wifely smile.

We went home in time for tea, and the evening was a near replica of the one before. I had survived a whole weekend with my family intact, my freedom uncurtailed, my future no darker than it had been on Friday. It was with a confused sense of gratitude that I collapsed into bed, giving no thought at all to Monday.

But Monday arrived all the same, and the phone started ringing. Three calls in half an hour left me with a scatter of important notes on my work desk and a return of the sharp pangs of guilt towards Mr and Mrs Kaplinsky, because she called to ask if we could try again. I grovelled and apologised repeatedly, until the poor woman lost patience with me. 'Just get over to the hospice, that's all I ask,' she ordered. 'If you can't guarantee a specific time, then just turn up and ask to see my husband.'

The hospice itself called about another inmate who had expressed an interest in my services. 'Better come today,' they warned me. 'She hasn't got long.' I began to feel less well disposed towards people who wanted to organise their own funerals. There was something to be said for the nice condensed time frame in which they had already died, and had to be buried within the week. 'I'll do my best,' I said, 'but things are a bit unpredictable at the moment. One of us will be there as quickly as we can.' I wrote the woman's name on a large sheet of paper, with 'Visit at hospice asap' underneath, and pinned it on the corkboard that Maggs and I used for important messages and the details of work to be done. I had already decided that my partner would get the job. She could go on her bike. Then I took the paper down and wrote 'Mrs Kaplinsky has forgiven me – also needs a visit, but make appt first'. It made perfect sense for the two hospice patients to be interviewed on the same visit.

The office was part of the same building as our house, but not directly connected from inside. I had to go out, along a little path, and in again. We had converted and enlarged a lean-to shed, giving it more robust walls and a tiled roof. The separate entrance was designed to give families and officials a sense of privacy, without the possibility of members of my family bursting in without warning. The space had been divided into two, with a tiny area for coffins to sit awaiting burial, and a second trestle, on which bodies might await their turn, on the rare occasions when we were handling two funerals at one time. We never did embalming, but there were still procedures that had to be performed before the final interment.

The post brought a welcome cheque from a recent customer, as well as information about a new supplier of willow coffins who sounded as if they had more realistic terms than the one I'd dealt with before, and another leaflet describing felt shrouds made by a local woman. I had the best of intentions concerning her wares – but repeatedly forgot to advise customers of their existence. Almost all of them opted for the standard cardboard coffin, thanks to the sample one I had in the office. Grandchildren would paint them and write farewell messages on them. They cost about a quarter of what the felt or willow things did.

Perhaps because of the school holidays, I had the feeling I would not be left long alone in the office with my paperwork. Maggs normally showed up by ten if there was nothing urgent to do, but she was unlikely to disturb me without good reason. The children might come and press their noses to the window, giggling and pushing each other, pretending to be afraid of my wrath. The days were long gone when Stephanie and I would work and play cosily together in the office. Now they were both firmly banned from entering.

But the interruption I was most braced for was further attentions from the Gloucestershire Police. It seemed impossible that they would not contact me in some way – impossible and unacceptable. I could not continue in limbo for long without demanding some sort of resolution. A good proportion of my thoughts were fixed on Broad Campden and the people there. That included Thea and Jeremy and the other Talbots, who, while not physically in the Cotswolds, were all part of the picture. The sense of unfinished business, of something crucial held in suspension, only increased as Monday morning crawled on. Not only was there an unsolved murder hanging over everything, there was also the uncomfortable trouble over Mrs Simmonds' grave and the attitude of the council towards it. A week on, and my worries seemed to be multiplying horribly.

Karen tapped on the door, a bit before ten, and asked whether she could take the car to the shops. 'Steph needs new shoes, and Tim wants to go to the library.'

'Fine,' I nodded. 'I might have to go to the hospice later, but I'm going to try to get Maggs to go instead. If I need the car for a removal, I'll call you on the mobile. Keep it switched on, OK?'

'Right. I assume I should use the credit card for the shoes?'

'How much will they be?'

She shrugged. 'Twelve or fifteen pounds, I suppose. Maybe a bit less.'

'Get good ones,' I said unnecessarily. 'There's still a bit of credit left.' I held up the newly arrived cheque. 'And somebody's just paid us, look.'

'Excellent. Bye, then. We'll be back by one at the latest.'

'Bye.'

I watched her reversing the car out, the children strapped into the back on their booster seats. It seldom occurred to me that there was anything strange about using the same vehicle to transport small children one moment and dead bodies the next. It was a long estate car, the seats constantly being folded down to make space for a body bag on a metal stretcher. It was sometimes necessary to use air freshener, and Timmy once told me a friend of his had said it smelt like mouldy sausages, but it was the way we operated, and we'd all got used to it long ago.

There was a letter still unopened on my desk, in an envelope with a handwritten address. I assumed it was a note of thanks from a customer, although there was faint chance it had a cheque inside. As far as I could recall, all recent funerals had now been paid for, and some sixth sense told me there was no such enclosure. Opening it inattentively, it took a few moments to register that it was actually quite important.

Dear Mr Slocombe,

Further to our telephone conversation earlier this week, I would like to inform you that I am now aware that you are under suspicion of murdering my husband, and that you are free on police bail. I am also informed that you spent Thursday night at Greta Simmonds' house with the house-sitter. While your morals are your own affair, I must say I am appalled at such behaviour. The whole village was discussing it this morning.

I have also learnt that Greta did indeed leave her house to you, which I knew she was considering, and which I think is a sign that she must have lost her mind. I am sure that if she had lived a little longer, she would have seen sense and altered her will again.

But it is my poor innocent husband that is obviously uppermost in my mind. I feel sure he was killed because of his attitude towards Greta's grave. There can be no other reason. He lived a quiet and blameless life. People liked him. He was very much at the centre of the church, and he took great care to abide by its teachings.

271

If it was you who killed him, I hope your conscience will never be easy again. I hope you will never have peace as long as you live. I have never cursed anybody before, but I believe this is what is needed now. Perhaps you will be clever enough to evade the punishment due to you – you certainly deceived poor Greta into trusting you – but in your own heart you know the truth, and I truly hope that it will always haunt you.

Helena Maynard

I was rocked by the force of it. The folly of spending the night in the cottage with Thea hit me powerfully. That had been a huge mistake, and I had known it, even at the time. The Watchetts must have spread the word up and down the high street on Friday morning, perhaps even contacting Mrs Maynard directly to give her the news. The police might well have shared the fact of my arrest with the local newspaper, making it common knowledge in the whole area. The furious widow must have written the letter sometime on Friday, catching the Saturday post. I tried to imagine the gossip, the anger at my apparent freedom to get on with my business and the insensitivity of my taking up with the pretty house-sitter in such a public fashion. Was Thea the object of similar opprobrium, I wondered?

I had to talk to someone – but not the someone who was at that very moment walking up to my office door. Maggs was definitely not the right person this time, which in itself was cause for acute regret. She had always been my sidekick, my reassurance and support through the dark times three years ago. Now, because of the fact of Thea

Osborne, I could not share anything with my faithful colleague. My technical innocence would not be enough for Maggs: she could see through to my core and knew what was in my heart. She would fight for Karen and the children, as any woman would. It was the right and natural line to take. I took it myself. But I knew I would be unable to tell the whole story about Mr Maynard and Mrs Simmonds and the Talbots and Ingrams and Watchetts and the way the police regarded me, without putting Thea at the centre of it all. After all, Maggs already knew the basics – that the police needed my help because I could have been the last person to see the murder victim alive. She knew I was under suspicion, but not that I'd been charged for the crime myself. If I revealed the letter from the vindictive widow, I would have to explain a great deal more than that.

I shoved the letter into my pocket and adopted a harassed expression as she opened the door. Before she could speak, I waved at the paper on the board. 'Two reasons to go to the hospice,' I said. 'I thought you might do them later today.'

She blinked and I noticed she looked somewhat subdued. Her nose seemed swollen and her eyes narrower than usual. 'What's the matter?' I asked belatedly.

'Just a cold,' she said thickly. 'Came on late on Friday and I've been getting worse ever since. My whole head feels stuffed with compost. A lot of it keeps coming out of my nose. It's disgusting.'

'You poor thing,' I said, thinking she would be deeply unwelcome at the hospice in that condition. 'Where did you catch it?'

'I have no idea,' she said crossly. 'What does that matter?'

'Has Den got it?'

She shook her head. 'Not yet. He didn't think I should come to work, but it's boring just staying at home.'

'At least the weather's quite nice,' I said fatuously.

She gurgled an inarticulate sound full of phlegm and self-pity. I tried to think of an easy task I could give her, but none came to mind. We were both accustomed to long days in which there was little to do but extract weeds from the paths between the graves, or prune some of the rose bushes that had been planted by grieving relatives. We would hypothesise about parallel businesses we could run in all the spare time we had, but nothing ever came to fruition.

I got up and walked around the room, aware of feeling trapped by this new development. I had somehow believed I could return to the Cotswolds whenever I wanted, because Maggs could handle everything for me. Now, if she was ill, I would have to do it all myself. 'I suppose I'd better go, then,' I said. 'To the hospice, I mean.'

'Mrs Kaplinsky forgave you?' she said, reading the paper on the corkboard. 'Wow.'

'I know. I expect it was all thanks to you.'

'And who's this other person? Sarah Williams?'

'Someone who's fading fast, apparently. Maybe she's been talking to the Kaplinskys. Anyway, they both want to see me, preferably today.'

'One in the eye for the opposition,' she smiled.

We both enjoyed stealing business from the mainstream undertakers in town. They were inclined to become altogether too complacent, if given half a chance.

'You'd better go home,' I worried. 'You're really not well.'

'I'm all right. It's only a cold. I'll stay out in the sunshine and do the nature cure.'

'You're a marvel,' I said, for probably the eight hundredth time. Maggs *was* a marvel. Everybody knew that. But she had left me with no choice but to visit the hospice myself, removing any possibility of heading back to Broad Campden to remonstrate with Mrs Maynard.

Because, I realised, this was definitely what I wanted to do. I wanted to meet her face-to-face and persuade her that I had nothing to do with the killing of her husband. I wanted to stand up to this angry woman and put myself on the same side in the effort to find who did kill him. I also wanted to quash the rumours about me and Thea, if possible. Neither task would be easy, and if I was caught up with arranging funerals and handling the business single-handed, I'd have no chance of even making a start.

Breathing deeply, trying to remain calm, I began to organise the day in my mind. Working for a large busy undertaker had taught me the necessity of a firm schedule. Despite the absence of many acute pressures, such as having to arrive at a crematorium at the precise right moment, it was still incumbent upon me to do what I'd agreed to do, and be where I'd agreed to be. The lapse on Thursday, forgetting all about the Kaplinskys, was

275

unforgivable and must never ever be repeated.

'Karen's got the car this morning, but I'll go straight after lunch,' I said. 'Whatever happens.'

'What's going to happen?' wondered Maggs innocently. Something in her look made me feel very lonely.

The drive to the hospice gave me time to think without fear of disturbance. The mobile was turned off, so even if the police wanted me, they'd have to wait an hour or two. A good portion of my thinking revolved around what I knew and guessed about their investigations. Now that they had charged me, in the belief that there was enough evidence to make a case against me, they would be working hard to establish that case. They would have questioned Mr Maynard's neighbours and work colleagues, and most of the local population, to discover his connection with my activities. They would have appealed for witnesses in the crucial period on Saturday. They would interview anyone who knew him and trawl through all his recent encounters with members of the public. They would read his private papers and examine his computer. His life would be peeled bare, his hobbies and habits all examined. And they would do all they could forensically, too. In theory there was no escape any longer for a killer. Everybody shed DNA and fibres everywhere they went. However, on a windy day in a damp little clearing, finding such evidence was never going to be easy. Besides, all those tests cost a great deal of money, and were therefore employed with some caution. Defence lawyers would cast doubt on apparently solid findings, speaking of contamination and misguided conclusions. I knew, from direct personal experience, how facts did not always support what they appeared to support. Even police investigators sometimes saw what they expected to see, and not what truly lay behind the evidence.

Like me and Mr Maynard. If traces from my person were discovered on his person, this would be because I had indeed met him that day. I had Officer Jessica to endorse the time and the place where this had happened. Beyond that, it was nothing more than circumstantial. I had gone for a walk and made phone calls from a spot quite near where he had been killed, soon after having a heated argument with him. It was enough to persuade the Crown Prosecution Service to send me to trial for the deliberate killing of the man from the council – unless new evidence materialised to exonerate me, or incriminate somebody else.

I tried to convince myself that our visit to the co-housing place had thrown up enough new information to warrant a closer analysis. I needed to sit down with Thea and talk it through. She and I should be drawing up flow charts, listing connections and questions and making logical deductions. If the police could do it, so could we. Nothing was worse than simply pretending to myself that it would all come right in the end, that I could not possibly find myself in court on a charge of murder. As I understood it, I was already well along the road to that very situation. But I also had a job to do, and while I was free, I had no choice but to get on and do it.

I conducted my interviews at the hospice with all due sensitivity, threaded with the businesslike approach that the dying patients expected. Other people were there to provide sympathy and pain relief and counselling. My role was to take down their wishes and assure them that it would happen just as they envisaged. I was in the same category as a solicitor would have been, and to waste time with expressions of regret at their plight would not be welcomed. Indeed, I liked to think that most people found it refreshing to be treated as a client with ordinary needs, instead of in some uniquely special situation simply because their time on earth was coming to an end. Mr Kaplinsky was initially scratchy because of my failings the previous week, and I readily agreed with him that I had let him down and did not entirely deserve the second chance. But he had heard about Peaceful Repose, and despite some misgivings about the name, which he characterised as 'slushy', he had chosen to have himself buried there. 'If I can't be taken home to the fields of Poland, then this will do almost as well,' he said. On questioning, it turned out that he had in fact been born in Wiltshire, so to refer to Poland as home was more wistful sentiment than anything real. He had visited his parents' one-time native village in his youth, and dreamt of it ever since.

But he signed his contract with me, and selected a mountain ash tree as his grave marker, and I left him relatively contented, or so I hoped.

Sarah Williams was fifty-nine, and dying rapidly of pancreatic cancer. She had an irritable manner, born of the pain that could not be completely kept at bay, as well as the necessity of 'putting her affairs in order' as she phrased it with some irony. 'I get so dreadfully *restless*,' she complained. 'I don't want to be in here at all, to be honest, but there isn't anyone at home willing to put up with me, so there it is.' She gave me a look that I had seen before – bewilderment overlaid with a kind of bravado. By definition, those dying individuals I encountered had come as close as possible to an acceptance of their fate. But at some level, they passionately wished they had not been forced to do so. The self-awareness of human beings was a recognised curse – why couldn't we be like animals, and have the whole business left obscure?

But, as always, I liked and respected the two new future inmates of the burial ground behind my house, and went home well satisfied with the service I had provided for them.

There was a message on my mobile when I turned it on again – which I did before driving home. It was breathless and excited. 'Drew? Sorry to bother you, but I think you'll be contacted again by the police today. Maybe you have been already? It's Mrs Maynard – she's causing a lot of trouble, and not just for you. Half the village has got involved, apparently. I can't tell you all of it in a message. Call me back when you get this.' She hadn't bothered to say who she was – there was no need for that.

I wanted to phone her right away, but restrained myself. First I should get back and see if there was anything else waiting for my attention. Karen, the children and Maggs all had every right to assume

279

that I would be there when required. Thea Osborne had no such right, and despite my earlier
desire to confront Helena Maynard, yet another
trek to Broad Campden was both impractical and
frightening.

Chapter Twenty-One

Everything at home was deceptively calm when I
drove in through our gate and parked the car.
The westering sun was throwing shadows across
the burial field, the different little trees at various
stages of growth marking the graves that had
been created so far. Officially, it was possible to
accommodate almost a thousand burials to an
acre, but I had opted for a more spacious alloca-
tion, aiming at less than half that density. With
ten acres at my disposal, I expected the space to
last until I retired, even if that wasn't until I was
eighty. I paused, as I often did, to admire and
relish the haven of natural restfulness that I had
brought into existence.

Karen met me at the door. 'Maggs has gone
home,' she said. 'The poor thing could hardly
breathe. She probably won't come in tomorrow.'

Flickering apprehensions assailed me. I was
going to need Maggs by Wednesday – perhaps
sooner, if Thea's message was as urgent as it
sounded. 'She'll soon shake it off,' I said optimis-
tically. 'Did she get any calls while I was out?'

Karen looked uncertain. 'I didn't hear anything,'

she said. Knowing how vague my wife could be, Maggs would have been sure to flag up anything that required my attention. So far, so good, I thought.

'Well, I'm desperate for some tea,' I said brightly. 'Have the kids been good?'

'Steph won't take her new shoes off, and Timmy brought four books home from the library. I tried to tell him he was only allowed two, but the stupid woman there told him he could have six. I said six was too many so we split the difference.'

'We should be glad he likes reading,' I said.

'I suppose so. I don't expect it'll last. It's a novelty, that's all.'

For a teacher, Karen had often seemed surprisingly uncommitted to the virtues of literature. I still clung to the idea that books were desirable for their own sake, though could not have formed a particularly effective argument to support my position.

'Let me just put these notes away, then,' I said, flapping the folder containing the new customer details, 'and I'll be with you in ten minutes.'

I had not quite reached the office door when the police car arrived. I turned to meet it, feeling resigned and not at all surprised. It was not unlike those split seconds before a car crash, when all resistance is gone, and you simply await your fate with no emotion at all.

It was a uniformed officer I hadn't seen before. 'Mr Slocombe?' he asked, with a serious expression.

'What now?'

'We've had a call from Gloucestershire, wanting us to escort you there as soon as possible.'

'Escort?' Yet again, the logistics took prime place in my thoughts.

'We'll take you,' he clarified.

'Right.' That was an improvement on the previous occasion, I supposed, despite the implication that I was an unreliable criminal who needed to be kept under supervision. Already the nervousness implicit in the situation was abating. I had been arrested and questioned before – I knew what it felt like. And Thea's phone message had already alerted me to the probability of a return to Broad Campden. The working day was almost ended anyway, and although I was permanently on call, the needs of my business were slipping rapidly down the list of priorities.

Karen and the children were a different matter altogether. 'I'll have to go and speak to my wife,' I said.

'Five minutes, sir.' The urgency was unsettling, but I assured myself that nothing too dreadful could happen if I delayed by a few extra minutes.

'I have to go in here first,' I said, indicating the office. 'Then I'll tell my wife, and get a bag of things, if that's allowed.'

'Quick as you can, then,' he encouraged.

As we sped up the M5, me in the back seat behind two police officers, I tried to stay abreast of probable developments. Mrs Talbot, friend, no doubt, of Mrs Maynard, had perhaps made some sort of complaint or demand that had, in Thea's words, caused a lot of trouble. My immediate assumption was that Jeremy had reported seeing us at the community farm, and that had led to some sort of unfortunate interpretation on his mother's part. The Talbots had no cause to like me, once they realised that I had snatched their inheritance from beneath their noses. The police already believed that the legacy proved me guilty in some way – although it was still far from clear how that linked with the killing of Mr Maynard. Thea and I had incriminated ourselves in the village, and produced the dreadful letter from Helena Maynard – which I still had in my pocket, I suddenly realised.

So far, so predictable. Things continued to make a kind of sense that I found reassuring. The worst thing was sudden surprises, new facts or accusations that came out of the blue and rendered logical thought impossible. The news of my inheritance had been just such a bombshell. Seeing Jeremy at the farm was another, though a lesser one.

We arrived in Broad Campden at about six, with the sun almost set, and the temperature quite chilly. I took close note of our route, and understood that we were going to the small field where Mrs Simmonds was buried. The associations that came with this realisation were more alarming than my conscious mind could explain. I found myself reliving my earlier journey to meet Mr Maynard at this very spot, and my shock at hearing that the field had not been Mrs Simmonds' legitimate property.

There were three cars already parked crookedly on the verge, leaving very little space for a fourth.

One was modest and red and contained a small head with long black ears, peering out of the driver's window. A surge of complicated feelings and questions went through me – why was Thea here? Was she in trouble? Had she offered to come because she thought she could help? Deeper than this brain activity was the thrumming of my blood at the prospect of seeing her again.

Somehow we joined the assembly ranged around the grave. It struck me as macabre and unseemly, the way everyone was giving it quite the wrong kind of attention. The helpless corpse beneath the soil had had her say, and expected to be left in peace for the rest of eternity. Instead, she was plainly the subject of heated argument. I did a rapid scan of the people present – a crowd slightly larger than the original funeral, at first assessment. Two Talbots, two Watchetts, a woman I had never seen before, a man in a suit likewise new to me, Thea, an old man leaning on a stick and a uniformed policeman all turned to watch as I approached with my escort. In the fading light, everyone had a greyish appearance, like an old photograph, the trees behind them casting more shade on the proceedings.

The unfamiliar woman strode towards me, her chin jutting. It took only a second to work out who she must be. 'Drew Slocombe?' she accused. 'I'm Helena Maynard.'

I did not offer her a hand to shake. The letter she had sent me was still sitting warmly in my pocket, emanating malicious vibes like the opposite of a talisman. 'Oh ... Mrs Maynard,' I said feebly.

She was tall and powerful, with short iron-grey

hair fitting around her head like a helmet. She wore a coat that stopped mid-thigh, and leather boots. I tried to imagine her in conjunction with her husband, the scrawny Gavin, in vain. I tried to hold on to the fact that she might well have been the one who ought to be under arrest instead of me. She certainly looked strong enough to have inflicted the fatal blow on the man's unprotected head.

The next person to approach me was Charles Talbot. His face seemed to be grooved around the mouth and between the eyes. 'We've been waiting for you,' he said menacingly. I was beginning to feel glad of the policemen on either side of me. If necessary, surely they would shield me from any violence. So far, both those who had addressed me were bigger and stronger than I was.

The moment had clearly passed for formal introductions, but I was still unsure of the identity of the man in the suit. He was apparently attached to Judith Talbot, and I wondered whether he might be a solicitor. I could hardly ask who he was, in my role as scapegoat and thoroughly despicable worm. Besides, the parade of random thoughts flitted through my mind too rapidly for anything like lucidity to emerge. All I could do was react and try to maintain a few shreds of dignity.

Thea was standing alone, very obviously removed from the main action, as if waiting for her cue that was still some way off. There was a sudden hiatus, where everybody continued to stare at me in silence, and the light seemed to disappear almost completely. What must we look like, I thought murkily – a crowd in a dark field, nobody saying anything? Were there owls and foxes watching from the sidelines, thinking how strange a manifestation this was?

The suited man finally spoke up. 'Mr Slocombe, there has been a request for an exhumation of this grave. Protocol demands that you be present, as the officiating undertaker.'

'You're the coroner's officer?' I asked, remembering something of the procedure.

'I am the coroner,' he corrected, with a glance first at the policeman and then at Thea. 'George Wilson.' He did not proffer a hand for me to shake.

'Are you doing it now?' There ought to be screens, if so, and a digger, and a receptacle for transporting the body. 'Isn't it a bit early in the evening?' Again, procedure ordained that such ghastly events take place at midnight, with discretion verging on secrecy.

Mrs Talbot gave a strangled cry, suggesting distress and rage and something like disgust. Still Thea Osborne said nothing.

'Later this evening. The relatives have come to pay their respects before the body is disturbed.'

I eyed the Watchetts with some scepticism, wishing I had the nerve to say, *What are they doing here, then? They're not relatives.* Ghouls, I concluded, eager not to miss anything.

'Why, though?' I finally asked. 'Why are you moving her? Is it at the request of the council?' If so, I thought, where was the relevant official, another little Maynard clone? Was his wife here in that capacity, I wondered wildly?

286

The first policeman spoke up. 'Because there is a question about how she died,' he said stiffly. 'DI Basildon will see you shortly, and brief you about it.'

'But ... there was a post-mortem. She died of natural causes.'

'Police investigations suggest this might not be the case,' he said.

Judith Talbot found her voice. 'You murdered her, you bastard!' she shouted. 'You murdered both of them, to get your hands on her house. It's sick, that's what it is. All you care about is your own pocket, and setting up your empire. *You* killed her.'

The word *empire* echoed so ludicrously in my ears that I gave a very unwise guffaw.

At last, Thea was at my side, competing with the policeman on my left. She peered around him, her face only just above his shoulder level. 'Drew – they have to act on such an accusation. I've been speaking to my brother-in-law about it. Mrs Talbot has produced some material that can't be ignored.'

She spoke quickly, as if fearing interruption. I tried to grasp the import of her words. Was she warning me to stay quiet? Was she simply being kind and keeping me abreast of developments? Was she letting the police know that she was somebody to be reckoned with, well connected and firmly involved?

'Poor Greta,' murmured a woman I could barely see in the gloom. It could only be Susan Watchett.

'Yeah,' came the strangled tones of Charles Talbot. 'Poor Aunt Greta.'

I wondered where young Jeremy was, and whether he knew what was being proposed. He, of the whole family, would surely be the most deeply distressed by what had been proposed.

And lying at our feet, silently reproachful and very much present, was the grave. The heaped soil had settled slightly in the ten days since it was piled over the coffin, but it still looked like a fresh wound in the grassy field. If left alone, by the end of the summer it would be almost invisible. The grass and wild plants would quickly cover it, and although it would remain a mound for a while, when the coffin collapsed under the weight of the damp soil it would be almost impossible to detect. I had urged the Talbots to erect a small fence to mark the position, for this very reason. The law demanded that all human burials be marked in some way, as well as being left undisturbed. The precise manner of marking was not specified, but I had made it clear that the mere planting of a small tree or shrub would not suffice. Wild creatures, or even stray sheep, would all too readily destroy something so flimsy. A little wall of stones, a chain fence, even kerbs of some sort – something like that was required.

'What's the depth of the grave?' asked the coroner.

'Four feet,' I said.

'Hmm.' He looked frustrated, as if hoping for a different response. Then he seemed to assert his authority, as the most senior official present.

'Well, then,' he said, 'I think we've finished here for the moment.' He moved to face Judith Talbot and her son. 'If I may, I suggest we all leave now,'

288

he said gently. 'You'll be kept informed of the results of our examination, of course. Probably tomorrow afternoon – at least with any initial findings.'

Charles shuddered. 'This is horrible,' he groaned. 'Mother – I wish you hadn't insisted on it.'

'I can't think what good it can do,' said Helena Maynard. Out of the blue I remembered the insinuation that Oliver Talbot had made that she was rather too close to Graham Ingram for propriety. Neither man from the altercation in the pub was present. But Thea had said in her message that it was Mrs Maynard who had been making trouble, not Judith Talbot. Obviously, I sighed inwardly, both women were gunning for me. I was burning to question Thea. Why was she even in Broad Campden again, when I had assumed she was going to go back to Witney and stay there?

'Good point,' I said, rather loudly. 'If all this is based on the idea that I killed her, then it's a complete waste of time. It's also an insult to my client and what she wanted.' I was finally finding a seam of indignation, which had been submerged under all the other emotions. 'She came to me of her own accord, and gave clear instructions as to the disposal of her remains when she died. All I did was carry out those instructions in good faith.'

'So why did she die so soon afterwards?' demanded Mrs Talbot. 'She wasn't ill. And why the *hell* did she leave you the house? You must have swindled her into it, telling her a pack of lies.'

'Yes,' echoed Helena Maynard. 'I've thought that all along, ever since I saw the will. I said to Graham–' abruptly she fell silent, a hand over her mouth. Nobody picked her up on it, but Thea made a small hissing sound, which I thought indicated some kind of confirmation of a thought or theory. The presence of Miriam Ingram would have been useful, I reflected. Any wife would surely have reacted. As it was, there was no one present who was likely to care what might have been going on between Helena Maynard and Graham Ingram. Foolishly, my mind snagged on the rhyming names – Graham and Miriam Ingram – repeating them to myself like a nursery rhyme, wishing Maggs were there to chuckle over it with me.

They were all looking at me. I threw up my hands in defeat at the unjust accusations. 'Well,' I addressed the grave, 'I did what I could.' It was obvious that I was the only real representative of the dead woman, and the opposing forces were just too strong for me.

It was not yet quite dark, but we could not properly see each others' faces, and there seemed a sudden collective desire for some illumination. 'Where do we go now?' asked Charles of the coroner. 'There's no way we can go home with all this going on. We want to be on the spot, but...' he sagged helplessly. 'Greta's house is no good.'

The coroner showed no sign that this was his problem. Charles persisted, hungry for information. 'Who's going to be here for the actual ... thing?'

'Myself, two police officers, a police doctor and

Mr Slocombe,' came the ready reply. 'Normally there would also be a minister of religion, but it seems in this instance that won't be appropriate.'

Good for Greta, I thought. At least she was spared that final indignity.

'Who does the digging, then?' asked Frank Watchett.

'There'll be a mini digger and an operative,' said the coroner tightly.

'What happens in the meantime?' asked Thea, whose mind I could almost hear whirring. From about ten minutes earlier, I had gained the strong impression that she had a purpose, a plan, that was dictating her words and actions.

'I suggest you all go home,' said the coroner, as if this was self-evident.

'We can't do that,' said Mrs Talbot. 'We live the other side of Oxford. We're staying right here in the village until we get some answers.' She looked at Charles. 'Susan says we can stay at her house for the night.'

It occurred to me to wonder why Mrs Maynard was there in the first place. What role was she playing in this strange little melodrama? I suspected that Thea knew the answer.

'Good old Susan,' Helena said now, with some bitterness. 'Always there in a crisis. Always shoving her nose in where it isn't wanted.'

'Oh, Helena,' murmured the abused Mrs Watchett. 'What a thing to say!'

'It's true, though. Except, of course, when my Gavin was bashed to death. Where were you then? Why weren't you snooping around when this ... *swine* ... was attacking him?' The swine, of course, was me.

'Helena, I'm really not going to discuss this. You have your views, and the police are obviously thinking along the same lines, but it certainly isn't for me to express an opinion about it. Gavin did what he felt he had to, and somebody felt they had to stop him. Beyond that, none of us can say.'

'And I don't know why you're here, when you were so against everything Greta wanted.' It was Judith Talbot speaking up, calling over her shoulder to Mrs Maynard as her son marched her determinedly away. 'It's a pity your Gavin didn't stay out of it, that's all I can say.'

I wondered what the police were thinking about the many reckless utterances flying around, and whether they were noting every word for use as evidence later. I took great care to say nothing as we all left the field. I half expected to see Jessica Osborne and her detective boyfriend, in another echo of the funeral that had begun the whole miserable business.

The cars belonged respectively to the Talbots, Thea and the coroner. Evidently the Watchetts had walked from their house in the village, and the police had no visible transport other than the car which had brought me from Somerset. I automatically headed for Thea's red Fiesta containing the long-suffering spaniel, before being checked by the coroner. 'Mr Slocombe!' he called, more loudly than necessary. 'We'll need you here promptly at midnight. Is that understood?'

I considered making some remark to the effect that I surely had no choice in the matter, but it seemed superfluous. Having made the journey yet again to Broad Campden, I could see no sense in disobeying orders. 'I'll be here,' I said.

Thea started the engine before I had shut the passenger door. 'Oi!' I protested. 'What's the hurry?'

'We've got four and a half hours,' she said. 'You're not going to let them exhume Mrs Simmonds, are you?'

'I hadn't thought of trying to stop them,' I admitted. 'I'd be terribly outnumbered.'

'They won't do it if they change their minds about her being murdered.'

'That could be true, although I'm not sure the process is reversible, once it gets started. And what could possibly change their minds, anyway?'

'A confession by the person who killed Mr Maynard, of course. And an assurance that Mrs Simmonds wasn't involved in any way.'

My head was spinning. 'For goodness' sake – how can we hope to manage that? I don't understand what you're talking about.'

'I'll try to explain it, then. It's been a very busy day my end, let me tell you. I must have made a dozen phone calls, and driven about three hundred miles. You see ... I got an idea...' And she proceeded to tell me, as we drove up an unfamiliar road into Chipping Campden, and parked in the small square in the heart of the town.

Chapter Twenty-Two

She talked for forty-five minutes, as we sat in the dark car, the dog curled quietly on the back seat. Very few people passed by – the town had closed for the night, the street lights transforming the medieval buildings into a scene from a painting. It was, I noted abstractedly, impossibly beautiful. The proportions were perfect – the use of space, with odd levels, could hardly have been improved. The main street had been built on a slope, so that one side was higher than the other, which might, I thought, have given rise to ancient rivalries and disagreements about status. The open-sided market hall, set bang in the middle, was of modest size but great antiquity. All the shops were small, some extremely so. All this I observed subliminally, the vast bulk of my attention on the story Thea was telling me, and munching the sandwiches she had very thoughtfully provided.

She had begun, it seemed, on Saturday evening, having dropped me back at home after our visit to the commune, after hearing much the same account of Mrs Simmonds from her old friend as I had from Roger. 'They didn't like her. She was a troublemaker, always complaining. But she did have one or two allies, who argued her case when she was asked to leave.'

She had enlisted PC Jessica in the project,

checking legalities concerning alternative burials, for one thing. 'But I could have told you all that,' I protested.

'I know. But there were several reasons for not asking you.'

A cold finger prodded my heart. 'You thought I might have killed her, and then lied about the rules?'

'I thought that others might think that, so you would be contaminated.'

I mused on this. 'But facts are facts,' I objected.

'Yes, well. You were busy. There wasn't time to talk it through with you.'

'We had the car journey.' To my recollection, we had spoken little during that half-hour or so on Saturday afternoon.

'I wasn't ready then. I had to think about it.'

She went on with her debriefing. She had looked up the Land Registry on the computer, and discovered that there were indeed anomalies in the ownership of Mrs Simmonds' house, going back to the middle of the twentieth century. 'It is still under review,' she said. 'The boundaries are very unclear, for one thing.'

'And she really didn't own the field?' It was a frail straw that I was clutching at, but just then anything seemed possible.

'Sadly, no. She didn't.'

'Did you check the legality of burying a body in someone else's ground?'

'I tried, but couldn't get a proper answer. It's some sort of trespass, that's all I could discover. There are conflicting laws, and I don't know which trumps which. Then I went to see the

Talbots,' she said. 'That was this morning.'

Another unpleasant suspicion struck me. 'So ... did you have anything to do with this new idea that I killed Mrs Simmonds?'

'I'm afraid so. But trust me, Drew. It's all for a good reason.'

I was poleaxed. Was this woman mad? Did she in fact hate me and want to see me thrown into prison for decades? Her calm request that I should trust her made me feel I was completely at her mercy.

'How *can* I trust you?' I said. 'How could anybody?'

She heaved a sigh. 'I thought you might. I know what I'm doing, honestly. Just listen and I'll explain.'

I did listen and she did at least partly explain herself, although I remained shaken and confused. Her logic was based on a very dubious theory of human nature, to my way of thinking. 'You've been reading too many Agatha Christie stories,' I said, when she paused.

'No, I haven't. I've been here before, Drew – that's the point. I know how people behave under pressure. You have to push them into a corner, make them desperate.'

'Isn't that the police's job?'

'Yes, it is. That's what interrogation is all about. Make them think there's nowhere to hide, catch them out in lies and contradictions. Confront them with their own guilt – force them to recognise it.'

'Nasty,' I shivered. 'Cruel.'

'Definitely. It's a cruel world.'

After all, I told myself, she did have relatives in the police, not least her assertive young daughter. She had been the girlfriend of a senior detective, and joined in a few of his investigations. She had glimpsed the cruel world that I could barely accept as real, despite my own brushes with violent crime. I had made excuses for people, even when they were shown to be killers. I had even tried to understand the man who had shot my innocent wife. 'Yes,' I said, 'maybe it is.'

'You don't sound convinced.'

'I'm not. I suppose I think cruelty is what gets forced to the surface under this pressure you're talking about. It's not a natural human trait.'

'It is, though. Of course it is. It's about power and hierarchies and maintaining your position. Just watch any playground.'

'I thought we were short of time,' I said, ducking the issue.

'Don't worry. We've got to wait here until half past eight.'

I had begun to understand that she really did have a plan in mind, that she was orchestrating a series of events designed to avert the exhumation at midnight. And that in her own thoroughgoing way, she was bringing me up to speed with what was going to happen.

'So you went to the Talbots?' I prompted.

'Charles and Judith were there. I had a long talk with them, going over what they told us last weekend, and a lot more. I can't tell you all of it now, but it was very interesting.'

'Why did they agree to talk to you? What business was it of yours?'

297

'I began with a grovelling apology for staying the night in the house with you, and telling the Watchetts that you'd been left the property. I guessed they had reasons for not wanting that particular fact to get out, and it turned out I was right. Anyway, that easily led into what I wanted to know.'

'Which was?'

'Oliver and Judith are very much in disagreement over the house, and whether or not to contest your inheriting it. Charles is on his mother's side. Oliver ... well, Oliver is an extremely important player in this game. We should have paid him more attention from the start.'

'Do you think he killed Mr Maynard?' I asked eagerly. 'Something to do with old rivalries – her carrying on with the Ingram chap?' I thought back to the argument in the pub. 'Or something about that girl, Carrie, who's such a mystery.'

'Wait,' she insisted. 'I have to tell it to you in the right order.'

'But what about Charles Talbot?' I could not resist asking. 'He didn't look too happy just now.' I thought again of the grooves in his face, suggesting inner torment as well as anger.

'No. There's some business between him and Helena Maynard, which I haven't entirely fathomed.'

'Business? Not an *affair*, surely? She's his mother's age, isn't she? And I thought we'd decided it was Ingram, not Charles.'

'We don't know that for sure – it was only Oliver making a wild accusation. And she's not so much older than Charles.'

298

'Yes, she is. She must be. She went to school with Judith, remember.'

'We haven't time for this,' Thea shook her head impatiently. 'Let me tell it in my own way.'

She went on to describe her visit to the Watchetts, again ostensibly to apologise for offending them by sleeping in the cottage. 'They weren't so easy to mollify,' she confessed. 'She ranted about betrayal and loose morals.'

'I hope you convinced her we didn't do anything immoral.'

She laughed. 'I didn't have that much time to waste. It was easier just to let them believe what they liked, and get onto the important stuff.'

I groaned, thinking my reputation and marriage were actually fairly important to me.

'Anyway, once I got Susan on her own, it all became very interesting. When she stopped to think, she wasn't surprised that you'd been left the house – typical of Greta, she said, always trying to have the last word. She still rather likes you, apparently, in spite of everything.'

'That was my first impression, when she came to the burial, but I thought she'd gone off me since then.'

'And Greta's choice of funeral was typical as well. Everybody says that. She'd have done it as much to upset the maximum number of people, as from any real concern for the environment or whatever.'

'That can't be true,' I objected. 'She really believed in ecological funerals and simple living. Look at that co-housing business. She must have joined them for strong personal reasons. She's

299

made the best provision she could to ensure that a natural burial ground be established here. Although,' I added sadly, 'if she didn't own the field, it's never going to happen, is it?'

She seemed to be vaguely aware of what I was talking about, but made no direct response.

'She was a nice woman,' she mumbled unhappily. 'I wish I'd known her better.'

I nodded. 'Have you seen young Jeremy again?' I asked, from an automatic association.

She shook her head. 'But I gather he's back here now. Somehow or other, his mother persuaded him.'

'Does she know he's been at the co-housing place?'

'No idea. Not relevant,' she said, with a quick flip of her hand.

The clock on the dashboard was approaching eight, and I wondered how much more she had to disclose. I concentrated hard on the information she was imparting, trying not to interrupt or divert her from the thread she was following. I was still very far from grasping the final import, the logical conclusion of what she had discovered. Gradually, I found myself believing and, yes – *trusting* her. She seemed so clear and sure about it all. I began to feel hope and excitement instead of dread and despair.

'But how did they rush through the demand for the exhumation so fast?' I wondered at one point. 'I'd have expected it to take weeks.'

She smiled, her face a strange shade of orange from the street lights. 'Well, that's where my influence with certain people came in handy. It helped that DI Basildon had come round to taking me seriously. That was mainly due to my friend Sonia Gladwin, actually. I called in one or two favours, as they say.'

I had an impression that she could have told me more – that her acquaintance with the police was even deeper and wider than I realised.

'What a very tangled tale,' I summarised, when she'd finished. 'People lying about their ages, fighting over a house, neglecting their own children. And yet they all seem perfectly pleasant when you meet them.'

'Right. I've learnt, from recent experience, that things that happened ages ago still rankle enough to make them do terrible things years later. People get stuck in certain positions, and never seem to be able to forgive or forget. And events from schooldays loom larger than most. It's all so passionate and overwhelming when you're sixteen.'

'How on earth have you found all this out? It's mind-boggling.'

'Friends Reunited, for a start. And Facebook – that's fantastic for linking people together. Everybody blithely reveals their entire past history for all the world to see. It makes me despair, usually, but for once it came in very handy. I think they've all been keeping in pretty close touch for years.'

'But there are no huge secrets. For example, I assume Oliver really is the father of both Charles and Jeremy?'

'Oh yes. Plus a daughter who has a degenerative disease and is in a care home.'

I had forgotten the invisible sister. 'Ah, so that's

it,' I said. 'It sounds like a very sad story.'

I wondered how much of this was directly pertinent to our campaign. Surely Thea would know better than to waste precious minutes on idle gossip, and yet I couldn't see where it was leading. 'So?' I asked.

'So now I think I've built up the complete picture.'

'And what happens next?'

'We recruit an assistant,' she laughed gaily. 'And I think this must be him, right on time. Look – it's half past eight.'

As if on cue, there was a rap on the driver's side of the car, bringing Hepzie to her feet, with a few startled yaps. 'OK, Heps, settle down,' said Thea, opening the window. 'Hello, Harry. What fantastic timekeeping!'

Chapter Twenty-Three

Harry was the elderly bearded bloke from the co-housing place, who had sat next to Thea at lunch. It took me some time to recognise him, and even longer to grasp that they had already started to hatch their devious plot over the soup on Saturday. I felt sidelined and even more betrayed. 'Couldn't I have helped?' I whined. 'If you'd explained it to me?'

'Yes, I'm sure you could. But I wanted to keep it to myself for a bit. I'm sorry if that sounds bad, but there it is. I mean, I hardly know you really, do I?'

I swallowed. It felt to me as if we knew each other rather well – that we had meshed almost from the outset, easy together and on the same side. But it was true – we had not spent many hours in each other's company. We had no real knowledge of how each other reacted under pressure – although I guessed that Thea had an idea that I might not be entirely reliable.

Harry was in the back seat with Hepzie and we were driving back to Broad Campden. Thea began to give instructions, like the top man in a bank robbery. The plan was bold and simple and terrifying. 'They're all in the same house, which is extremely handy,' she said.

I found myself running through the story again, increasingly aware of the many gaps Thea had left in her reasoning. One major omission was Helena Maynard. I was still ignorant of how or whether she fitted into the picture, apart from speculation as to whether and with whom she had been unfaithful to her husband. But it was too late to ask any further questions, so I tried to concentrate on the tasks allotted to me by our leader, far from fully understanding precisely how everything was going to work.

The house was ablaze with light, upstairs and down. The Watchetts lived in a row of houses on the Chipping Campden side of the village, that looked as if they had once been owned by the council: solid, unimaginative, built to last, with good-sized gardens at the front, and no doubt also at the back.

Harry went first, while we waited in the car. He

was to introduce himself as a close friend of Mrs Simmonds, from the co-housing group, come to express his regrets for not being at the funeral. He was to manifest total ignorance of the proposed exhumation, shock, horror and then a display of dawning understanding as he absorbed the idea that Greta might have been murdered. "Well," he would say, "I suppose I'm not entirely surprised, when I come to think about it – but from what I know of Greta's life, it wouldn't have been the undertaker who killed her. She had enemies far closer to home than that." This was designed to cause flurries of mutual suspicion amongst those present, and a heightened atmosphere.

'Won't the atmosphere be quite high already?' I asked. 'Under the circumstances.'

'The higher the better,' said Thea.

Harry had a scant fifteen minutes to achieve his objective, at which point Thea and I would enter the fray, claiming that we could not settle, knowing they all believed that I had killed their sister, aunt and friend. I would proclaim my innocence in a near hysterical mode – further heightening the atmosphere, hoped Thea. She would disclose her intimacy with senior members of the police force, and hint that she was aware of many aspects of Mr Maynard's murder that had not been publicly revealed.

'That gives us an hour or so in which to get what we want. Should be plenty,' she said.

'Thea – I ought to tell you,' I began hurriedly, 'you ought to know that I have been involved in something rather like this before. People behave with serious violence when they're under pressure. I've seen it happen. You need to know what you're doing.' She seemed like a barely credible character at that moment – something from a comic strip: Nancy Drew or Lara Croft. Not a small English widow in her forties.

'I like to make things happen,' she said, with a ridiculously sweet smile. 'It usually works.'

'But what if it goes wrong? What if Charles or Mr Watchett has a gun? Or a knife? I mean – *everyone* can get a knife easily enough, can't they? There'll be a drawerful of them in the kitchen.'

'Why would they want to knife anybody?' She gave me a wide-eyed look that didn't fool me for a moment. 'All we're going to do is talk to them.'

I gave up. Beneath all the plans and instructions thrummed the constant question – who killed Mr Maynard? He had certainly been deliberately coshed by somebody, even if they hadn't meant to kill him. I thought I understood where the guilt must lie, but to my slow-moving brain, the proof was flimsy and the whole exercise fraught with hazard.

'It's simple,' she said impatiently, when I stammered out my confusion, without explaining precisely what it was that was so plain and obvious.

I did my best to concentrate on the present moment, trying to trust that Thea knew what she was doing. At least there was no sign that Harry had blundered too badly, so far. No screaming or slamming doors or gunshots issued from the house. No wailing police sirens attending an alarm call. At exactly nine o'clock, Thea opened her door, told the dog to stay where it was, and said, 'Come on, then,' to me. Feeling rather like a second spaniel, I did as I was bid.

We were admitted to a living room that seemed uncomfortably crowded. The bright overhead light left nowhere to hide, and all the faces, as I looked from one to another, displayed varying emotions, from irritation through impatience to boredom. There wasn't much of a heightened atmosphere, as far as I could discern.

Thea made her opening speech and then waited for me to deliver mine. 'I know you all think badly of me,' I began, 'but I came to try to convince you that I truly did not harm anybody. Not Mrs Simmonds or Mr Maynard.' I stood up straight and met any eye that fell in my direction. 'It has all been a complete mix-up, and it's time we straightened it out before any more damage is done.'

Seven people stared at me. Charles Talbot was standing by the fireplace, in a pose that seemed deliberately calculated to suggest the final act in a play from the Thirties. He ought to have been smoking a pipe for maximum effect, I thought crazily. His young brother was slumped in a corner of a big green sofa, his mobile phone in his hand, as if just about to compose a text message to someone, taking no notice of me and my announcement. Did he have a girlfriend, I wondered? Someone he was relaying all this family turmoil to?

Judith Talbot was beside her friend Susan Watchett, slightly squashed on the remaining sofa space. Mr Watchett was in an armchair, his head and shoulders pressed back as if trying to withdraw from the proceedings. His stare came and went – more a snatching of quick glances than a sustained attention to what I was saying. Oliver Talbot squatted incongruously on a leather pouffe close to his elder son, his expression sulky.

Harry and Thea had gravitated to a point behind the sofa, leaning over it like latecomers to the drama. A big grey cat was curled on a rug in front of the unlit fire, ignoring the whole performance.

'Poor Greta,' sighed Harry, apparently not quite done with his own presentation. 'She was her own worst enemy, of course. Would never give an inch in a disagreement. I never expected her to be murdered, but I sometimes wondered how she escaped a good smack.'

Thea gripped his arm. 'What do you mean? How well did you know her? Who *are* you, anyway?'

It struck me as deeply unconvincing, but nobody else seemed to spot a piece of bad acting when they saw it.

'Oh, I do beg your pardon,' he gave a quaint little bow. 'The name's Harry Richmond. I knew your Mrs Simmonds for six months before she left the cooperative. I actually took her side once or twice in an argument, just for the sake of fair do's, but it never seemed to help. She was such a very *abrasive* woman.'

A protesting snort came from the boy on the sofa, but nothing more articulate emerged.

'So you agree with us that she was murdered?' said Judith Talbot, in far less belligerent mode than earlier in the evening. 'But you don't think

307

it was Mr Slocombe who did it?'

'Of course I didn't do it,' I shouted hotly. 'How many more times?'

'Be quiet,' ordered Charles Talbot. 'Please be quiet. We just might be getting somewhere at last.' He eyed his mother. 'Ma, you've already heard what this man has to say. It doesn't really change anything, when you think about it. At least – it confirms what you thought.' He frowned, and chewed his lower lip. 'Although–'

'If I understand him, it means Drew's in the clear,' Thea interrupted. 'And *that* means she wasn't murdered at all, and there shouldn't be an exhumation.'

I hadn't expected her to reach this point so soon. She was deviating from the script, leaving me to flounder.

'Or ... someone we know did it,' said Charles, again giving his mother a thoughtful look. 'And we might be sorry to have it brought into the open.' He might be slow, but he was certainly functioning more effectively than most people in the room.

I caught Harry Richmond's eye. He seemed to be feeling something close to triumph, his eyebrows twitching manically.

Time was passing far too rapidly for comfort. If everyone was to have a say, and the goal achieved of averting the exhumation, a lot had to happen in the next half-hour.

'Helena Maynard sent me a very nasty letter,' I said, hoping to shift things along a bit. 'Completely out of order it was.'

'But the police are convinced that you killed

Gavin,' Susan Watchett said, speaking for the first time. 'You're only out on bail because they're still collecting evidence. As I understand it, you've already been charged with murdering Gavin. I don't know how you can have the gall to come amongst decent people, you two-faced creature. Swindling poor Greta out of her money and then bashing Gavin to death when he threatened to expose you for what you are. It's all quite clear to me what happened. You made that stupid mistake about the field, which obviously meant you wouldn't inherit the house as you expected. So you thought if you could shut Gavin up, it might not be pursued by anybody else. It might all be hushed up and you'd get what you'd wanted all along. Of course, you killed Greta as well. That much is perfectly obvious.'

She spoke without drawing breath for most of this speech. Her face was pushed forward, with red cheeks and wide staring eyes.

'That's right,' endorsed Judith Talbot, with scarcely less passion. She proceeded to repeat much of what Susan Watchett had just said, which was quite unnecessary, to my mind.

The melodrama was finally getting going, it seemed, in accordance with Thea's plan. Furthermore, she was stating the received wisdom about what had happened, in a summary that was both painful and frustrating to hear. I wondered whether I would ever see myself in the same light again, after being so directly accused of a double murder. For some reason, my glance fell on young Jeremy, still fiddling with his phone. Wasn't he too young for all this adult hysteria, for accusations about murder and greed? Feeling my eyes on him, he looked up and met my gaze. He smiled tightly, embarrassment evident on his face, and something that suggested shame. He might well feel ashamed of his raving mother, I thought. Any boy would.

I was grateful for the smile, at least. Here was someone who apparently did not believe I had committed murder, who had not recoiled from me as everybody else had done when I first entered the room. I was something close to monstrous in their eyes – or at least in the eyes of all those who had not themselves killed Mr Maynard. Perhaps this, too, was part of Thea's plan – to observe which person failed to react that way, knowing I was actually quite innocent. Trying to visualise that initial scene again, it seemed to me that it was the women who had been outraged and vituperative, while all the men showed varying levels of fatigue or exasperation. Except Jeremy, who seemed to care for nothing but his phone.

In the brief silence following the two female tirades, I wondered about motivation. What could be so bad that it drove a person to kill? Mrs Watchett thought it was basically about property and business expansion. Plus an element of face-saving, perhaps. 'You're wrong,' I told the women. 'Completely wrong.'

'Why would it mean he wouldn't inherit the house?' asked Thea slowly. 'Why would the mistake about the field lead to the loss of his inheritance?'

'It's in the will,' supplied Judith Talbot. 'A condition of him getting the house is that he establish a natural burial ground in that field.'

'Didn't you know that?' I asked Thea. 'Surely I told you?' I remembered our fractured conversation in the car. 'I thought you knew about it.'

'You didn't tell me,' she said. 'I had no idea.'

It was one reason why I had decided that honesty was the best policy, very early in my career: I could never remember what I had told which person. The deliberate evasions over the past week where Karen was concerned had been one of the most unpleasant aspects of the whole affair. I could only cope with it by telling her almost nothing. She still had no idea there had been a murder, never mind that I was the chief suspect. But I did think I had been completely frank with Thea. 'I meant to tell you,' I said.

She was clearly thinking hard. 'Hmm,' she said, unhelpfully. Only then did I realise she was acting for the benefit of her byzantine plan.

'So, what now?' came a new voice. Finally, Jeremy had spoken from the corner of the sofa.

I remembered that he and Harry must surely know each other. How had the boy reacted when Harry first showed up at the Watchetts' door? Had he contributed when Thea's friend had delivered his little speech about enemies at the commune? He had, after all, told Thea and me that his aunt had effectively been killed by the people there – *like dogs*, he said. Jeremy, at least, did not believe that I was in any way involved.

I addressed him directly. 'Jeremy – you don't think I murdered your aunt, do you?' Before saying more, it struck me that he might not want his mother to know about our conversation on

311

Saturday. Evidently, he had decided to return to his family, instead of hiding away in Somerset.

'Nah!' he said carelessly. 'Course you didn't. The whole thing's daft.'

'Jeremy!' His mother looked as if she would like to smack him.

'Well, it's true. You've got it all wrong, as usual. You never did understand Auntie Greta, did you? None of you understood her.' He looked around the crowded room, his gaze finally resting on Charles, his much older brother. 'But she put one over on you all, in the end. She got what she wanted, exactly the *way* she wanted it.'

'Except now it's all going to be ruined,' said Thea softly.

The effect on Jeremy was galvanising. 'No!' he shouted. 'It's not gonna happen. This bloke never went near her. How could he have killed her? You should get your facts right before going off to the police with your rubbish ideas.' He switched his attention to Harry, twisting round to look at him where he still leant over the back of the sofa. '*You* know,' he hissed. 'You tell them.'

Reprieved from the full glare of a room full of people, I found my brain starting to function more effectively than it had done for some hours. I had understood that Thea was not divulging every detail of her plan, but a startling suspicion took root, germinated by Jeremy's words. I checked it from all angles, but it held fast.

Harry reached out to lay a hand on the boy's shoulder. 'Sorry, lad, but I think it is. If we can't convince the police that your mother's accusations are groundless, then they'll be forced to do another postmortem examination.'

'It's rubbish,' insisted Jeremy. 'And you all know it is,' he challenged the whole room.

His mother seemed to become more aware of him than she had so far. 'Jerry – who're you texting?' she suddenly asked.

'Who d'you think?'

'It's not your sister, is it?'

'Christ, Jeremy!' exploded big brother Charles. 'You're not, are you?'

'None of your business,' snapped the boy, closing the front of his phone. I caught a fleeting look of pain cross his face, as if his mother and brother had somehow wounded him. I gave the phone a closer examination, wondering just what functions it possessed, only dimly aware of the speed at which technology was moving, and the dinosaur nature of my own elderly gadget. This one looked more like a tiny computer than a telephone.

'Can it do pictures?' I asked.

He gave me a withering glance. 'Does a bike have wheels?' he said with impressive sarcasm.

Susan Watchett stood up, moving fluidly. She spoke to the gathering in general. 'Well, I don't know about you lot, but Frank and I are almost ready for bed.' She gave her husband a meaningful look. 'Can you put the cat out?'

As far as I could tell, they had all four Talbots as house guests. One of them was very likely to be sleeping on the sofa. I tried to catch Thea's eye, for instructions as to what happened next. As far as I could figure out, her plan had failed. The high stakes had been called, and if my hunch was right – a hunch that Charles Talbot evidently

313

shared – she was about to be unmasked as a troublemaker with no rights, and every reason to be thrown out of the house.

My idea took a knock as I tried to think it through to its source. 'When did you go to the police with your accusations against me?' I asked Mrs Talbot.

'She did it for me,' she said, indicating Thea. 'She knows some high-up bloke in the police, who could pull the right strings.'

Aha! 'Oh, yes, I see,' I said, carefully avoiding Thea's eye. More rapid thinking threw up new difficulties.

'I'm very sorry, Drew,' said Thea. 'It must feel like a terrible betrayal to you. But I felt that justice had to be done. I knew Greta Simmonds, after all. I couldn't just let it go, if she really had been murdered.'

'You never have completely trusted me, have you?' I accused her.

'I didn't *know* you,' she defended. 'And when I heard that you'd inherited the house – well, you must see how bad that looks.'

'You've got it all wrong, I tell you!' cried Jeremy, thumping a fist on the arm of the sofa. 'You're not *listening* to me. Nobody ever listens to me.'

'For God's sake,' growled Charles, who had clearly lost the thread some minutes ago. 'Grow up, why don't you.'

'But what about Gavin Maynard?' asked Oliver Talbot, who had apparently been half asleep for the past twenty minutes. 'Where does he fit in?'

I almost laughed at having my line so helpfully stolen.

'Well, I think your wife has got that part right,' said Thea. 'He threatened to forcibly remove the grave from that field. And that put him against the whole family.' She looked hard at Judith Talbot. 'Who at that point had no idea of what was in Greta's will. The trouble and notoriety that would arise from the whole messy business would reflect badly on them, and probably reduce the value of the house. It might also raise inconvenient questions about actual ownership of the whole property. That's why they were in such a hurry to find a buyer. Naïve, perhaps, since the searches would have thrown up the anomalies, but since they've never actually had to buy or sell a house, they probably wouldn't have known that.'

I waited, in some confusion. What was she trying to say?

'You think my parents killed Gavin Maynard?' queried Charles, on behalf of us all.

'Right!' asserted Thea, with rock-solid certainty. 'That's absolutely right. It all fits.'

Judith, her artificially red hair glittering in the bright light, drew back her lips in a snarl. 'How dare you!' she spat. 'You bloody interfering little bitch.'

At which point, in true melodramatic style, a loud knock came on the door.

Chapter Twenty-Four

Harry Richmond went to answer the knock. Helena Maynard came in slowly, startled at finding so many people, obviously in the middle of a heated argument. 'What's going on?' she faltered, losing much of the aggression that had so far characterised her.

'Mrs Osborne just accused my mother and father of killing your husband,' said Charles in a neutral tone. 'And Ma's not pleased.'

Jeremy snorted, apparently highly amused by this summary. Given the matter under discussion, everyone seemed remarkably relaxed, except for Mrs Talbot, who continued to glare at Thea and flare her nostrils. Her husband had his face in his hands, his knees uncomfortably raised, a low rumbling sound emerging from him.

'Judith?' Helena said. Then, 'Susan?'

It was, after all, the Watchett's house. It must have been them she wanted to speak to. The three middle-aged women began to gravitate together, forming the core of the assembled group, leaving the men on the outside. They all had Thea in the full beam of their attention.

'You're not seriously accusing Judith, are you?' Mrs Maynard demanded. 'After what we talked about this afternoon?' She threw a contemptuous glance at me, and I wondered whether Thea had actually reinforced the widow's certainty as to my guilt. It wouldn't have surprised me.

'I believe she has a lot of questions to answer,' said Thea. 'Now, we can't stay much longer. The police want Drew at the grave quite soon, and I dare say it's almost Jeremy's bedtime.' Two or three people glanced at the clock on the mantelpiece, registering amazement at the lateness of the hour.

'What?' The boy regarded her with outrage. 'I'm seventeen, not seven, you know. Bedtime!' He flounced back on the sofa, oozing indignation.

'Although ... don't you think it would be the right and decent thing to call off the exhumation?' Thea went on, looking first at Charles, then at his brother. 'After what's been said, does anybody really believe that Mrs Simmonds was murdered? Drew really couldn't have done it. He was busy with a funeral on the day she died – and the post-mortem was absolutely clear as to the cause of death. It's a wild and silly idea.'

'The police didn't think so,' said Judith. 'And *you* didn't think so this afternoon, either.'

'Well, I do now. I've spoken to Harry since then, and he's convinced me it's all completely untenable. And when the second post-mortem comes to exactly the same conclusion, you're going to be asked to foot the bill for the whole thing.'

'My fees alone will be five hundred pounds, at least,' I said, daringly. 'As I understand it, I'll be there in my capacity as funeral director, not murder suspect.'

'Come on, Ma,' said Charles. 'They're right, aren't they?' He gave me and Thea a slow discern-

317

ing look.

But Judith held firm. 'We can't back out now,' she insisted. 'And what harm can it do?'

'It's no light thing, to disturb a grave,' I said.

Thea waited quietly, her silence more effective than any words. One by one, everybody looked at her.

'There's no getting around it, then,' said Harry Richmond.

'I'm afraid not,' she said. 'There's been special Home Office permission, which was quite difficult to obtain at such short notice. Nobody's going to want to cancel it now, even though it would obviously be the best thing. Official wheels don't go into reverse very easily.'

'I'd better go, then,' I said, on the verge of adding that it would be a lonely walk in the dark down the deserted country road. Before I could say it, Harry stepped forward and offered to drive me, using Thea's car. This had apparently been decided between them in advance, much to my admiration.

'Thanks,' I said, gratefully.

'Not got your motor?' asked Jeremy. 'Where're you staying tonight, then?'

Touched by his concern, I rolled my eyes ruefully. 'Police cells, probably.'

He winced, as if I'd said something offensive. 'Tough luck,' he sympathised, seemingly sincere.

They all saw me off with varying degrees of anxiety. The solemnity of the imminent procedure had quietened them down, and despite suspicions as to my criminal behaviour, they remembered that I was also an undertaker, with special connections to forbidden and frightening worlds.

Harry and I got into the red Fiesta, greeted joyously by the spaniel, who seemed quite unconcerned at the absence of her mistress. 'I'll drop you, and then go back for Thea,' he said. 'The police will watch out for you.'

We manoeuvred around the other vehicles parked outside the house, and drove off through the village. 'Are we really going to the grave?' I asked.

'Oh yes,' he assured me.

'Is there really going to be an exhumation?'

'Oh no,' he chuckled. 'Well spotted.'

'Thea set it all up with her police cronies? It was all a pretence – is that right?'

'Absolutely correct. She's a wonder, that woman. An absolute marvel.' It was the word I always used about Maggs. I felt blessed.

'So what happens now?'

'Wait and see,' he advised. 'It could still all go horribly wrong.'

The sky was clear and a three-quarter moon shed enough light to see by, so long as you didn't want to read anything, or recognise the nuances of a human face. For anybody knowing their way around, it was more than adequate for a midnight walk.

Harry drove me to the field with the grave, and almost pushed me out of the car. It was completely silent and deserted. 'What do I have to do?' I asked.

'Go and sit by the grave, and wait,' he ordered me. 'Oh, and take this.' He reached over to the back seat and produced a kind of lantern.

I took it awkwardly. 'How does it work?' I asked.

He showed me quickly. It could be adjusted, from a faint light to a dazzling beam.

I found myself obeying instructions without any demur. It was no hardship, despite my bewilderment as to what was meant to happen. Of all the people around me on that overcrowded evening, one person above all the others had a hold on my conscience. It was whimsical, and probably counterproductive in several ways, but the more I thought about it, the stronger her claim seemed to be. I acknowledged to myself that I had something to answer for, a duty of care and concern that had not been properly fulfilled.

She hadn't gone anywhere, of course, since we had all stood around arguing over her remains. The soil was now damp, and deep black in the strange light. I set down the lantern without turning it on, then occupied myself with tidying the edges of the grave where small clods had rolled down from the dome at the top and made a ragged line. It was heavy stuff, and I wondered how difficult it had been to dig out. Ignoring the effect on the knees of my trousers, I knelt beside the grave. 'Well, here we are again,' I muttered aloud. 'Can't stay away, can I?'

It was never easy to simply walk away from a grave. The separation was always painful, even after a short acquaintance. It felt wrong to just abandon the poor, cold body to its fate below the earth. This was why I did the work I did. I wanted everything to be brought to a proper conclusion, for people to have every chance to do and say what they needed to for that separation to be as smooth as was humanly possible. Much of it had become automatic, from the repetition and familiarity. I had learnt that it was good to follow gut instincts: to rush away without looking back was just as valid as to sit for half a day at the graveside. Some people came every day for weeks. Others never once returned. Either way was fine.

I discovered that I needed this last little communion with Greta Simmonds, in order to gain her absolution for the mess I had made of her funeral. However I wriggled, I could not evade the knowledge that I ought to have checked ownership of the field. I had not even asked her the simple question. And that crucial omission had led to all the subsequent trouble – or so my upsurge of guilt persuaded me out in the midnight field, when I should have been speeding home to my family.

I was so quiet and still that I should have heard when somebody came to join me, but maybe I was too deep in thought to notice. I had forgotten why I was there, for a moment. Whatever role I was confusedly playing in Thea's grand plan, those minutes by the grave were genuine, and all-consuming. But finally I became aware of a companion.

Stumbling over the rough grass, his infernal mobile still in his hand, Jeremy was within five yards of me before I looked up. His face was impossible to discern, but I had no doubt as to who had joined me.

'You cheat!' he shouted. 'You've been lying and cheating all along. And I *trusted* you.'

Within seconds he was on me, hitting wildly at

my head and chest, the mobile phone connecting painfully with the bridge of my nose.

'Stop it!' I panted, struggling to get to my feet. I pushed him hard, and took the momentary respite as my chance to stand up. He whirled back to the attack, but now I had height on my side, and a cooler head, I could see that he was presenting me with much less of a danger than I'd first thought.

'Stop it, Jeremy,' I said again. 'There's no need for this. Behave yourself.'

I had slipped into parental mode by accident, but it worked. My face was bruised and throbbing, but no real harm had been done. The boy paused, looking doubtful. 'You're not going to dig her up, are you? It was all a trick.'

'I suppose it was,' I said, frowning down at him. 'Did you come here on your bike?'

'Right. I told them I was going out for a walk, and came over the fields.'

'You know all the paths,' I realised.

'Used to come here when I was small, and again when Auntie Greta came back to the cottage. She took me for walks.' He laid a protective hand on the grave and I felt sudden tears welling, as the truth hit me.

'You're the only one who really cares whether or not she's exhumed,' I said. 'Jeremy – were you here when I was arguing with Mr Maynard that Saturday? Did you overhear us? You followed him and...' It was all too obvious, and yet still impossible to believe.

'You'll never prove anything,' he blustered.

'Well, I'm going to have to try. Otherwise they'll

charge me with it, and I'm not taking the blame for what you did.' Even as I spoke, I found myself thinking that perhaps I should. That perhaps it would be the truly noble line to take, saving the boy from wasting his prime in a miserable prison.

'She hated him – that Gavin. He was a right little toerag. Charles has a thing with the wife, as well. I reckoned I was doing everybody a favour.'

'Oh, Jeremy,' I moaned.

'I never meant to drop you in it, though. You were decent enough. She thought you were a star. Leaving you the house, and wanting you to start up some natural burial business here. She was all happy and excited about it. Said you might let me work for you.'

This echo of my own idea moved me even more. I slumped beneath the sadness of it.

'Who do you keep texting?' I asked.

'Carrie – just as Ma said. Don't know where she got the idea, though. She forgets all about her most of the time.'

'Carrie? Your sister?'

'Right. She's in a special hospital. But that doesn't make her stupid. *She* understands about Auntie Greta and the grave.'

'How old is Carrie?'

'Nineteen.' He gave me a look of pure misery. 'She's only nineteen, but she looks like an old woman. She hurts all the time. Her bones never grew right. She won't live much longer – and then she'll be buried here as well.'

I tried to keep my expression neutral, while wishing heartily that Mrs Simmonds had mentioned this potential second grave a year ago. Two burials in the open countryside were a very different proposition from one. And then I remembered my inheritance. Suddenly it made considerably more sense. 'I see,' I said slowly. 'That's terribly sad.'

He stared at me earnestly. I could see the whites of his eyes, the urgent angle of his body. 'The council won't make us move her, will they? Not now.'

I lowered myself once more to the wet grass. 'Jeremy – you're in awful trouble. You know that, don't you?'

He smiled painfully. 'Not bothered,' he asserted. 'That lady said I shouldn't be upset.'

'Thea? You mean Thea? Surely she doesn't know–?'

'That I cracked his head open with a spade? Course she doesn't. She thinks it was Ma and Dad.'

'A spade?'

'Yeah. The one I used to help here, after the funeral. I never gave it back to the old bloke. He went off and left me on my own. Said he'd collect it another day, if I wanted to finish off. Nice old man, talked to me about bodies and souls and stuff.'

'And you came back the next day, when I was here arguing with the man from the council?'

'Couldn't hear all of it, but it was obvious what he wanted. Then that woman showed up in her car...'

I had to think. 'Jessica! She's Thea's daughter. She's in the police.'

He shrugged. 'She was a nuisance. But I had

324

the bike, and waited till you'd driven off – it was for Carrie, d'you see?' Much of his bravado had slipped, and he sounded close to pleading.

'When did Thea tell you not to be upset?'

'At the co-housing place. She told Harry to have a word with me, saying I ought to come back here today because something important was happening. Tricked me, didn't she?' He spoke wryly, and I thought I could see a shadowy grin on his face.

'And have you told Carrie what you did?'

He nodded. 'Had to talk to someone. She's ace on the mobile – texts me the whole time. I sent her a picture of the bloke – not too close up – the blood didn't really show. But she told me I did the right thing. She said the grave was the only bright thing in her life, thinking she'd be lying here next to Auntie Greta for ever. I sent her pictures of that as well.'

'I expect you did,' I said, thinking that Carrie Talbot's phone was all that would be needed to convict young Jeremy of premeditated murder.

While I was wondering whether he would accompany me quietly if I made a citizen's arrest, and if so, where we would go without any transport, his telephone warbled at him.

He answered it without hesitation, its little screen lighting up in an eerie glow. 'Yeah?' he grunted into it. Not sweet sister Carrie, then, I concluded. 'Yeah, Ma, I'm OK. What d'you want?'

He listened for a moment, heaved a long sigh, and said, 'Whatever,' before closing down the call. I was left very little the wiser. The only immediate consequence was that I remembered that I too had a phone, and could call for assistance whenever I chose.

'We have to go,' I said. Clouds had obscured the moon, so I reached out and switched the lantern Harry had given me to its lowest setting. 'Turn it off,' growled Jeremy, but I ignored him.

'We'll need it to find your bike,' I said.

'Don't be daft,' he spoke softly, distractedly. 'I'm not going anywhere. This is my place now. Mine, and Carrie's and Auntie Greta's.'

I was unforgivably slow to react. He had taken a knife from his pocket, pushing a catch to produce a vicious blade that glinted in the soft beam of the lantern, before I had any notion of what he intended. Perhaps, subliminally, I couldn't believe a person could kill himself, leaving his last word to his mother a laconic *Whatever*. That simply could not happen.

But it did. He turned away from me, facing his aunt's grave, and drew the blade firmly across his own throat, starting just below his left ear.

Without thinking, I flicked the light to full beam, watching in horror as the unnaturally purple fountain gushed from the boy's throat.

He couldn't die. This single thought shouted itself at me, over and over. The carotid artery was severed – one of the quickest and most certain ways to bleed to death. It was extremely difficult to stem the flow, to find the right pressure point. But failing a highly trained paramedic, I was a good person to be on the spot. I knew about this stuff.

In the darkness, my clothes soaked by the spurting blood, I found the right place, and exerted the right pressure. I murmured soothingly, hoping to slow his heart rate from the high panic mode it was liable to be in. It would be working overtime to keep his brain and lungs supplied with oxygen. But instead it was sending the precious blood uselessly out into the open air.

I had no idea of the passage of time, but it seemed quite a while before people came running to my side with bright torches. I ignored them, never even asking myself how they knew to come when I hadn't made any effort to summon them. 'What did he do?' asked a man, repeatedly. 'What's he done?' They shone their lights onto Jeremy's neck and made appalled noises. Nobody tried to elbow me aside until eventually I caught sight of a blue flashing light out in the road, and then there was a woman with an equipment case and needles, and finally a stretcher.

'Don't let him die,' I pleaded. 'He's only seventeen.'

'You did the right thing, mate,' said a man. 'The flow's slowed right down already. He'll survive.'

I was too shaky to even try to stand up. Everything was sticking to me, the terrifying hot smell of blood all around me. The lights were all on me, so I couldn't see who was holding them, couldn't make out the voices as coming from anybody I knew. There was, in truth, only one voice that I was listening for.

It came, at last. 'Come on, Drew, we can go now. You were amazing. We never *dreamt*– I mean, it didn't occur to us that he'd do something like that. That is – we were expecting one of his *parents* to follow you, not Jeremy.' She sounded almost as shaky as me.

'Were they watching us, then? Listening to what he said? We were under *surveillance?*' The idea enraged me beyond all reason. After all, they would feel perfectly justified, the clever way the whole thing had been set up, the satisfactory outcome. They'd claim, no doubt, that they'd saved the boy's life by being on the scene so quickly.

'I'm afraid so.'

'And you *knew* about it?'

'It was my idea,' she said proudly.

I staggered to my feet, walking stiff-legged from the clotting blood that seemed to coat me from head to foot. I had to fight off tears that had gathered at the back of my nose. I felt no sense of achievement, no pleasure at being exonerated from Mr Maynard's murder. I felt sick and sad and defeated.

'He did it for his sister,' I muttered, when I was in Thea's car, making a terrible mess of her upholstery. 'Carrie. He did it for her.'

'They'll have got it all on tape,' she said, as if that was some sort of consolation.

'He's only seventeen.' This was another persistent thought that I couldn't shift. 'And he wanted to die.'

'He couldn't see any other way out.'

'That wasn't it. He wasn't trying to escape. He was trying to be with his aunt, and maybe blazing a trail for his sister. That field – it was much more important to them all than we realised.'

'So why didn't Mrs Simmonds check more carefully as to who owned it?'

I sighed. 'Because she trusted me to make it all right.'

We had nowhere to go. Thea had been driving through the lanes for ten minutes before I started to wonder where we were heading. It was one in the morning, and I needed a hot shower more than I ever had in my life. 'Where are we going?' I asked.

'Cirencester,' she told me, as if it was obvious.

'Why?'

'The police have got a flat ready for us to use. We're VIPs now. They've pulled out all the stops for us.'

I was too traumatised to argue or enquire any further. Nothing seemed to matter very much.

I slept deeply for about three hours, and then woke while it was still dark. My first thoughts were about the spring equinox, the perfect balance between night and day, the subtle delight in the slowly lengthening evenings, the burgeoning life in my vegetable plot, the discarding of bedcovers and warm clothes. And then I reproached myself for this escape into the cosmic when individual people were suffering so badly. Nothing was actually concluded – Judith Talbot burnt herself into my consciousness: the twice-bereaved mother, with her dying daughter and murdering son. She was an ordinary inoffensive woman, capable of the normal range of emotions, guilty of nothing more than an inability to watch her girl disintegrate before her eyes. Charles and Jeremy both seemed to feel she was a coward, a failed mother, because she carried on with her life and let other people cope with Carrie.

And Helena Maynard – would she understand why her husband had died? Would it separate her from Charles Talbot, or would they grow closer now that both were free and available? It would be a neat recompense for the miserable times ahead.

Because I knew, better than most, that the bad times were still in front of them. Jeremy would recover, only to be charged with murder and confined in some special prison for minors until he was eighteen. They would live with the stigma for ever.

And the grave. What was the future for the grave?

Thea came into my room, wearing a large green dressing gown that looked as if it'd wrap around her two or three times. She carried two mugs of tea, and put one down carefully beside my bed.

'Morning,' she said.

I looked at her for a long moment. She was pale, with mauve shadows under her eyes. She hadn't brushed her hair and it stuck up in funny places. There was a slightly dusty smell about her, that I thought must come from the dressing gown. 'Morning,' I replied.

'Drew...' she began, and I spotted one of those exhausting female conversations about to begin. One of those analytical, emotional speeches which said far too much. I gave her no invitation to continue.

'I've been lying awake all night, thinking,' she went on. 'Trying to analyse myself, mostly. Things

330

could have gone dreadfully wrong last night, all because of me. I wasn't fair to you, letting you get into such a horrible situation.'

I hauled myself more upright, wanting to get out of bed, but belatedly aware that I had fallen into bed after the hot shower wearing nothing whatsoever.

'It's OK,' I said. 'You had my best interests at heart, I'm sure.'

I had no reason to absolve her from her manipulative ways, apart from her obviously good intentions, and her disarming apology.

'I did,' she said. 'But it wasn't actually any of my business, was it?'

'Go,' I ordered her. 'Take your tea and leave me alone.' Then I remembered I had no clean clothes, other than a shirt – if my bag had somehow miraculously caught up with me. 'What am I going to wear?'

She pointed to a cupboard in the corner. 'There are things in there. It's all very well equipped.' She spoke almost normally, just a tight little catch in every other word betrayed her.

'The police will want to talk to us.'

'I expect they will.'

'Where's your dog?'

'On my bed, where she always is.'

'And where did you say we are?'

'Cirencester.'

'Oh. I've never been to Cirencester.'

'Well, I can show you around, if you like. It's got a very splendid church.'

'Just what we need,' I said, with heavy emphasis.

331

She laughed, and went downstairs.

We were debriefed by DI Basildon, who had evidently fallen for Thea pretty heavily. What man wouldn't, I asked myself.

The news about Jeremy was as reassuring as possible, in the circumstances. He would survive with no permanent physical damage. There were no loose ends left to tie – the Talbots were miserable, Mrs Maynard was mildly apologetic, Harry Richmond was energised by his role in Thea's plan, returning to the co-housing group with quite a tale to tell. I reviewed Thea's part in the whole business in small stages. She had kept so much concealed from me, either not trusting me to remember my lines, or still very slightly unsure as to whether I had indeed bashed Mr Maynard to death. Or had she believed herself to be protecting me? That, when I thought of it, seemed the most convincing explanation.

The solicitor who had handled Mrs Simmonds' affairs contacted me – rather late, it seemed to me, on reflection – and offered to conduct a legal battle to secure ownership of the house.

'What about the field?' I asked.

He paused. 'I'm only guessing, but I suspect there wouldn't be much objection from the council to selling it for a fair figure.'

'But I don't have any money,' I protested.

'You have assets,' he corrected me. 'I think you'll find it feasible, once all the excitement has died down.'

The excitement turned out to be considerable over the next few days. The story made headlines in several local newspapers, and was mentioned in the nationals in their turn. The boy who only wanted to save his beloved aunt's grave was given a cautious approval, despite his arrest for murder. Even I could see that Gloucestershire Council might be reluctant to have any more to do with the infamous grave. I began to view it from a more businesslike angle. Maggs, when she finally grasped the complete story, was loudly enthusiastic.

'There'll be *loads* of people wanting to be buried there!' she crowed, with a highly premature delight.

'But we have to *live* there,' I objected. 'How do you think that's going to work?'

'It'll work,' she said confidently. 'And when that boy comes out of prison, he can join us.'

A whole new life offered itself temptingly to my gaze. Perhaps I could move to the Cotswolds, start a new business, leaving Maggs to run everything in Somerset. It might just work, given enough luck and goodwill. I dreamt this seductive dream for all of five minutes before the complications crowded in and I felt weak at the prospect of so much change.

I went home, and spent a week strenuously chasing up business, sending out leaflets, even approaching a few groups such as Probus and Inner Wheel with a view to doing one of my talks, which had fallen into abeyance after Karen's injury.

Thea Osborne phoned me after a week or so, asking how I was feeling, and whether I'd made any long-term decisions.

'Certainly not,' I said. 'It's far too soon. How about you?'

'I've agreed to do another house-sit in Cranham, in July,' she said. 'It's in a lovely old manor house, apparently. I'll go and see them next week. I'm really looking forward to it.'

Karen never asked for details about my Broad Campden experience. I abandoned the blood-soaked clothes and never told her where they'd gone. I did tell her I would have to give testimony in a murder trial, at some future stage, but not for several months. Then I carefully broke the news that I had inherited a house, with some very stringent conditions attached.

It showed how changed she was, the way she failed to grasp the implications. Her headaches were becoming more severe and more frequent, and we had an appointment for a brain scan within a few days. 'We can't move house, though, can we?' she said, her expression bland and open. 'The children wouldn't like that.'

I thought of the wide fields and the footpaths and the lovely Cotswold buildings, and wondered. On the face of it, Somerset had just as much natural freedom as did Broad Campden, but the roads were bigger and faster, the crime rate was increasing, and the weather turning wetter. If Maggs could take charge of the burial ground, I thought a move might just work out. I could not shake myself free of Greta Simmonds and Jeremy Talbot and the story I had blundered into.

'We'll have to see, then, won't we,' I said.

This Large Print Book for the partially sighted, who cannot read normal print, is published under the auspices of

THE ULVERSCROFT FOUNDATION